THE PARFIT KNIGHT

THE
PARFIT KNIGHT

JULIET BLYTH

St. Martin's Press
New York

For
JOHN PAWSEY
without whom. . .

Library of Congress Cataloging in Publication Data

Blyth, Juliet.
    The parfit knight.

    I. Title.
PR6052.L9P37   1986   823'.914   86-13793
ISBN 0-312-59664-2

First published in Great Britain by Severn House Publishers Ltd.

First U.S. Edition

10 9 8 7 6 5 4 3 2 1

He nevere yet no vileyne ne sayde
In all his lyf unto no maner wight
He was a verray parfit gentil knyght

Geoffrey Chaucer
THE CANTERBURY TALES

THE PARFIT KNIGHT

Prologue

The day was hot and the sky a vast, uncharted ocean of blue. Beneath it, only the brook seemed awake while, quiescently tranquil and lulled by the sun, the rest of the world spun languid dreams or was shrouded in sleep. Curving down from the quiet post-road, the lane was a dappled haven of hypnotically swaying foxgloves and the shimmering air was disturbed by nought save the whispering murmur of leaves and the silver song of the water.

The child on the bank rolled lazily over to gaze into the clear, bubbling stream, so close that her shining fall of hair brushed its surface. A dragonfly hovered nearby and she lay very still, smiling as if it shared her joy in this very special day; for the dragonfly, the full sum of its brief existence, and for the child, her very last day in single figures.

Tomorrow she would be ten years old; and that was exciting, of course – birthdays always were – but it *did* seem that once you arrived in double figures you stayed there for a very long time. Even Great-Aunt Maria had not managed three yet and she was very old indeed. The girl gave a tiny, rippling laugh as she tried to imagine herself with a skin like a little, wrinkled apple and a toothless grin. Then she felt a twinge of conscience for surely it was not at all funny for Aunty who had to be helped wherever she went and could not even read her own letters any more. Not that she seemed to mind it particularly – but perhaps that was something to do with having had so many adventures on account of Bonnie Prince Charlie; and *that* just went to prove that Aunty hadn't always been an old woman. A fact that was as hard to believe as the other.

The sun beat down on her back through the leaf-green taffeta of her gown and she wondered idly where she had left her hat. She supposed that she should retrace her steps in search of it since its loss would make the third in as many weeks and Mama would undoubtedly scold; but on such a lovely day a hat seemed a matter of small importance and Mama never scolded for long. She closed her eyes and, laying her cheek on her arm, dabbled the fingers of her other hand in the cool water.

'Rosie-rose is a lazy doze! Come *on*, you sluggard – or are you going to lie there all day?'

The taunting call shattered the afternoon's peace and the girl's eyes flew open. Then, without even glancing round, she closed them again and said, 'Yes. Go away.'

There was a mocking laugh and the next instant a wooden billet sailed over her head to land in the water with a splash.

'Ugh!' The girl leapt up in a flurry of laughter and damp taffeta. 'Just you wait, you beast! I'll . . .'

'Who's waiting?' teased the boy as he vanished into the trees on the far side of the lane. 'If you want to catch me you'll have to run.'

It was unnecessary advice. Almost before the words were out, she had snatched up her skirts in both hands and was racing across the springy turf.

'Faint-heart! But I'll catch you – see if I don't!'

Weaving his way into the heart of the copse, the boy heard her shout and in the same moment became aware that the gradual crescendo of distant sound was distant no longer. He stopped and swung round, struck by a sudden premonition.

2

'No, Rose – *wait*!'

The girl neither answered nor checked her pace but darted up the lane, skirting the trees. It was silly of him, she decided, to think he could dupe her so easily; a coach and travelling fast – but on the post-road, never this lane.

It was her last conscious thought as the team of blood chestnuts swept round the bend on top of her. There was a sensation of falling through aeons of painful, swirling blackness, and then nothing.

Plunging wildly back in the direction he had come, the boy emerged in time to see the horses being dragged to an abrupt standstill while a man jumped down from the inside of the still-moving chaise; and then his horrified gaze took in the crumpled leaf-green form at the roadside and he felt suddenly sick. His legs refused to obey him so that, instead of running, he could only stumble across the intervening space, dumbly terrified of what he would find.

The gentleman from the chaise was before him. Heedless of silks and laces, he knelt in the dust, one hand seeking the child's pulse whilst his eyes anxiously scanned her still, white face. Then he laid her wrist gently down, the sun striking sparks from the emerald on his finger, and looked up at the equally white-faced youth beside him.

'Your sister?'

The boy nodded, his eyes fixed on the girl and his brain obsessed by the foolish thought that there was no blood. She could almost have been asleep except that she was so pale. She did not *look* hurt. It should have made him feel better but somehow it didn't.

'It's alright.' The gentleman saw the question in the frightened blue eyes and answered it. 'She has been very lucky, I think – but will be the better for seeing a doctor.'

Blinking back an unexpected rush of hot tears, the lad said baldly, 'Are you sure she isn't dead?' And was ashamed of the tremor in his voice.

'Quite sure.' Younger than his powdered head made him appear, the gentleman tactfully affected not to notice the tremor. The coachman hovered behind them, wringing his hands.

'I tried to swing over, sir,' he said unhappily. 'But I had no warning – her being round the bend as she was. No one'd have stood a chance of avoiding her; not at . . .' He stopped abruptly.

'Not at that pace,' finished his master with a sort of grim placidity. 'Yes, Pierce, I know.' He lifted the girl very carefully in his arms and directed a briefly reassuring smile at her brother. 'Which is nearer – your home or the doctor's house?'

'The – the doctor's. It's that way.'

But mere directions, it seemed, were not to the gentleman's taste and young though he was, he had the habit of command. Dazedly allowing him to take charge, the boy found himself perched on the box beside the coachman while his sister lay on the seat within and he did not demur until they drew up outside the doctor's house and he was told not to get down.

'I don't want to leave her,' he said mutinously, preparing to descend.

'No. I daresay you don't,' agreed the gentleman with crisp amiability as he lifted the girl gently out of the coach. 'But your parents should be informed and Pierce will need you to guide him. Pray convey my compliments to your father and beg him to make use of my chaise.'

'My uncle,' the boy corrected automatically. Then, 'Sir, it's all very well, but . . .'

Already half-way to the door with his fragile burden, the gentleman turned with a swiftly controlled loss of patience.

4

'It is *not* very well if you persist in wasting time in worthless argument,' he said deliberately. 'There is nothing you can do save that which I have bidden you. Now go. And if your uncle requires to know my name, you may tell him that it is Ballantyne – Denzil Ballantyne.'

Chapter One

Although it contrived to appear very much as usual, the gaming-room of White's wore a faint air of disapprobation. Beginning as no more than a watchful glint in the eyes of some of the older members, it had gradually deepened to something approaching scorn and finally found expression in low-voiced murmurs of contempt.

'The stakes are up again. By God, I'd not have thought it of Amberley!' Colonel Harding stared balefully at the large table where a game of dice was in progress.

'Nor I,' replied Mr Cardew, following his gaze. 'But if a year in France has taught him nought but how to pluck a pigeon, then he'd best have stayed there.'

Viscount Ansford adjusted the position of his elaborate wig and gave an irritating titter. 'Perhapth my Lord thuffered ill-luck in Parith and theekth the meanth to mend hith fortuneth.'

Not for the first time, Jack Ingram wondered how it was that the decorative Viscount never failed to construct sentences filled with the one letter he was incapable of pronouncing. Annoyed, though not because of the lisp, he allowed his eyes to dwell appreciatively on his Lordship's blue-powdered head and said sweetly, 'Utter nonsense.'

Gripped by a moment of horrid doubt, the Viscount was too stricken to reply.

'Well, I hope so,' said Mr Cardew with blunt significance. 'But you can't deny that it don't look well. The play is devilish deep and Amberley has been accepting the boy's vowels for the last hour and more.'

Jack spared a brief glance for the youthful person of Robert Dacre, observing his flushed cheeks and the slight unsteadiness of the hand engaged in writing yet another promissory note. His mouth tightened a little and he turned back to Mr Cardew with a sardonic smile.

'It has perhaps escaped your attention that Mr Dacre's presence at the table is due solely to his own rather heated insistence,' he said evenly. 'Amberley did not invite him.'

The Colonel snorted. 'No – but he's damned quick to take advantage! The boy's little more than twenty – still green. And Amberley knows it!'

A look of distaste crossed Mr Ingram's pleasant face as he rose unhurriedly from his seat and shook out the full skirts of his brocaded coat.

'He also knows – as do we all – that this is not young Dacre's first season. He has been on the town a full two years and is therefore old enough to know better.' He sketched a slight bow. 'Your servant, gentlemen.'

Viscount Ansford watched him go with a distinct feeling of resentment.

'No fineth,' he said peevishly. 'Doubtleth he and Amberley are prodigiouth well-thuited.'

Apparently oblivious to the comment and feelings of animosity that his play was arousing in the conservative breasts of his fellow-members, the most noble Marquis of Amberley pushed a fresh pile of guineas to the stock already in front of him and called serenely for the next bet.

To the casual observer, he appeared much like any other gentleman in the room; a thought more modish, perhaps – but in one so recently returned from Paris that was easily explained. No London tailor had fashioned that exquisitely-cut coat of moss-green velvet, extravagantly laced with gold, or designed the elegant floral vest that lay beneath it. The folds of snowy lace that adorned both throat and wrist were the finest Mechlin.

Yet the quiet air of distinction that clung to the Marquis had little to do with his apparel. It was, perhaps, most obvious in his rejection of wig or powder, rouge and patches. Instead, he wore his own hair neatly but simply tied in long ribands of black, against which it gleamed pale as silver-gilt in the candlelight; and innocent of cosmetics, his face was lightly but undeniably tanned – as were the well-shaped tapering hands, half-hidden beneath their foaming ruffles. And there were other differences for the discerning eye and ear accustomed to fashionable boredom – for no cynical gleam shadowed the bright, grey-green eyes and no languid drawl marked the pleasant tones. Indeed, both eye and voice held more than a hint of lurking amusement and the firm-lipped mouth as much humour as resolution.

The Marquis of Amberley was rich, assured and thirty-four years old, with the reputation of being a law unto himself; and, in addition, he was possessed of a certain elusive charm which even his well-wishers were inclined to regard as frankly disastrous.

Just now his careless dismissal of public opinion was causing his nearest well-wisher a good deal of disquiet and, from his position at the side of the room, the Honourable Jack Ingram stared irritably at his friend's face. As if aware of his scrutiny, the Marquis suddenly glanced across at him, laughter tugging at his mouth and brimming wickedly in his eyes. Then he lifted one brow in quizzical sympathy and restored his attention to the game. Jack relaxed; whatever else Amberley was, he was certainly not a fool.

'Why so thoughtful, my dear?' asked a soft, almost purring voice from behind him. 'One would almost think you minded to see the bantling lose a few of his feathers.'

Jack turned his head to meet the Duke of Rockliffe's mocking gaze.

'Hardly,' he said lightly. 'Though I could wish it were some other collecting them.'

'Ah yes.' The Duke raised his glass with characteristic languor and levelled it at Amberley. 'But you cannot deny that it has a certain . . . er . . . poetry. And he does it so well.'

'Practice makes perfect, in fact,' snapped Jack sarcastically. 'You have only to add that both Amberley and Paris are expensive and you will have said what everyone else is saying.'

'Unworthy, Jack.' His Grace lowered his glass to make a haughty sweeping gesture. 'I never run with the herd, you know.'

Mr Ingram gave way to unwilling laughter.

'I do, of course.' He paused for a moment. 'Very well. If you don't believe Amberley is fleecing young Dacre in an attempt to recoup his fortunes – what *do* you think he is up to?'

'The same as you, my dear,' drawled his Grace, lazily amused. 'He believes himself – erroneously, in my view – to be teaching the boy a useful and well-deserved lesson. And the Honourable Robert, of course, joined the table for much the same reason.' He produced an enamelled snuff-box and offered it to the other man. 'Aurora – by Ravenet of Battersea. Quite pretty, don't you think? Though not, perhaps, best suited for evening use.' He sighed. 'How vexing. More an afternoon box, wouldn't you say?'

'Yes,' said Jack, used to and undeceived by this by-play.

'Yes,' repeated Rockliffe with a faint smile. 'Now . . . where was I? Ah yes. Friend Robert, you must be aware, has neither forgotten nor forgiven Amberley for succeeding where he failed with the so-delectable Fanny.

One cannot but see his point. But his dreams of retribution – so melodramatic! – have gone sadly awry; for instead of breaking Amberley's bank, I would estimate him to have lost some three thousand guineas.'

'Hell!' said Jack, startled. 'As much as that?'

'Oh easily. Experience, as they say, is not bought cheaply.' The Duke turned to go and then looked back to say softly, 'Amusing, isn't it?'

The Honourable Robert Dacre did not think so and neither, if his expression was any true guide, did the tall young gentlemen in blue who stood behind him, one hand resting on the back of his chair. Robert had left sobriety behind him and with it any clear idea of his losses. Only one resolve remained and that grew stronger with every bottle – a fact which was beginning to dawn on his watching companion. The blue-coated gentlemen cast a dubious glance at the Marquis, unknown to him before this evening, and encountered a look which made him suddenly very angry. The fellow knew; he knew he had only to pass the bank to another for Robert to stop playing – had known it all along and yet done nothing.

His fingers closed hard on his friend's shoulder and he said urgently, 'For God's sake, Bob – come away. Haven't you lost enough?'

Robert shrugged the hand away and over-bright brown eyes swivelled to meet worried blue ones. 'No. No, damn it. I haven't,' he replied thickly. 'But you don't have to stay, Ver. Quite ca . . . ca . . . I can manage without you.'

Captain Lord Philip Vernon, late of his Majesty's army, had more than one reason to doubt this but nothing in his four-month experience of London society had taught him what might be done to alter the situation. He was, however, familiar enough with Mr Dacre to be fairly sure that the morrow would see him seeking a loan to cover tonight's losses; and he was also uneasily aware that his betrothed might well expect him to come to her brother's assistance.

Philip was not, as yet, very well-acquainted with his future bride. The match had been hatched between her father and his uncle; and when Uncle Rowland had died, forcing him to resign his commission and take his place as head of the family, Philip had decided that he could do worse than follow the old gentleman's wishes and offer for Isabel Dacre. But Uncle Rowland, he thought grimly, could never have foreseen the possibility of Robert who, though pleasant enough in the ordinary way, was wildly extravagant and bidding fair to become a hardened gamester. Not that Robert's excesses were any excuse for the Marquis, whose honour should recoil from the thought of winning large sums from a foolish boy.

Help was at hand and from an unexpected source. Even as Lord Philip debated the wisdom of appealing to Amberley's better nature, always supposing that he had one, the matter was taken out of his hands by a tall and rakishly elegant gentleman in purple who strolled to the Marquis's side to gaze down at him out of darkly mocking eyes. Then he made a deeply flourishing bow. 'My Lord Marquis – your most obedient servant!'

Grey-green eyes laughed back at him as Amberley rose from his chair to respond in kind. 'And yours, my Lord Duke!' Then, raising one eyebrow, he said pleasantly, 'Well, Rock? You interrupt the game, you know.'

'Indeed,' drawled Rockliffe softly. 'Indeed. It was my intention.'

Somehow – and Philip was not at all sure just how he did it – the Duke was commanding everyone's attention. Gradually the room's companionable chatter faded and died until every man there had his eyes fixed on the two facing each other beside the Hazard table. And as Philip watched, he was struck by a strange sense of likeness between them. Something that had nothing to do with parity of height or age but was more a similarity of type; of affinity in experience and character. Then he shrugged the ridiculous notion aside. The Duke was languid and smooth-spoken with, apparently, some sense of honour; and at least his hair was conventionally powdered.

Amberley, it appeared, was waiting with unabated good-humour for his Grace to continue – and eventually he did so.

'I've a mind – if you will permit me – to try a throw for your bank.'

If the atmosphere had been tense before, it was now positively electric. Philip glanced down at Robert and perceived from his glazed expression that he no longer had any clear idea of what was happening.

The Marquis spread eloquent hands and smiled.

'For myself, I have no objection. But perhaps these gentlemen . . ?' It was a courteous appeal to the table and one by one, as if some master puppeteer had pulled their strings, each signified his consent. All save Robert – who was fast coming to resemble a glass-eyed effigy.

Like all moments of eagerly anticipated crisis, it was over in a flash, leaving the company silent and faintly dissatisfied. And the one man amongst them who ought, by rights, to show some disappointment – or shame – apparently felt none.

'Behold, your Grace,' announced Amberley, with what Philip privately considered to be unnecessary theatricality, 'the bank is yours.'

Amusement lurked in Rockliffe's eyes. 'Behold also,' he replied suavely, 'that Mr Dacre has fallen asleep.'

As he glanced quickly down to see that it was, alas, all too true, Philip heard the Marquis give a tiny choke of laughter and say unsteadily, '*Pique, repique* and *capot* – and let that be a lesson to you!' – which made no sense whatever. He would have liked to thank Rockliffe for his

13

intervention which, though it had turned out to be unnecessary, he was convinced to have been well-meant; but his acquaintance with the Duke was of the slightest and he therefore had no idea of how such an overture would be received, so he gave a faint sigh and turned his attention to the tedious task of getting Robert home.

He was in the vestibule, engaged in keeping his future brother-in-law upright against the wall whilst waiting for the porter to summon a hackney-carriage when he heard a now-familiar voice say lightly, 'Shades of Milo and his ass! Do you need any assistance?'

It was the last straw and Philip, who had spent a trying and wholly unenjoyable evening, cast the Marquis a look of blazing scorn.

'Thank you, no. I think you've left it a little late, don't you?'

Amberley met the angry blue gaze sympathetically. 'You would naturally think so. Have I quite spoilt your evening?'

'Oh no! I *enjoy* watching a boy being fleeced by a hardened gamester fifteen years his senior,' snapped Philip sarcastically. 'But that is beside the point. I don't know if you make a habit of this kind of thing, but . . .'

'No, indeed. How should you?' enquired the Marquis cheerfully. 'Forgive me, but I am afraid I really have no intention of explaining myself to you – nor do I have the remotest interest in your opinion of my character.' He smiled suddenly. 'Permit me to point out that Mr Dacre is slipping.'

Philip stifled an oath, caught swiftly at Robert's coat and jerked him upright. When he turned round again it was to find that Mr Ingram had appeared and was regarding them with mild anxiety.

The Marquis strolled unhurriedly to the door, pausing to cast a knowledgeable eye over Robert before addressing himself once more to Philip.

'When your friend has recovered what little sense God gave him, I should be obliged if you will desire him to wait upon me before noon on the day after tomorrow. Without fail.'

'Duns after you, my Lord?' taunted Philip before he could stop himself.

The grey-green eyes surveyed him with resigned patience. Then, 'You would do well to acquire a little tolerance, my fledgling – and to recollect that you know me not at all. This matter is between Mr Dacre and myself and your interference in it does me no harm and you little credit. As for my message – you may believe that it is in Mr Dacre's best interest to do as I ask.'

No longer amused, the voice held a crisp authority that was vaguely familiar but Philip was in no mood to consider it. Burningly aware that his anger had betrayed him into a gross lack of conduct – a fact that naturally did nothing to improve his temper – he put a rigid curb on his tonue and said coldly, 'I doubt we are likely to agree on that, sir. But you need have no fear. I will see to it that Mr Dacre is made privy to your wishes.'

'I am glad to hear it.' The ice melted and after a second's shrewd appraisal, the Marquis asked abruptly, 'Hussars or Grenadiers?'

Philip's jaw dropped. 'G-grenadiers. I sold out.'

Amberley smiled. 'I see. You should try persuading Mr Dacre to sign up for a time – it would do him so much good.' And with a slight, graceful bow he was gone, leaving Mr Ingram to follow helplessly in his wake while Lord Philip stared after them in complete bewilderment.

Strolling up St James Street in the direction of Piccadilly, Jack caught up with the Marquis and began with the question that took rather ridiculous precedence over all others.

'How did you know he was an army man?'

'Impressed, Jack?'

15

'Very. I had thought you left omniscience to Rockliffe.'

'And so I do,' came the laughing reply. 'No – I am afraid it was merely something in his bearing. That and the severity of his tailoring. Do you know who he is?'

Mr Ingram shook his head. 'No. But then, I've spent very little time in town this winter. Rock could probably tell you.'

'Not a doubt of it.' Amberley paused and then said thoughtfully, 'Quite a pleasant young man when he's off his high ropes, I should think – but I can't imagine what should lead him to spend his time with Robert Dacre. Quite apart from the fact that there must be five or six years between them, I doubt very much if they've anything in common.'

'No.' Jack thought for a moment and then said abruptly, 'I suppose you know what everyone was saying back there?'

'Why, yes.' Amusement rippled through the light voice. 'They think that I lost my fortune in the wicked flesh-pots of Paris and am come home to repair it; that I'm a ravening wolf, preying on the innocent – a villainous fleecer of youths – a leader of lambs to the slaughter. And worse, they're not at all sure I'm not a Captain Sharp.'

'Don't be an idiot!' snapped Jack, patently unamused. 'No one thinks you cheated – though if they did think it, you'd have no one to blame but yourself. It's one thing not to care what's said of you but quite another to deliberately create a false impression. There are times when I think you're a candidate for Bedlam!'

The Marquis eyed him with mischievous concern. 'Be calm, my loved one. You're likely to suffer an apoplexy. And you should know by now that I never deliberately create anything. I simply let things take their course.'

Grasping his arm, Mr Ingram pulled him to a halt. 'Den – how much does that young fool owe you?'

'I'm afraid I wasn't counting,' replied Amberley, his attention plainly elsewhere. 'If I promise not to run away, do you think you might cease mauling my favourite coat?'

'Rock thinks it to be over three thousand,' said Jack, letting go of the coat but not of his argument.

'Does he? Well, well – he *has* been busy.' This with a certain acidity. 'And there I was thinking that he only interfered out of a desire to steal the stage.'

'You know perfectly well that he did,' responded Jack dryly. 'It's a habit with him. He no more thinks you a flat-catcher than I do.'

'I thank you both.'

'Don't mention it. I take it you've no intention of letting the boy pay you?'

The Marquis crossed northwards into Berkeley Street. 'Do you? Now why should you think that?' he enquired sweetly.

'Oh bloody hell!' breathed Mr Ingram, disgust getting the better of him. 'I wonder if you know just how irritating you can be?'

'Well, I *think* I do,' came the meek reply.

'I doubt it! I've known you for fifteen years and . . .'

'As long as that?'

'Yes. And you've never been any different. For . . .'

'Really? Well that *is* a comfort.'

Jack was forced to smother a grin. 'Who for?' he retorted. And then, without waiting for a reply, 'You know that *I* know you won't take Dacre's money – but for some lunatic reason you'd sooner bleed to death than admit it. Well? Correct me if I'm wrong!'

'I wouldn't dare!' said the Marquis amicably.

There was an explosive silence and then Mr Ingram said carefully, 'I sometimes wonder why I put up with you.'

'Surely not?' His Lordship laughed. 'It's because I can

give you the entrée to Richmond. Can you doubt it? And, by the way, I'm driving there tomorrow. Do you care to come with me?'

This was obvious bait but none the less tempting for that and it was with very real regret that Jack recollected a previous engagement. Invitations to the Dowager Marchioness of Amberley's charming retreat were all too rare and the Dowager herself (though anyone less like a dowager Jack had never met) rarely left it.

'I can't,' he said. 'I'm promised to Gilmore.'

They had reached Bruton Place where lay Mr Ingram's lodging and the Marquis turned to face him with a teasing grin.

'Just as well, perhaps. I've really no ambition to acquire you as a father-in-law.'

Jack grinned sheepishly. 'Don't be an idiot. It's just that she is so . . . so . . .'

'I know,' interposed Amberley helpfully. 'And, like you, I've never met a woman who could hold a candle to her. And if, and when I do, I shall take the greatest care not to present the lady to you.'

'Wise of you!' laughed Jack. And then, 'Do you stay in Richmond or shall I see you in the club on Friday?'

'Neither. I leave for Amberley when I've settled matters with young Dacre.'

Mr Ingram stared at him. 'You're mad! It's January and there's more snow on the way if I'm any judge!'

'I'm only going to Hertfordshire,' the Marquis protested. 'It's not entirely beyond the realms of civilisation, you know – and I haven't seen the place in over a year. My agent writes of a dozen matters requiring my attention and if I don't go now, I doubt I shall be there before the spring. Only four days back in London and already the tentacles of society are beginning to close round me.'

'You may find they unclose again fast enough after

tonight,' warned Jack, reverting to his original theme. 'I know Robert Dacre is a spoilt and mannerless young cub sharply in need of a kicking but he already resents you more than is reasonable and, given the opportunity, I believe he'd be glad to do you a mischief.'

'Content you, Jack. He shall *not* be given the opportunity.'

'Well, I hope not.' Mr Ingram eyed his friend with resigned exasperation. 'You're not going to discuss it, are you?'

'No. I had hoped, you see,' replied the Marquis with a very faint note of wistfulness, 'that I didn't need to.'

Jack was not proof against that tone. 'Oh devil take you, Den – you're impossible! Go home to bed!'

Amberley laughed. 'Is that a blessing or a curse? Either way, I feel I should sympathise with you.'

'Cold comfort!' retorted Jack. And then, 'By the way – what happened to Fanny? I take it you didn't bring her back with you?'

His Lordship turned back to survey him mockingly from the middle of the road.

'No. I didn't bring her back. I think, like you, she found my levity rather trying – especially when relating to such vital necessities of life as emerald tiaras and Mediterranean villas. At all events, she hurled a coffee-pot at my head one morning, favoured me with a sadly unflattering description of my person, my character and my . . . er . . . capabilities – and finished with a graphic hypothesis on my genealogy. Then she ran off with a Genoese Count. A very *rich* Genoese Count, so I believe.'

'Good God!' breathed Jack reverently. 'And what did *you* do?'

'The only thing possible,' replied Amberley gravely. 'I am very much afraid that I laughed.'

Chapter Two

The clock was just striking noon when the Marquis of Amberley's valet informed him that the Honourable Robert Dacre had arrived and was waiting to see him. Still gorgeously attired in a frogged silk dressing-gown, the Marquis raised his eyes from the absorbing task of polishing his nails and said gently, 'Already? Well, well.'

Saunders met the guileless stare stoically. 'Yes, my Lord. Shall I get your Lordship's coat?'

'My coat? Ah yes.' His Lordship leaned back in his chair and surveyed the garment pensively. 'Do you know, Jim – I believe I will not wear grey after all. It has an appearance of austerity that I feel will not appeal to Mr Dacre. I shall wear . . . claret.'

'Yes, my Lord.' Well aware what game was being played, a sardonic gleam replaced Saunders's wooden expression as he turned to restore the grey coat to the clothes-press.

'Or should it be blue?' mused the light voice behind him. 'Blue . . . with the cream broidered vest.'

The valet turned back with every appearance of helpfulness. 'There's the purple you haven't yet worn, my Lord.'

'Mn . . .' Mischief danced in the grey-green eyes but his Lordship's mouth was prim. 'But it seems a pity to waste it on a mere . . . on a journey. Don't you agree?'

Saunders's impassivity became a trifle forced. 'As you

20

say, my Lord.' He fixed his gaze on a point some six inches above his master's head and said disinterestedly, 'I quite forgot to tell you, my Lord – Barrow did happen to mention as how he'd left a bottle of the best Chambertin in the library with Mr Dacre. He hoped he'd done right, sir.'

There was a brief silence and then the Marquis succumbed to long, infectious laughter.

'You should have been a General, Jim. Such tactics are worth a better cause,' he said unsteadily. And then, getting up, 'Oh – very well. You may get out the blue coat. But if Barrow finds out how you impugned his honour, you'll be thoroughly ditched and so I warn you!'

By the time the Marquis entered the library, Robert had been waiting a full half hour and his angry flush and smouldering gaze spoke volumes for the state of his temper. He was a good-looking youth and mercifully unaddicted to the extremes of fashion favoured by the Macaroni Club but his face was constantly overlaid with an expression of petulance and his manners frequently careless to the point of rudeness. Just now he swept round to fix Amberley with a scorching stare and said impetuously, 'At last! I daresay you think it funny to order me here and then keep me kicking my heels . . .' And then he caught the look in the other man's eye and the words seemed to wither on his tongue.

'Not at all,' replied Amberley equably. 'You are merely a little more punctual than I expected.'

Robert cast him a glance of acute dislike. It was true that he had intended to be late but Lord Philip had nipped that idea in the bud by handing over the wad of banknotes and then personally driving him to Grosvenor Square to deliver them.

The Marquis had no difficulty in interpreting that look and a mocking smile played about his mouth. 'Just so. I did not, however, invite you here to discuss your views on punctuality. Sit down.'

21

'Invite?' flared Robert. 'I understood it was more in the nature of a command! And you had absolutely no right to behave as though I could not be trusted to come and pay you of my own accord. I don't forget my debts and if you'll be so good as to produce my vowels, I'm more than willing to redeem them! I . . .'

'Sit down,' said Lord Amberley again and this time his voice was stripped of both amusement and patience.

Robert swallowed convulsively – and sat.

'That's better. I have no taste for lengthy rodomontades – nor do they impress me,' the Marquis went on crisply. 'Neither do I care for ill-mannered young cubs who habitually play with money they don't possess. Yes – I know you have apparently found the funds to pay me but that merely means that you owe someone else – unless your father has been persuaded to bail you out yet again. And I doubt that very much because I imagine that it would puzzle him to do it.'

Robert's hand clenched on the arm of his chair and he said furiously, 'Damn you! That's no concern of yours!'

'No. It isn't. But it ought to be a concern of *yours*. And though I would have been very happy to remain outside your affairs, you made that impossible when you indulged in what I can only assume to be an ill-judged attempt to wreak vengeance on my head. Do you really think that I derive pleasure from winning large sums from such as you?'

'Are you telling me that you don't?' sneered Robert. 'You certainly didn't try very hard to prevent it.'

Amberley sighed. 'And just how would you have wanted me to do that? By a point-blank refusal to have you at my table – or by allowing you to chase me from it? The first could surely have occasioned you no satisfaction whatever and the second is possibly a little too much to expect.'

'I expect nothing from you – except that you go out of your way to make a fool of me!'

'You are mistaken. You achieve it quite successfully without my help and I have better ways of passing my time.' Amberley's face was stern and his eyes held a glint of steel. 'I know that you fancy the exquisite Fanny to have been a victim of my rank, my wealth, and my Machiavellian wiles designed to thwart your happiness but it isn't so; and while I make full allowance for your natural disappointment at the time, you should by now have contrived to master it.'

'You don't understand!' It was the resentful cry of youth. 'She loved *me* before you turned her head!'

'I assure you that I understand only too well,' came the calm reply. 'And though I doubt you will believe it, she was by no means the blushing little flower of virtue you apparently believed her – and quite shockingly expensive.' Amberley surveyed Robert's face of implacable but frustrated fury and then gave a tiny shrug of resignation. 'All this is beside the point. You think I called you here to pay me. I didn't. I leave town this afternoon and I wished, before I left, to inform you that the only use I have for your vowels is to light the fire with them.' He opened a drawer in his desk and then tossed a small packet into the younger man's lap. 'Here – take them.'

For a second Robert was dumbstruck and then he lifted his eyes from the bundle of papers to look suspiciously at the Marquis.

'Why?' he asked baldly. 'What do you want of me?'

An expression of mild contempt darkened the grey-green eyes. 'I don't want anything of you. It would, of course, be pleasant if you refrained from making the same mistake again but I imagine that it's too much to hope for – at least until you exhaust the good-nature of your friends.'

Robert flushed, suddenly conscious of Lord Philip's bills nestling comfortably in his pocket.

'As for why,' Amberley went on scathingly, 'it is a

23

matter of honour. And for the sake of some future young idiot, as yet in the nursery, I can only hope that you come to understand it for yourself.'

'All you care about is what will be said of you,' retorted Robert nastily.

The Marquis wished that Mr Ingram had been privileged to hear that remark and his laugh held real amusement. 'Hardly – though you would naturally think so.'

The brown eyes narrowed. 'You mean you don't intend to tell everyone?'

'No. You really shouldn't judge everyone by your own standards, you know.'

Robert ignored this. An idea was taking shape and the ridiculous simplicity of it stopped his breath. Two birds with one stone – and all he need do was keep his mouth shut and trust Amberley to do the same. He subdued an impulse to smile, the first he had known in two days, and got up, cramming the vowels into his pocket.

'Very well – I accept your word,' he said gracelessly. 'And if there's nothing else you wish to say to me, I'll take my leave.'

The Marquis pulled the tasselled cord that would summon his butler and said dryly, 'I can think of several things but I am quite sure it would be a waste of breath.' The bright gaze became thoughtful. 'I take it that your military friend is new to town?'

'My military friend?' echoed Robert blankly. And then, 'Oh – yes. He's to marry my sister – though I can't conceive why it should interest you.'

Amberley smiled slowly. 'It doesn't. But it explains a lot.'

Walking away from Grosvenor Square in the direction of the Cocoa Tree, it never once occurred to Robert that he had neither contemplated refusing Lord Amberley's offer nor made even a token gesture of gratitude. It occurred to the Marquis – but being precisely what he expected, he did not allow it more than a passing thought. Indeed, he considered the episode both trivial and finished and would have been very surprised had he known then how much trouble was still to come from it.

By two o'clock the Marquis's elegant travelling-chaise was bowling north towards Ware and at a half after four it halted at the Green Man in Waltham Cross for a change of horses. After one glance at the rapidly darkening sky, his Lordship declined to enter the inn but stayed only while the change was completed, for though he had known before leaving town that he had no chance of reaching his destination before nightfall, he certainly hoped to do so before the promised snow became a reality. The weather, he thought resignedly, was already responsible for his making the journey inside the chaise with Saunders instead of perched behind his greys in the curricle – and that was more than enough. He had no wish to be benighted.

In the eyes of those who served him, Lord Amberley was possessed of only one eccentricity and that but a minor foible that did no harm save to establish a lively rivalry between his head coachman and his chief groom. It was simply that he preferred, whenever possible, to drive himself – which meant that while the coachman sat behind the kitchen table staring morosely into a pint of ale, the groom sat behind the Marquis and enjoyed the freedom of tap-rooms the length and breadth of the country. And today, as he hauled himself back on to the box, Chard could not help dwelling bitterly on the fact that life was demonstrably unfair.

Inside the chaise the Marquis leant back against the velvet squabs with closed eyes. His breathing was even, his body swayed easily with the motion of the carriage and anyone seeing him could have been pardoned for thinking that he slept.

25

Jim Saunders, though he rarely travelled in his master's company, knew better. Amberley was not asleep and neither was he as relaxed as he appeared. It was almost as though the very fact of being driven was sufficient to make him tense – and certainly he consistently forbade Chard to spring the horses which was an odd trait in one otherwise so rational; and who drove fast himself. There did not seem to be any accounting for it.

By the time Ware was reached it was pitch dark and sundry dancing flakes of snow were beginning to settle playfully on the coachman and his attendant groom. The groom folded his arms tight across his chest in an attitude of endurance; Chard was audibly unhappy.

'Rot it!' he muttered as the off-leader stumbled in a rut. 'Rot the lousy road and rot the lousy weather! But ain't it always the same?'

The groom did not reply. He might be young and new to his position but he was able to recognise a rhetorical question when he heard it.

'Do I ever get a nice little trip in the sun?' Chard went on, warming to his theme if nothing else. 'Do *I* ever go to Merton or Richmond or get a day at the races? Oh no! It's Keele as gets all that. *I'm* just the poor sod as has to keep us out of the ditch in the dark – and if that ain't enough, I have to catch me death while I'm adoing it! Come hail, come rain, come thunderstorm, here I sit driving his perishing team – and now here we are heading into a perishing blizzard! It ain't *fair!*'

'Why don't you leave him then?' asked the groom.

'Leave him? *Leave* him?' Chard swelled with indignation. 'I've been driving him for ten years – and afore that I drove his father. And afore *that*, my *father* did it!'

This was confusing. 'But if you don't like him . . .' the groom began.

26

'Who said I didn't?' demanded Chard, incensed. And then, 'Idiot!'

Startled, the groom begged pardon, dropped his chin on his chest and retreated into the comparative safety of silence while he pondered the incomprehensible complexities of human nature. And then he was jerked suddenly upright by the sound of a shot passing over his head.

'What the . . ?'

'Fool!' yelled the coachman. 'Use your blunderbuss!'

While the groom fumbled with nerveless fingers for the weapon lying at his feet, Chard whipped up his horses to run down the two mounted figures in the road ahead. Then there was a second explosion and the reins fell slack as the coachman slumped heavily against his terrified companion.

At the sound of the first shot, Saunders had leant swiftly across to drop a hand on the Marquis's arm.

'Yes, Jim. I heard it.' His Lordship did not move but his eyes were open and alert. 'I'd say the new man was a little slow, wouldn't you?'

And then came the second shot and the vehicle came to a shuddering standstill.

The Marquis discouraged his valet from jumping down with a brief shake of his head, while his right hand slid unhurriedly into his pocket. Aside from that, he still did not move.

There was a good deal of confused noise outside. Two rough voices were raised – one commanding the groom to throw down his weapon and the other berating someone called Joe for not shooting wide of his mark. Amberley's mouth tightened into a grim line and then the door of the coach was wrenched open and the muzzle of a large pistol inserted through it.

'Empty your pockets and be quick about it!' It was the voice responsible for disarming the groom.

'Go to hell,' replied the Marquis calmly. And his hand came swiftly out of his pocket.

There was a sharp report; a little tongue of flame momentarily lit the darkness and the shape at the door dropped where it stood. Almost before it hit the ground, Amberley was out of the chaise and left-handedly levelling a second pistol at the other highwayman who, equally quick to react, dived headlong into the cover of the trees.

The Marquis lowered his arm and turned round to find his valet dispassionately regarding the still body of Joe.

'He's dead, my Lord. Shot through the heart by the looks of it.'

Nodding curtly as if the matter held no interest for him, Amberley focussed his attention on his coachman.

His arms still frantically clutching Chard's still figure, the young groom looked down into his employer's unusually stern countenance and hurried into speech.

'My Lord – I swear I did my best. But we was took by surprise and Mr Chard wouldn't . . .'

'Is he dead?' The cold question cut across the boy's faltering excuses.

'I – I d-don't know.'

The Marquis lifted his foot to the step and swung himself lightly up to examine Chard as best as he could in the dark. His fingers located a sluggishly-beating pulse and then, having opened the man's coat, came back darkly stained. The groom looked on horrified and began excusing himself again.

'Be quiet and help me get him down,' his Lordship commanded crisply. 'Jim – come and lend a hand.'

'Is it bad?' asked Saunders, panting a little from the exertion of lifting the coachman into the chaise. Chard was not a small man.

'I don't know.' The Marquis folded his handkerchief

into a pad and then, finding it insufficient, pulled off his ruffled cravat to press it over the wound. 'The bullet's high in the shoulder but he's bleeding very heavily and needs better attention than we can give him here.' He cast his cloak over the inert body and stepped back onto the road. 'Where the devil are we?'

'I'm not certain, my Lord,' offered Saunders cautiously, 'but I think we're three or four miles short of Hadham Cross.'

'Oh hell!' For once the Marquis was plainly unamused. 'And nothing behind us for the same distance back to Ware. Well, it won't do. He'll bleed to death before we get him there. Damn it, there *must* be something closer – even if it's only a cottage!' He picked up the abandoned blunderbuss and tossed it up to the groom. 'Here – and try to keep it ready this time. Jim – get inside with Chard and hold him as still as you can. I'm going to drive on and see what I can find.'

The first gentle flurries of snow had by now become a good deal less spasmodic and within minutes Amberley's hair and coat were lightly powdered with white. The groom, huddled inside his thick frieze coat and nervously clutching the gun, wondered how his Lordship could drive without gloves – for even with them his own hands were freezing.

But if the Marquis felt the cold he gave no sign of it, tooling the chaise expertly down the road whilst keeping a watchful eye over the top of the hedgerows. Suddenly he found what he had hoped for; a pair of wrought-iron gates and a lodge with lights at the windows. Swinging his team in off the road, Amberley sent his groom to rouse the keeper and within minutes they were on the wide, curving drive which led up to the house. Lights showed here too and the arrival of a chaise-and-four outside the colonnaded entrance was enough to bring the butler to the door before the Marquis had even reached the top step.

'Good evening,' said his Lordship briskly but with a hint of his charming smile. 'I must apologise for the intrusion but I have a wounded man who needs shelter and medical attention – preferably from a doctor. Will you ask your master if I may bring him inside?'

The butler gave a slight but very stately bow. 'That will not be necessary, sir.' The man in front of him might be excessively dishevelled and have arrived on the box of his carriage but Josiah Lawson was a man of considerable experience and he knew a gentleman when he saw one. Waving a lordly hand at a pair of matching, green-liveried footmen, he said, 'Thomas, Claud – your assistance will be required.' And bowing again to Amberley, 'If you would care to step inside, sir?'

'Thank you – in a moment.' His Lordship was already on his way back to the chaise with Thomas and Claud. 'Lift him carefully and mind his left shoulder. Gently now.'

Once inside the house, Chard was lowered full length on a satin-covered sofa while the butler addressed himself once more to the Marquis.

'My mistress has been informed of your arrival, sir, and has instructed me to have your man put to bed and to send a groom for the doctor – subject, of course, to your approval.'

'I would be most grateful.' Amberley's eyes were on the coachman's ashen face. 'It's a bullet-wound. The doctor may wish to know.'

'I will see that he is informed of it, sir,' replied Lawson. He motioned the footmen to resume their burden. 'The yellow chamber – and you may undress him before summoning Mrs Reed.'

Amberley looked round at his valet. 'Go with them, Jim and give what help you can. I shan't need you.'

Saunders, his professional and artistic soul in torment over the picture his master presented, would dearly have

30

loved to voice his disagreement with this statement but he knew better than to attempt it. With a small, wooden bow which he hoped conveyed some small part of his disapproval, he followed in the wake of Thomas and Claud.

A gleam of humour flickered in his Lordship's eyes but his mind was occupied by matters a good deal more important than the state of his dress and he turned back to the butler, saying rapidly, 'I am afraid that I shall have to impose on your mistress's hospitality at least until I hear what the doctor has to say – but after that I shall naturally remove myself to the nearest inn. Meanwhile, perhaps my groom could take my horses to your stables? They will need rubbing down if they are not to take cold.'

Lawson bowed but, before he could answer, the Marquis added one final request, palpably an after-thought. 'Ah yes – and while your man is out fetching the doctor, it might be possible for him to deliver a message to either the parish constable or the magistrate. My coachman was shot when we were set upon by two highwaymen. One of them made good his escape but the other is lying on the road about a mile south of your gates. He ought, I imagine, to be removed.'

'Is he dead?' a musical and undoubtedly feminine voice enquired interestedly from behind him.

'He is most certainly dead,' responded Amberley, swinging round to face the speaker. 'I am afraid that I . . .' And there he stopped, his breath deserting him with an impact that was almost physical.

She stood at the foot of the stairs, gowned in amber silk and cream lace, one small hand resting lightly on the carved newel. She was the most beautiful creature that he had ever seen. Softly gleaming hair, black as night, rippled back from a smooth, white brow and left tiny, curling tendrils around a heart-shaped face of ineffable

31

sweetness. Eyes, heavily fringed with sweeping lashes and so dark that he knew not if they were blue or black, gazed steadily at him from beneath narrow, winging brows while a faintly teasing smile tugged at soft curves of her mouth.

'Yes?' she prompted. 'You are afraid that . . ?'

'That I shot him,' replied the Marquis mechanically. He was aware that he was staring at her like a doltish schoolboy but there seemed to be every excuse. Then, collecting his scattered wits, he smiled and made her a deeply elegant bow. 'I am very grateful for your kindness to my servant. Without it I fear he may well have died.'

'It is nothing,' she said pleasantly. Strangely, she did not curtsey in response to his bow but started to cross the hall, her walk slow and infinitely graceful. 'We are pleased to be able to help.'

The butler moved to open the doors in front of her and then stepped back to let her pass.

'Thank you.' She paused, half-turning towards Amberley. 'Do come in to the fire, sir. They tell me that it has begun to snow and you must be quite frozen.'

The Marquis was suddenly acutely conscious of what five minutes ago had bothered him not at all. His hair was wet and windswept, his coat creased and bloodstained and his cravat upstairs with Chard. A faint flush stained his cheeks and he hesitated, casting a glance of comic appeal at the butler.

It went unanswered. Lawson merely bowed and ushered him into the uncompromising light of the parlour, leaving his Lordship feeling quite un-accustomedly foolish as the doors closed softly behind him.

Chapter Three

'Please sit down and get warm,' the girl invited as she moved away across the room. Her fingers trailed lightly along the back of a gessoed sofa and she came to rest beside a handsome sideboard upon which stood a decanter and glasses. 'Will you have some claret? At least, I *think* it's claret – though it seems only fair to warn you that it may be burgundy.' She gave a little gurgle of laughter. 'Are you prepared to take your chances, sir?'

An answering gleam leapt to Lord Amberley's eye. 'Only provided that you, madam, are prepared to assure me that there is no possibility of it being ratafia.'

Again that deliciously husky laugh. 'You have my word on it,' she replied, unstopping the decanter and carefully filling a glass. 'Lawson would die sooner than permit such an atrocity.'

'Quite right,' approved the Marquis. 'I knew he must be a man of no little discernment.'

She turned and one dark brow lifted mischievously as she held out the glass. 'Naturally. He let you in, didn't he?'

It was his Lordship's turn to laugh. 'True,' he said, crossing to her side. 'I must apologise for my disreputable appearance and confess that I feel lamentably out of place.'

Her smile was replaced by a look of doubt. 'I'm sorry?'

The Marquis felt vaguely baffled. Her composure was

33

remarkable, her manner refreshingly natural and she seemed anything but a fool – so why did she affect not to understand his meaning?

'Well, it's true that I'm not exactly dripping on your carpet,' he said lightly, 'but Chard's bullet-hole and a short spell on the box of my chaise have done little to improve the elegance of my coat.'

'*You* drove your coach here?' she asked blankly.

'Yes.' Her eyes, he noticed, were neither blue nor black but actually an exquisite shade that he could only describe as violet.

They widened suddenly and, instead of handing him the glass, she set it down again with a little snap. 'And you are wet! Oh, I *do* beg your pardon – you must be desperately wishing to change. Lawson should have told me.'

She sounded mortified and Amberley, who was beginning to feel as though some vital point had eluded him, said weakly, 'It is really of very little moment, I assure you – merely that I am not fit to grace your parlour.'

Something must have given him away for he heard a tiny sound as the breath caught in her throat and then she said quickly, 'I'm sorry. You see, I so rarely meet people who don't know that I tend to forget . . .' She stopped, but only for a second. 'If your appearance has caused you embarrassment on my account, you may disregard it. I am blind.'

The Marquis experienced an unpleasant lurching sensation in the pit of his stomach and a dozen muddled thoughts jostled through his brain; that it was a tragedy in someone so lovely; that her words suggested an isolation that was little short of criminal, and that, for all her careless tone, it must have been damnably hard for her to tell him.

For a second he stared at her helplessly, instinct

34

warning that his first words were critical. Then, with a hard-won indifference, he said, 'Are you? I'm sorry. It is by no means apparent.'

The suggestion of tension left her shoulders and she gave a tiny shrug. 'Practice – though, of course, it only works here where I know every piece of furniture intimately.' She stretched out her hand, felt delicately for the glass and held it out to him again. 'Please drink your wine and I will have Lawson see your luggage is taken upstairs so that you can get out of those wet things.' She smiled suddenly. 'You can't possibly go to the Pheasant, you know. Lawson will tell you that the food is dreadful and they water the brandy. You'll be much more comfortable here – and I expect you will wish to look in on your coachman later.'

Amberley found himself smiling in response and then trying to come to terms with the fact that she could not see him. 'It is extremely generous of you – and if you are quite certain that it will give no trouble, I shall be pleased to stay.'

'No trouble – indeed, you will be doing me a favour for I rarely have company,' she informed him with cheerful unconcern. 'Will dinner in an hour suit you?'

'Well, that depends,' replied his Lordship, the laughter back in his voice.

'Upon what?'

'Upon whether I can set aside my scruples and dine with a lady to whom I have not been introduced.'

A dimple peeped roguishly beside her mouth. 'A difficult problem, sir.'

'But not, I hope, insurmountable,' replied Amberley gallantly. And then, openly coaxing, 'Madam, I am very hungry!'

Her lips parted on a ripple of laughter and then she swept him a magnificent curtsy. 'Very well, sir. I beg leave to present Mistress Rosalind Vernon of Oakleigh Manor.'

Setting down the glass, his Lordship took her hand in his

and, bowing very low, raised it to his lips. 'Mistress Vernon – the Marquis of Amberley is delighted to make your acquaintance and entirely at your service.'

She flushed a little but said teasingly, 'My goodness – are you really a Marquis? I had no idea I was in such exalted company!'

'I expect that's because I was very badly brought up,' he apologised untruthfully. And then, his tone utterly commonplace, 'I wonder what I have said to put you out of countenance?'

The flush deepened. 'Why nothing. It's just . . . do gentlemen usually kiss ladies' hands? I don't know, you see.'

Just for an instant, an emotion not unlike anger held Amberley in its grip. Then he said regretfully, 'I'm afraid I can't speak for gentlemen – but Marquis do it all the time.'

Rosalind was seated at her dressing-table, striving to conquer a childish desire to change her gown again when Mrs Reed, otherwise known to the household as Nurse, bustled into the room with the news that the doctor's gig had that minute arrived at the door. 'And though I've made all ready for him, I can't stay above a minute for I daresay he'll be needing me.'

A tiny smile touched Rosalind's mouth. 'Then perhaps you shouldn't have left the sickroom?' she suggested innocently.

'Oh yes, I should!' averred Mrs Reed grimly. 'Mr Lawson says you've asked this so-called Marquis to stay and *that* I'll admit you couldn't well avoid. But whatever was you about, Miss Rosalind, to ask him to dine with you?'

Miss Rosalind yielded to the promptings of her particular devil. 'Well, he said he was hungry, you know – and so am I, come to that. On the other hand,' she continued dubiously, 'he also told me he'd been badly brought up. Do you think that means he eats peas with a knife?'

Mrs Reed snorted. 'No, I do not and neither do you – so give over with your play-acting! What worries me is that you didn't ought to dine unchaperoned with *any* man – let alone that brass-faced gypsy as says he's a lord!'

This description proved too much for Rosalind's gravity. 'Oh *Nurse*! How unkind – and when you haven't even seen him!'

'Well I have,' replied Mrs Reed, not without satisfaction. 'He came up to see how his coachman did – and a fine sight he looked too, with his neckcloth gone and his good coat ruined! That valet of his – who's got more sense than you'd expect – was downright ashamed of him. And all his precious Lordship could do was laugh. Not that he laughed when he saw the state of that poor man's shoulder,' she admitted grudgingly. 'Seemed quite upset for a minute – but that was the only proper feeling he showed, mark you!'

Rosalind toyed idly with a carved tortoiseshell comb. 'How old is he?'

'Turned thirty at least,' sniffed her mentor. 'Old enough to know better than think he can get round *me* with a saucy smile and a hug.'

'He didn't!' breathed Rosalind, awe-struck. 'That *was* brave of him.'

Pleased but unwilling to show it, Mrs Reed ignored this piece of provocation and said coaxingly, 'Be a good girl and eat your dinner up here.'

Rosalind stood up, smiling oddly. 'I'm not a girl. I'm twenty-two years old, and well and truly on the shelf so I don't need a chaperone,' she announced with characteristic candour but no hint of bitterness. 'And that being so, I intend to dine downstairs with Lord Amberley.'

Mrs Reed followed her to the door, torn between her duty to her patient and anxiety for her nurseling. 'You may be two-and-twenty but you've no more idea than a week-old kitten when it comes to the snares of the ungodly.'

Rosalind chuckled. 'And you think that the Marquis is one of them?'

'Mark my words,' came the dark reply. 'He's a philanderer. I know the signs.'

'Do you?' asked Rosalind, impressed. 'I wish I dared ask you what they are – and, better still, how it is you know them. Indeed, Nurse – I am surprised at you. I never realised that you were a Woman with a Past!'

Watching her float serenely down the stairs, Mrs Reed contemplated with mixed feelings the knowledge that the light of her life was possessed of a new glow. As if someone had lit a candle in her, she thought. And then, swallowing savagely, 'And if it's you, you honey-tongued Lordship, you'd better not do anything to put it out again – because if you cause my lamb even a minute's upset, I'll cut out your black heart and fry it!'

When the Marquis entered the room to which Lawson had directed him, it was to find his hostess ensconced beside the fire, patiently awaiting him and never, he thought, could a jewel have been placed in so appropriate a setting. For a moment he remained where he was, words of apology for his tardiness forgotten, as he breathed in the scent of pot-pourri and simply stared.

The room bore every appearance of having been specially furnished to form a bower for her. The walls were hung with amber brocade only a shade lighter than her gown and the colour was echoed in the richly textured carpet where it was interwoven with tones of amethyst and violet. Curtains of violet damask were closed across windows flanked on one side by an ebony escritoire and on the other by a delicately inlaid harpsichord; there were shelves full of books; a frame holding a half-worked tapestry and a large, gilt cage housing a brightly-coloured but decidedly sulky-looking parrot; a group of seventeenth-century miniatures were hung over a lacquered cabinet containing a collection of Chelsea figurines and from above the mantel, a dark-haired child laughed down from her frame with a vividness that was almost uncanny.

His Lordship's gaze travelled from the painted face to the one of flesh and bone seated below it and was startled to find that it was turned in his direction and alight with teasing amusement.

'Well, sir – do you like my room?' she asked.

For an instant, the resemblance between child and woman was so strong that the Marquis was stunned into silence. Then he said simply, 'It's charming. And it suits you,' before realisation dawned and he smiled ruefully. 'I'm sorry. You knew I was there, of course.'

'Yes.' Mercifully, she did not seem offended and was even half-laughing. 'I heard you cross the hall – and no one in this house wears heeled shoes. But let me guess . . . you were comparing me with myself – and finding me lacking, I should think.'

'Yes and no – in that order,' he replied, as he strolled across the room to her side. Suddenly everything became crystal clear and the doubts which had beset him upstairs vanished. In any other woman her remark would have been an open invitation to a compliment of a flirtation but in Mistress Vernon it was neither. Her tone was one of prosaic amusement but her words, whether she realised it or not, and he rather thought that she didn't, were a sort of test. An odd gleam lurked in his grey-green eyes and he went on deliberately, 'You may not be able to see your face but you must surely have been told how beautiful it is.'

The blood rose swiftly beneath her skin and he heard her catch her breath.

'Well? Am I not right?'

'Yes.' Her face grew pensive. 'And so, I suppose, was Nurse. But indeed I did not mean . . . to . . .'

'I know.' But you did think I'd skirt round your blindness, didn't you? was his instinctive thought. 'I gather that Nurse is the redoubtable dame I encountered above stairs?'

'Yes.' The dimple peeped and was gone. 'She says you are a philanderer.'

There was a brief, incredulous pause and then his Lordship gave way to appreciative laughter.

'*Merci du compliment*! That *has* given me my own again, hasn't it?'

'I thought so,' agreed Rosalind sweetly.

Neither was aware of Lawson's presence in the doorway until he coughed discreetly.

'I am sorry to disturb you, Mistress Rosalind,' he said with an air of gentle reproof that accorded ill with the benevolence in his eyes, 'but dinner has been ready a full half hour and Mrs Thorne is becoming a trifle distraught over the beef.'

This intelligence was all that was needed to overset Rosalind's gravity.

'Oh dear! I . . . is she?'

Perceiving the need to intervene, the Marquis said pleasantly, 'My fault, I am afraid. I stopped to consult with the doctor and was rather late in coming down. Please convey my most sincere apologies to . . . Mrs Thorne, I think you said?'

'Certainly, my Lord.' Lawson bowed and withdrew, leaving them to follow.

Amberley took Rosalind's hand and laid it on his sleeve. 'That was handsome of me, wasn't it?' he remarked virtuously, leading her into the hall.

'No – merely truthful,' she retorted. 'You *were* shockingly late and, what is more, I would not be surprised if you used speaking to Dr Dench as a pretext for showing Nurse your fine velvet coat in an effort to improve your standing.'

His Lordship grinned. 'How did you guess? After all, I have my reputation to think of.'

'As a Marquis?'

'Not at all. As a philanderer.'

When they were seated in the green and gold dining parlour and the door had closed upon them, Rosalind said resignedly, 'I suppose I should have known that you had formed a partiality for Nurse when she told me that you had been hugging her.'

The Marquis drew a long sigh of relief and said fervently, 'As long as that is *all* she told you!'

'You mean there is more?' The violet eyes were wide with demure wonder slowly changing to liquid sympathy. 'But I doubt your case is hopeful, sir, I distinctly recall hearing her describe you as – as "a brass-faced gypsy as s-says he's a Lord!"'

His Lordship narrowly avoided choking on a mouthful of ham. 'But *that*,' he pointed out swiftly, 'was before she saw me dressed to kill. I'll warrant she's now prepared to admit that I am a Lord – though certainly brass-faced.'

Mistress Vernon laid down her knife and dissolved into laughter again.

'D-don't!' she begged unsteadily. 'Are you never serious?'

'Less often, perhaps, than I should be,' he admitted ruefully. 'Are you?'

'Me?' She gave a tiny crooked smile. 'More often than I should like.'

He sensed a wealth of things left unsaid and wondered why it should touch him; but their acquaintance was too

41

slight, and he was too wise to probe, so he passed it off by launching into an account of the accident that had brought him to her gates and finished by telling her what he had learned from the doctor. 'He says – and I believe him – that Chard should not be moved for at least a week. And although I hardly like to ask it of you . . .'

'Then don't,' interposed Rosalind decisively. 'There is no need, for he is most welcome to remain here. Indeed, I doubt that you could persuade Nurse to let him go for she dearly loves an invalid.'

'There – I *knew* I should have driven myself!' said the Marquis, vexed.

The soft mouth quivered. 'You could always develop a fever,' she suggested.

'If the doctor is to be believed, I may have to,' he replied. And this time the humorous tone held a hint of grimness.

'Oh?'

'It's snowing thick and fast,' he explained, a faint frown creasing his brow, 'and if it continues to do so you may find that it isn't only Chard who is forcibly quartered on you.'

'Oh,' said Rosalind again, but with a very different tone.

There was no mistaking the pleasure in that single syllable and the Marquis knew a crazy impulse to admit that his own first thought, after only ten minutes in her company, had been much the same. He repressed it, forcing himself to recognise the feeling that he had known her all his life for what it was – an illusion – and to remember that there were other considerations. A cautious man, he reflected wryly, would at this point remove himself to the inn while there was still some chance of doing so. But he was not cautious and, furthermore, to do so might well cut him off from Chard for some days and would undoubtedly put a stop to his unvoiced intention of allowing Saunders to get some rest by sitting with the coachman himself for a part of the night. And then, of course, the snow might stop after all.

At the heart of his Lordship's nature, and constituting a large part of his charm, lay a streak of recklessness and even now he could not wholly subdue it. While one part of him said, 'Careful, my friend. This one could take you out of your depth,' the other was saying 'Risk it.' Inclination leaned to the latter but he could not quite bring himself to follow it; and the sensation was unfamiliar.

Rosalind was also undergoing a novel experience – that of guarding her tongue. She wanted to urge him to stay, to confess that as far as she was concerned it might snow for a month; but a reservation entirely new to her warned that this was somehow wrong. So she contented herself with politely informing him that he would be welcome to remain should the need arise and then, when he did not reply, said quickly, 'But of course you cannot wish to do so and doubtless you are expected.'

Quick to catch the faint note of wistfulness, Amberley cursed himself for his silence and reached a decision. 'It's not that,' he said crisply. 'The truth is that I am becoming increasingly aware that I should not be here at all. What the devil are your family about to permit you to live alone in this fashion?'

The disapproval in his voice brought forth a characteristically literal reply. 'But I don't live alone. I have Lawson and Nurse and Nell, my maid and . . .' She appeared to lose interest, her right hand delicately exploring the various dishes in front of her, '. . . and so on. Your presence would appear to have put Mrs Thorne on her mettle. Is there a bowl of fruit amongst this lot?'

The Marquis placed it within her reach. 'That was

43

not what I meant and well you know it.' He watched, fascinated, as the graceful hands selected an apple and began skilfully to pare it. 'I was referring to the absence of a gentleman to protect and a lady to chaperone you.'

'I have no need of either. I rarely go beyond the grounds and within them Lawson heads a team of protection which would probably astonish you. And since the only man who calls here is the rector, a chaperone would find life very dull.' She laid a coil of peel on her plate and began carefully to slice the fruit into quarters. 'I live very quietly, you know.'

'I don't – but I am beginning to do so,' said his Lordship, a green spark lighting his eyes. 'Are you telling me you have no family?'

'Only my brother,' she replied, puzzled and a little wary. 'You seem a trifle put out, sir.'

'I believe that I am,' he said slowly. 'Or at least, I anticipate the possibility.'

A shuttered look came into the beautiful face and she stood up abruptly. 'And I believe that *I* can guess why.'

'I doubt it,' said Amberley, lazily watchful.

'You are about to start feeling sorry for me,' she challenged, half scornful, half disappointed.

'Hardly,' came the cool reply. 'Why should I?'

'Because I am blind.' It was out before she realised it.

'So?' His tone was flippant but his eyes showed the cost of it. 'It would take more than that, my dear. And I can't conceive what possible use sympathy would be to you – or why you should expect it.'

'I don't expect it!' she snapped, her eyes darkening wrathfully. 'No, nor want it either – but save for embarrassment, it's the only puling emotion I seem able to inspire!'

Lithe as a cat, he was out of his seat and at her side, laughing. 'Not so, Mistress Vernon, not so! I know of at least one other.' And then one hand was round her waist and the other beneath her chin as he dropped a brief kiss on her parted lips.

'*Oh!*' Blushing hotly, Rosalind thrust him away, 'You . . . you . . .'

'Brass-faced gypsy?' obliged the Marquis, his voice brimming with gay mockery. 'Now you can go and tell Nurse how right she really was. But just one thing, my dear; you may call me a hypocrite if you choose or accuse me of taking unfair advantage of your situation – but what you may *not* do is to assume that I regard you as an object of pity because you can't see. If I feel any sympathy for you at all – and as yet I'm not sure that I do – it's because you appear to be living the life of a recluse.' He paused and then said casually, 'It seems to me to be a waste – but for all I know you may be an anchorite by choice. Or you may simply be a coward.'

Words of blistering denial hovered on Rosalind's tongue and the Marquis waited hopefully. Then an arrested expression crept into her eyes; she hesitated, tilting her head consideringly, and finally, incredibly, the dimple quivered into being. 'Do you find quarrelling quicker than question and answer – or are you merely possessed of a tortuous, not to say unscrupulous, mind?'

'Neither.' If he was surprised, it did not show.

'But you *were* hoping for an orgy of self-justification?'

'Something like that, perhaps. Am I doomed to disappointment?'

'You certainly deserve to be,' she said severely. 'And worse.'

He gave a rueful laugh. 'I know it – and beg your pardon. But the truth is that I thought I had a point to make.'

One dark brow lifted in sardonic amusement. 'It is seen. And one, moreover, that words could not make for you?'

Already uneasily aware that save for her own good sense, his careless impulse might have wrought unintentional harm, Lord Amberley hesitated before replying truthfully, 'They might have done so – but I'll admit to having an uncommonly low resistance to temptation.'

Irony vanished and a rippling laugh issued from the slender throat. 'You are shameless, sir!'

'Indeed, I fear it – but not, I hope, unforgivable? You have my word that it shall not happen again.'

And despite the now-familiar note of levity, Rosalind knew instinctively that this, at least, he meant. She held out her hand and felt him take it in a cool, friendly clasp. 'You have no need to promise. I know that it will not,' she said simply. And smiled.

Behind his silver-brocaded vest, a number of strange sensations took place and unconsciously the Marquis's fingers tightened on hers. Then, pulling himself together, he laid her hand on his arm and said lightly, 'I hope you don't intend to leave me here in solitary state with my port.'

She shook her head. 'To tell the truth, I had quite forgotten that I should. And besides – you asked for a chaperone and I am determined that you shall have one.'

'Oh?' He smiled down into the flower-like face as they moved out into the hall and back towards her parlour. 'And who is it to be?'

Again that wicked laugh. 'Wait and see.'

One glance was sufficient to inform the Marquis that the room was empty but Mistress Vernon was plainly waiting for him so he closed the door and allowed himself to be led over to the gilt cage.

'My Lord Marquis – pray allow me to present my most jealous guardian,' she said demurely. 'His name is Broody.'

My Lord Marquis examined the bird with interest. 'I had a feeling that it might be,' he responded gently. And then, to the parrot, 'How do you do, sir?'

Broody eyed him with marked disfavour and sat on one foot.

'I don't think he likes me,' observed Amberley plaintively.

'Well, that is nothing new,' replied Rosalind. 'I should be amazed if he did.'

'I thank you!'

She laughed. 'Don't be absurd! What I meant was that he doesn't like anyone – except possibly me. Thomas and Claud won't touch his cage if he is in it because he bites them and when the maids come into this room to clean it, he swears at them.'

The Marquis uttered a little choking sound. 'Does he indeed? And who taught him to do that?'

'If you mean was it me – the answer is no,' she chuckled. 'My brother bought him from a sailor and was sadly confounded when he heard the extent of his vocabulary. Indeed, he was only persuaded to let me keep him on the strength of my most solemn promise never to use any of the words myself. Not that I could, of course, because I don't understand half of them.' And on this faintly regretful note, she turned back to the cage. 'Come Broody – say hello to our visitor.'

Broody stared unwinkingly back at the Marquis, apparently reviewing his repertoire. Then, in accents of pure disgust, he said, 'Scabby pirate!' before turning a disdainful back on his mistress's improper laughter.

'Well, that disposes of me, doesn't it?' grinned the Marquis. 'But I suppose I should be grateful it wasn't worse.'

'Very grateful!' Rosalind sank weakly on to a sofa. 'You should hear some of the things he calls Philip!'

His Lordship seated himself opposite her. 'Philip is your brother?'

She nodded.

'Then since he is reponsible for endowing you with

that unsociable bird, I withold all sympathy,' he said firmly. 'Mr Vernon is well-served.'

'You are out, sir,' she told him, lifting her chin with would-be haughtiness. 'My brother is not *Mr* Vernon but Captain Lord Philip – late of his Majesty's army.'

Amberley accepted the rebuke stoically. 'I beg his Lordship's pardon. I take it that by "late" you mean he has recently sold out?'

'Yes. He was forced to do so when my uncle died last year.'

'Your uncle? Not your father?'

'No. Papa died when we were children and Mama had not the least notion of how to manage without him so her brother became a sort of trustee until Philip came of age. Only by then Phil was army-mad so, of course, Uncle Rowland had to let him enlist while he himself continued to look after our affairs.' The expressive face clouded. 'He was very good to us. I miss him.'

'I am sorry,' said Amberley lightly. 'But now your brother has quit the army to assume his responsibilities he will doubtless spend a good deal of his time here with you.'

'Yes.' Her voice was dubious. 'He will certainly do so during the summer months but he may prefer to winter at the London house.'

'Is that where he is now?'

'Yes. He is enjoying his first real taste of society and furthering his acquaintance with Mistress Dacre.'

The grey-green eyes flew suddenly wide. 'Mistress Dacre? Viscount Linton's daughter?'

'Why, yes. Do you know her?'

'Not at all.' His Lordship's voice held a strangely desperate note. 'Your brother is not, by any chance, the gentleman promised to wed Mistress Dacre, is he?'

'Yes. How did you know?' she asked baffled. And then, brightening, 'Can it be that you have met Philip?'

48

'Oh Lord!' gasped the Marquis, dropping his head into his hands. 'I am afraid . . . I am very much afraid that I have. Unfortunately.'

And he dissolved into helpless sobbing laughter.

Chapter Four

Rosalind awoke to a sense of drowsy well-being, so pleasant that it seemed unnecessary to locate its source, and for a few minutes she lay relaxed in that limbo between slumber and wakefulness, savouring the moment's nameless content. Then it shifted and gradually, with her growing consciousness, changed into a sharp-edged, tingling awareness so that she sat up, suddenly alert, as she recognised its cause.

Excitement rippled through her veins and set the nerves vibrating beneath her skin, producing a tiny shiver of mingled fear and delight. A part of her that had not stirred for a very long time stretched its clamped muscles and began to wake, luring her from the safe harbour of her cultivated, hard-won tranquillity and setting her adrift in the alien, almost forgotten, seas of hope and doubt. Painfully, like one rousing from a state of prolonged catalepsy, she investigated each new sensation and greeted it with apprehensive pleasure until she found again the things so long mislaid; the bitter-sweet joys of youth and anticipation.

A bubble of happiness welled up and she clasped her arms around her knees as if to hug it close. Against all expectation, she had found a sort of kindred spirit whose mind ran with hers in laughter and companionship, and who, effortlessly as breathing, had taught her that if she wished him to forget her handicap, she must first forget it herself.

It was strange. For twelve years she had been surrounded with a wall of protective consideration that never alluded to her blindness. She had been loved, cherished and guarded with well-intentioned sympathy, shielded from every unkind wind and word; yet, despite all the devotion lavished upon her, she suddenly realised that she had never before had the feeling that someone truly understood. Never, that is, until last night.

It was suddenly impossible to be still and she reached out an impatient hand for the small silver clock that stood beside her bed. Flicking open the glass, her fingers told her that it was twenty minutes after seven; still early then, but not as early as the midnight-like stillness had led her to suppose.

Charged with compulsive energy, Rosalind slid out of bed, dragged a taffeta robe over her night-robe and pulled the bell for her maid.

Nell found her mistress eager to dress, determined to breakfast downstairs and in a mood that was by turn fussy and distrait. All three were unusual but Nell was not surprised by any of them. She had caught only a fleeting glimpse of the Marquis but it was her opinion that if his ways only half matched his looks, no girl could be blamed for losing her head a little. It was just a pity, Nell had confided to Mrs Thorne, that Miss Rose could not see him for herself. 'And him so fine in black velvet all silver-laced with his hair shining like the best gilt plate. And what's more, if you ask me that one's a proper man – none of your dandified beaus. He's handsome and elegant alright – but he's got a way of moving that makes you think of them big cats they have in menageries; sort of lazy and dangerous.'

Had she but known it, Rosalind had not yet spared a single thought for his Lordship's attractions or lack of them – had not even wondered what he looked like. There seemed no need. She knew the timbre of his voice and the light, cool clasp of his fingers on hers; and that, oddly, was enough.

'Nell – is it still snowing?' she asked urgently.

Nell grinned. 'Yes, Miss Rose. Has been all night by the look of it. And it's drifted too. You can't hardly see the front steps.'

Rosalind drew a long breath, tried hard not to feel quite so pleased and failed. A faint flush stained her cheeks and her eyes held a curious gleam. Nell surveyed her benevolently, thinking that, blind or not, it was only right and proper that anyone as pretty as her mistress should have a beau.

In fact, far from planning to enslave the Marquis, Rosalind was busily hatching dark schemes to make him explain precisely what had been so hilarious about his meeting with her brother. Naturally, she had asked him last night – when he had finally stopped laughing sufficiently for her to make herself heard – but he had steadfastly refused to tell her. Breathless and sobbing faintly, he had simply said that he doubted if she would appreciate the jest. And when she had threatened to ask Philip, his Lordship had merely dissolved afresh and managed to indicate that he doubted Philip would appreciate it either. It was all extremely provoking.

She sat down on the end of the bed and curled her feet up beneath her. 'What shall I wear today, Nell?'

The maid threw open the clothes-press and began to enumerate on its contents.

'There's the yellow cambric.'

'No. I wore amber last night and it's too similar. I want to look different.'

'The pink dimity then?'

'Too simple. I always think that it probably makes me look like a milkmaid.'

Nell laughed. 'Well, what about the 'broidered muslin?'

Rosalind thought for a moment, then shook her head regretfully. 'It's too thin. I'll freeze to death.'

The maid chewed one finger-nail and looked frowningly along the rack. Then her face brightened and she pounced. 'That's the one! You've never worn it and it would be a terrible shame to waste it on the rector.' And to herself she added, 'And if you don't knock his Lordship's eyes out in this, he ain't the man I take him for!'

While Rosalind thought she was making an early start to the day, the Marquis had made an even earlier one. Roused by a reluctant Saunders at four in the morning, he had dozed fitfully in a chair at Chard's bedside until just before six when the wounded man had woken in a state of high fever. For the next hour his Lordship was kept very busy indeed but since, like any other healthy young man, he knew very little of illness and what to expect, he soon became extremely harrassed. He managed, not without difficulty, to tip a measure of the doctor's potion down Chard's throat but when even this failed to make any notable improvement he felt somewhat at a loss and knew a rueful desire to admit defeat and call his valet. And then the door opened and Mrs Reed made a timely entrance.

'Oh, thank God!' said the Marquis devoutly. 'He's become acutely feverish and I'm damned if I know what the devil to do to relieve him.'

'Well, sir, you can begin by moderating your language,' replied Nurse tartly, in much the tone of one addressing a nine-year-old. 'And what you're doing here when you should be in your bed, I just don't know. Gentlemen don't belong in a sick-room at any time and as for you trying to nurse your coachman – well, it's neither right nor proper and so I tell you!'

Laughter stirred remotely in the grey-green eyes. 'Chard has been in my service for a long time,' he explained meekly. 'And I thought it only fair to let my valet rest for a few hours.'

'That's all very well, sir. But what you *should* have done was to have him call me.'

It was with a good deal of difficulty that Lord Amberley refrained from replying that he was not that brass-faced. Instead, he gave his singularly charming smile and said, 'Well I own that I would like to have done so – and that it would undoubtedly have been better for Chard – but having put you all to so much trouble already, I was loath to inconvenience you further.'

Mrs Reed thawed a little. 'As to that, my Lord, it's no trouble at all. And far better to have called me than to come yourself – and you with no more idea of what to do than Miss Rosalind's parrot.'

The Marquis noted with due apreciation that he had finally been accorded his rank and filed the rest for future use. 'Very true. And I own that I was never more glad to see anyone in my life.'

She cast an expert eye over the restless coachman and nodded decisively. 'Well, now you can go away and leave him to me, my Lord. This is no more than I expected and I know just what will quiet him so there's no need for you to worry. And I don't need you – indeed, you'll be no more use than ornament, if you'll pardon me saying so. Besides,' she eyed him critically, 'you'll be wanting to shave, I'll be bound.'

A shave was indeed Lord Amberley's most pressing requirement and, after that, a change of clothes, his sojourn in Chard's room having left him feeling distinctly crumpled. He accomplished both in record time, and without the aid of his valet, then went briskly downstairs to discover what chance there was of travelling at least as far as the inn.

One glance through the window was sufficient to dissuade him from opening the door and going out. The wind was driving the snow hard against the house and

54

the drift was already some four feet in depth. The Marquis cursed softly and turned round to meet Lawson's impassive regard. 'Have you any idea how bad conditions are likely to be on the road?' he asked crisply.

The butler bowed. 'My Lord, I sent a groom out an hour ago to discover it and he is of the opinion that no coach could travel as much as half a mile in safety and that the road to Hadham Cross is almost certainly impassable.'

Lord Amberley folded his arms and raised one quizzical brow. 'And what is *your* opinion?'

'That he is right, my Lord.'

'I see. So we are snowbound and I am stuck here indefinitely. Doesn't that worry you, Lawson?'

Lawson's stolidity did not waver by so much as a hair's breadth. 'No, my Lord.'

'Then it should.' His Lordship abandoned subtlety and faced the butler with a hint of grimness. 'In the absence of her brother, it is up to you to protect both Mistress Vernon's good name and her peace of mind. For aught you know I might be capable of either rape or seduction.'

'Yes, my Lord.'

'Devil take it, man – is that all you can say?'

A dry smile touched Lawson's mouth. 'No, my Lord. It is not. Have I your Lordship's permission to be quite frank?'

'Please do,' invited the Marquis sardonically. 'I should be glad of it.'

'Thank you, my Lord.' He bowed. 'The case is quite simple, sir. If I believed you in any way likely to cause distress to Mistress Rosalind, I should naturally contrive your speedy departure – no matter what the weather. As it is, I am satisfied that your Lordship's honour is to be relied upon.'

The Marquis bowed ironically. 'I thank you.'

'Not at all, sir,' demurred Lawson politely. 'Should you give me reason to revise my opinion, I shall have no compunction in ejecting you from the premises forthwith. Even, if necessary, by force.'

His Lordship grinned suddenly. 'Oh you think you could, do you?'

'Yes, my Lord,' came the placid reply. 'Though not, perhaps, without calling for reinforcements.'

'Allow me to tell you that there is no perhaps about it!' retorted the Marquis, amused. 'Very well. I'll admit that your mistress is safe with me but the mere fact of my presence here is enough to compromise her and I've no mind to it.'

'My Lord, what is not known can do no harm. That which keeps you here will keep others away and there is no one in this house who will gossip. We are all too much devoted to Mistress Rosalind's interests.' Lawson hesitated as though debating the wisdom of his next words and then said carefully, 'And in truth, sir, I would be pleased to see you stay.'

'Would you indeed!' The Marquis was a little startled. 'Why?'

'Because I like to hear Mistress Rose laugh,' said the butler simply, 'and I had forgotten how long it is since she last did so. Not,' he added quickly, 'that she is ever anything but cheerful, you understand, sir – far from it. But seeing her last night I suddenly realised that for all her smiles and teasing, there has been something missing.'

'And you think that I can supply it?' His Lordship's tone was faintly sceptical.

'My Lord, I *know* that you can for I have seen you do it.'

The elegant shoulders lifted in a tiny, careless shrug. 'What you have seen is no more than simple companionship.'

Lawson permitted himself a small smile. 'Yes, my Lord. Just so.' For a moment he looked steadily into the light, frowning gaze and then, with a slight bow, turned away.

'Good morning, my Lord,' said Rosalind from the curve of the stair. 'You are very early. I had expected to be before you.'

The Marquis flashed a quizzical glance at Lawson, then turned to confront a vision in cornflower quilted taffeta. And he smiled because, he thought, it wasn't possible to do anything else.

'Shall I apologise?' he asked, strolling across the hall and taking the hand she offered him. 'Or shall I simply plead the excuse of inspecting the weather?'

She smiled. 'Neither. Just tell me if it's true that the snow has covered the steps.'

'Quite true.'

'So the road may well be blocked?'

'That is a distinct possibility,' responded his Lordship unhelpfully.

'And a journey out of the question?'

'A long one, certainly.'

'A short one too, I should think.'

'That, Mistress Vernon, would depend on the skill of the driver.'

The dimple quivered and was gone. 'You are trying to provoke me, sir.'

'*I*, madam?' Somewhere in the affronted tone was a hint of the mischief dancing in his eyes. 'Surely not!'

'And now,' she said sternly, 'you are laughing and that is worse.'

He shook his head. 'I am maligned.'

'Are you so?' The violet eyes gleamed a challenge. 'Then no doubt you will be content to prove it?'

The Marquis swept a flourishing bow and laid one hand over his heart. 'In any way you care to choose,' he announced dramatically. 'You have but to name it!'

'Then I shall do so. It is a very small thing,' she said in a dulcet tone. 'You may tell me – without further prevarication – whether you consider it safe to travel *at all* today.'

'*Eh bien.*' He shrugged resignedly. 'No, Mistress Vernon. I do *not* consider it safe to travel today.'

She was suddenly radiant. 'Then you will stay?'

My Lord bowed low over her hand and raised it to his lips. 'Please. If I may?'

During the course of the morning Rosalind made three separate attempts to lure his Lordship into disclosing the nature of his acquaintance with her brother. The first two he skilfully evaded and the third he met with open amusement.

'Not again, Mistress Persistence! Why does it fascinate you so?'

'Because you won't tell me,' came the truthful reply. And then, severely, 'And if you weren't prepared to explain, you shouldn't have aroused my curiosity by laughing like that!'

The Marquis grinned. 'That is indisputably true. Very well, child – but I'll warrant that you will be disappointed. I have met your brother just once and that was last Wednesday. The encounter was not what you might call fortuitous and I rather fear that Lord Philip may have taken a dislike to me.'

Rosalind folded her hands and nodded wisely. 'You mean that Phil's particular demon prompted him to jump to conclusions and yours prompted you to let him?'

His Lordship gave a choke of startled laughter. 'Very shrewd! Though I would rather say that circumstances conspired against us.'

'And what do you think that Philip would say?'

The Marquis collapsed neatly into a chair. 'That I am an adventurer in search of a fortune. He thinks . . .'

58

'Yes?'

'That I'm more than half-way to the debtor's ward at Newgate,' he finished flippantly.

'My goodness! And why should he think that?' asked Rosalind, seizing an apparent advantage.

'Oh no, my dear! It's a nice try but you'll draw no more from me,' he said pleasantly. 'The rest of the story is neither mine nor Lord Philip's and I've no taste for idle gossip. Instead, you may tell me if you are acquainted with Mistress Dacre and her family.'

Rosalind gave a tiny sigh, then capitulated with a good grace. 'No. She's never been here and I, of course, have never been to London. I had hoped that Phil would bring her with him when he came at Christmas – but I suppose it would not have been proper. And, as things turned out, it would probably have been a good deal more bother than it was worth because Philip was only able to stay three days himself.'

The grey-green eyes narrowed and grew suddenly hard but the Marquis's voice remained levelly conversational as he said, 'Do I detect an element of doubt over this betrothal?'

'Just a little,' she admitted ruefully. "You see, it was arranged between Viscount Linton and my uncle and I don't think Phil really knows Mistress Dacre very well. I daresay it's foolish of me, but I would have preferred him to make a . . . a less *bloodless* alliance and the very nature of this one makes me wonder if Mistress Dacre isn't bloodless too. All Phil will say is that she is quietly-behaved and pretty – which could mean practically anything.'

Lord Amberley kept to himself the inevitable reflection that, since Lord Linton's finances were well-known to be at a perpetually low ebb, his daughter might conceivably believe it her duty to accept any offer from a respectably wealthy quarter; it was unlikely, he thought wryly, that

Rosalind would find this information comforting and he could scarcely ask outright if Philip was rich enough to qualify. Instead he said mildly, 'I appreciate your misgivings but such marriages are the custom, you know.'

'That's all very well,' she objected, 'but would *you* do it?'

His Lordship smiled and yielded to temptation. 'How do you know that I haven't?'

The violet eyes opened very wide. 'I don't. I must say that it never occurred to me. *Have* you?'

'Have I what? Made a marriage of convenience – or any marriage at all?'

'Both.'

He laughed. 'No. And the full truth is that Lord Philip's way would not be mine.'

'Nor mine either,' she replied thoughtfully. 'Not, of course, that it is at all likely to be asked of me.'

'Why not?' asked Amberley, deceptively casual. 'Or will your brother permit you to make your own choice?'

Rosalind appeared faintly surprised. 'Well I daresay he might, but, since it is doubtful that the question will arise, we've never spoken of it.' She smiled and went on with reproving dryness, 'You can't have considered, sir. Away from this house I should have to be constantly accompanied and watched – a thing which I would dislike quite as much as the person whose duty it was. That makes me something of a liability and I can't imagine any man in full possession of his faculties desiring such a poor bargain. As for the remote possibility of some gallant gentleman becoming so besotted that he would be willing to put up with the inconvenience – I'm unlikely ever to meet him.'

The stark truth of this succinct and dispassionately-stated evaluation seemed unanswerable and for a moment the Marquis stared silently across at her, his mouth grim. Then he said curtly, 'Have you never been away from here?'

'Not since . . .' She stopped abruptly and began again. 'Not for a long time. After Papa died, we stayed at my uncle's home in Surrey for a while to make it easier for Mama to accustom herself.' She paused and when she spoke again her voice held a hint of strain. 'That was when I was nine – the year the portrait was painted.'

His Lordship raised his eyes to encompass the vital, glowing face in the frame and made a sudden discovery, so obvious that he could not understand why he had not realised it before. The child in the picture could see. He looked sharply back at Rosalind and said lightly, 'And then you came back here?'.

'Yes.' The word had a curious flatness.

But by then you were blind. He knew it as surely as if he had been told. What he did not know was *how*; but that must wait, for she was clearly not ready to talk of it – yet. 'And your mother?' he asked gently.

Rosalind's hands lay tightly gripped in her lap but her voice was still perfectly controlled. 'She died when I was sixteen. Phil was twenty and already in the army so Uncle Rowland continued to administer the land and I took over the running of the house. That was six years ago.' She managed a tight little smile. 'And from that quite unnecessary piece of information, you will have gathered that I'm all of twenty-two years old.'

The effort behind that smile brought an unfamiliar ache to his Lordship's throat and for a moment the urge to take her hands was almost overwhelming. But holding him back was the knowledge that, to her, this emotion he could not name would appear to be the thing she most dreaded – pity, and that he had no right to break that rigidly maintained compsure which was her only defence. And so, because there seemed to be nothing else left, he took refuge in levity.

'Before you go any further,' he said mockingly, 'I feel that it is in my own interests to point out that *I* am all of four-and-thirty. And I absolutely refuse to be classed as a dotard!'

The tension vanished as if by magic.

'I wouldn't dare!' she assured him. And then, comfortingly, 'Besides – you must be very well-preserved because Nurse only put you at turned thirty. And no one could accuse *her* of flattery.'

The grey-green eyes dwelt on her appreciatively. 'No – nor you either! But don't stop there – I feel sure there is more.'

'No! Truly there isn't. I didn't ask, you see.'

The Marquis winced. 'Well, I asked for that one, didn't I?'

This produced a ripple of laughter. 'I'm sorry! It wasn't intended as a snub – I merely meant that it didn't seem important.'

'Worse and worse!'

'Oh you are impossible!' Her attempt at severity was a hopeless failure and she turned away in desperation. 'I don't *need* to ask. You would probably be astounded by how much I know without it.'

'Go on then,' invited his Lordship cordially. 'Astound me.'

'I will.' Rosalind tilted her head pensively and began a brisk and faintly teasing appraisal. 'You have a good voice. It's light and crisp and it – it *laughs*. And it's distinctive; I'd know it anywhere. Your hands are cool and you have long fingers. At a guess, I would say that they are a good deal stronger than they look. You are tall – but not heavily built because you move too quietly. Except, of course, when you cross the hall flag-stones in high heels,' she added wickedly. 'Am I right so far?'

A curious smile lurked in Lord Amberley's eyes but he merely said, 'Quite right. Is there more?'

'A little. Since your voice is rarely serious, I think that your eyes are probably the same. You don't use paint or powder – if you did I would be able to smell them; but something about you carries a mild scent of ambergris . . . I should think it is your handkerchief. You like wearing velvet and choose the best quality – which is also true of the lace at your wrists and if you wear any rings, they must be on your left hand.' She paused for a moment, deep in thought and then said triumphantly, 'Oh yes – I nearly forgot! Your wear your own hair without powder.'

There was a long pause and then, 'You are sure it's not a wig?' he asked lazily.

'Positive.' She sent him a provocative, slanting smile. 'Well? Are you impressed?'

'Impressed – and terrified!' was the laughing reply. "I had no idea, you see, that you were a cross between a bloodhound and – and a ferret!'

Rosalind choked. 'You say the nicest things to me!'

'Don't I though?' He paused meditatively. 'I feel peculiarly like a Chinese puzzle in urgent need of re-assembly . . and I hardly dare move for fear of what you will discover next. *Not* that there seems to be anything left.'

'Well there is,' retorted Rosalind cheerfully. 'I haven't a clue about your colouring or the cast of your features. And, of couse, I don't know if you are considered handsome or not. But I don't suppose you will tell me that, will you?'

Lord Amberley gave a tiny gasp and his shoulders began to shake. 'How right you are!' he said unsteadily. 'I'll tell you that my hair is fair and my eyes a sort of grey – but beyond that . . . beyond that you'll just have to ask Nurse!'

Chapter Five

All that day and far into the next the snow continued to fall, whirling down from a leaden sky in large, soft flakes until the manor was marooned in a silent and deserted wilderness of white. Hour by hour, the outside world receded further into the realm of things forgotten and unregretted while Time itself seemed to hang motionless in the frosty air; and the Marquis, strangely content to let it be so, spoke no more of departure.

Indeed, for him as much as for Rosalind, the days of effortless conversation and small, shared pleasures were of the stuff that fills the golden treasure-house of memory; but while his Lordship unconsciously recognised their implicit transcience, Rosalind lived only for the moment and gave no thought for the morrow.

Experiencing for the first time a companionship in which her blindness existed only as a minor obstacle to be largely ignored and occasionally overcome, she developed overnight a sense of dizzying freedom. But after twelve years of captivity, release can be a frightening thing and courage is as easily forgotten as lost; so there were times when, with the best will in the world, she found herself imprisoned anew by her own doubts – or would have done so had she been left alone.

But it seemed that the Marquis, having turned the key, had no mind to leave the door closed and Rosalind's regretful, 'I can't', met invariably with a coolly challenging, 'Why not?' that effectively turned acquiescence into the line of least resistance.

The first major instance occurred when the snow stopped. His Lordship discerned a few pale rays of wintry sunshine, simultaneously discovered that a team of grooms and gardeners were busily clearing paths around the house, and calmly announced that it was high time Mistress Vernon went out for some air.

Not unnaturally, Mistress Vernon, for whom present conditions made every step a hazard comparable to Theseus's progress through the labyrinth, responded with an instinctive denial; Amberley demanded reasons and, when she reluctantly provided them, proceeded to demolish them by means of laughter and wilful incomprehension. Ten minutes later they were outside.

And with his Lordship's arm to guide her, Rosalind made the intoxicating discovery that it was not hazardous at all – merely exhilarating; that, amazingly enough, it was possible not only to walk with him but alone; that by listening to the sound of his voice she could indulge in the deliciously childish pastime of snowballing and even – sometimes – hit him. They were out for over an hour and it was Amberley who insisted that they return to the house and Rosalind who did not want to go.

Oddly, it did not occur to her to wonder why Philip had never apparently thought that she might be capable of braving the elements and enjoying it, and if it had occurred to the Marquis, he elected not to mention it.

Not all their activities were so strenuous. There was music – for the harpsichord in Rosalind's parlour was more than a piece of furniture. Though she could play only by ear or from memory, she had a light touch and was quick to learn, and Amberley, who could not play a note but was possessed of a light, even tenor, ransacked his brain for all the latest Parisian airs and derived a good deal of pleasure from teaching them to her. In exchange, Rosalind attempted to pass on the rudiments of her skill but his Lordship proved an indifferent pupil, much inclined to let his concentration wander and seemingly unable to get past the stage of picking out *Rule Britannia* with one finger so that the lessons always ended in laughter.

There were books too. Rosalind explained that while Lawson usually read her the news-sheets, she had to rely on the rector's daughter for anything of a lengthier nature.

'She normally comes three times a week for an hour – but, of course, she can't get here while the snow lasts.'

Even at the hectic height of the social season, the Marquis read rather more than that and it was his considered opinion that for anyone living as Rosalind did, three hours a week was little short of paltry. He said, 'And what do you read?'

Rosalind sighed, 'Well that,' she admitted ruefully, 'is the problem. Rebecca is a dear girl and I'm fond of her and grateful. But she is full of scruples and so very *good* that she cannot bring herself to read most of the things I wish to hear.'

'Dear me!' His Lordshp grinned. 'Never say you asked her to read Rabelais?'

'No.' She exhibited signs of mild interest. 'Is it shocking?'

'Very.'

'Oh. Well if I did, she wouldn't – any more than she should read *The Canterbury Tales* or *Tom Jones* – or anything at all to do with ancient Greece or Rome.' A gleam of humour appeared in the dark eyes. 'On the other hand, she has nothing against the poetry of Herbert and positively enjoys Milton. We have had *Paradise Lost* twice.'

'All of it?' asked his Lordship weakly.

'*All* of it. Also *A Pilgrim's Progress* and Fox's *Book of*

66

Martyrs. We did start on some of Donne's verse but, despite being in Holy Orders, his work came as a terrible shock to poor Rebecca and we had to set it aside in favour of *Gulliver's Travels.* As for *Pamela* or *Clarissa* – she is afraid that Papa could never approve of her reading *novels!*'

Amberley ran his fingers along a row of leather-bound volumes and pulled out Wishart's *Life of Montrose.* Rather surprised that it had a place in Rosalind's select collection, he asked lightly if Mistress Rebecca had felt able to tackle it.

Rosalind's smile became distinctly sardonic and her voice held a note of bitter irony as she said, 'A man of the sword and an excommunicate Calvinist? Good Heavens, no – *most* unsuitable!'

The Marquis examined her with an air of mild discovery. 'That sounds like a cry from the heart.'

'It was. I particularly wanted that book and it took Phil months to find a copy of it – and all to no purpose. I wouldn't care,' she said wrathfully, 'if I thought that either Rebecca or her Papa knew the first thing about James Graham – but of course they don't. And although, in the main, I'm willing to tolerate their absurd strictures, I find that when their petty moralisms are applied to a man of Montrose's calibre, it makes me ill!'

There was a deathly hush and then, 'Bravo!' said the Marquis, trying hard not to laugh.

'It isn't funny!' Rosalind was indignant. 'Surely you know what I mean?'

'Peace, child,' he said, crossing the room to sit at her side. 'I not only know what you mean but will engage to prove it by reading you the tale myself.'

She was suddenly eager. 'Really? Oh *thank* you! But are you sure you don't mind?'

'Not at all. I shall be delighted to be of some small service,' bowed Amberley, exquisitely formal. And then with winning, if disastrous, candour 'Especially since *I* was less fortunate than Lord Philip and looked for a copy of it in vain.'

After frequent pauses for discussion, the book was finished late one night with the candles guttering in their sockets and for a long time after it was laid aside, neither of them spoke.

Then his Lordship stirred and said remotely, 'I always thought that he went to the block. He had the right.'

Rosalind turned slowly towards him. 'It hurts, doesn't it?'

The Marquis looked at her wet lashes and, without thinking, reached out and took her hand. 'It's damnable. But there are many things that Time doesn't change and not all of them are bad. Fortunately.' And wondered why, even as he said them, the words seemed to mean something else.

With Chard healing nicely above stairs nursed by Mrs Reed, and attendance on his master required only three times each day, Saunders found himself with very little to do and duly resigned himself to a period of rare inactivity. His fifteen years with the Marquis had covered everything from the boisterousness of army life and a number of mad escapades abroad, to the courts of Paris and London, but never once in all that time had he been bored. Excited, over-worked, entertained, annoyed and occasionally scared out of his wits – but never bored, and strangely, despite his expectations, he was not so now.

Since the butler was the only member of the household whose status could be said to match that of his Lordship's valet, it was only natural that Saunders should be invited into Lawson's inner sanctum on terms of equality. Within two days a curious friendship had sprung up between them in which little was said but much understood, and within three Saunders had absorbed the full measure of the manor's mood.

Between a gentleman's gentleman and a dignified butler,

both of unimpeachable professionalism, the question of gossip was unthinkable and while Saunders confined himself to the perfectly proper indications of Lord Amberley's wealth and position, Lawson made no effort to enquire further. But it speedily became plain to the valet that, apparently on no greater recommendation than his personal charm, the Marquis was favourably regarded by everyone in the house – not excepting the scullery-maid who was unlikely ever to have clapped eyes on him. Even the fearsome Mrs Reed, after a confidential word from Lawson, had lowered her defences and grudgingly admitted that his Lordship's frivolous manner concealed a surprising degree of proper feeling and that he appeared to have done her darling nothing but good. And eventually, in a flash of dazzling inspiration, Saunders realised what was behind it all.

The entire staff of Oakleigh Manor were romantically united in the belief that, though there could not be a man who was wholly worthy of their beloved mistress, the noble Lord Marquis would do very nicely. And, from Lawson downwards, they were all in the placid expectation that his Lordship would offer marriage.

From stunned disbelief at their presumption, Saunders passed to sardonic amusement for what was likely to prove a forlorn hope to a nagging concern that the Marquis was getting in a good deal deeper than he either intended or realised. This last caused the valet to subject his master to a discreet surveillance which finally served to convince him of three things; that Amberley and, as far as he could tell, Mistress Rosalind were blissfully unaware of the fond hopes surrounding them; that his Lordship, uncommunicative as ever, gave every appearance of knowing exactly what he was about; and, most significant of all, that, despite all this, a subtle change had gradually come over him in the course of the last few days.

Saunders was unable to put his finger on just what that change was, but it somehow suggested that this hope was perhaps less forlorn that he had previously supposed, and he settled back to await the end-game with interest.

There was, in fact, one inmate of Oakleigh who was not reconciled to his Lordship's presence. Contemptuous of mankind in general and outraged in particular by those members of it who were rivals for his mistress's attention, Broody sat on his perch and eyed the Marquis with growing malevolence.

At first he sulked, silent, hunched and glowering; then he took to turning his back on the room and giving vent to an occasional muttered squawk, and finally, in desperation, he started to talk. With verve, *élan* and distressing clarity, he uttered every possible combination from his mixed fund of dockside and Anglo-Saxon invective; and the Marquis, bombarded by expressions he had not heard since his army-days and others which he had never heard at all and whose meanings he could only guess at, listened in shocked fascination before succumbing, typically, to helpless laughter.

'That bird,' he announced to Rosalind, 'could out-curse the devil. It is totally unfitted for life in a genteel establishment and will undoubtedly come to a sticky end. I hope.'

Having exhausted both himself and his repertoire, Broody retired into undefeated silence while he devised new tactics. He discovered them when his enemy was alone and seated conveniently close-by. Broody seized a sunflower seed and spat; it was a hit and he chortled his satisfaction. His Lordship calmly retrieved the seed and continued to read his book without turning his head. Broody was annoyed; he spat another seed and then another. Lord Amberley slowly closed his book and turned round.

There was a pregnant pause while parrot and Marquis surveyed each other measuringly and then the Marquis, who, on his own admission, had been very badly brought up, picked up a seed and returned it with casual accuracy.

Broody jumped. 'Wark!'

'Quite,' replied his Lordship pleasantly. 'One to me.'

Broody waited, cautious but interested, and when the second seed was flicked his way, he sidestepped it neatly and put his head on one side. 'Lawks!' he said. And then, hopefully, 'Clear for action?'

And the Marquis, recognising that he had apparently made a major breach, laughed and shied his remaining seed. It was quite reprehensible and he knew it, for there was no telling who the wretched bird might choose to spit at next; but it was a definite improvement on being sworn at.

For five days the snow lay heavy and unmoving; then, as January merged into February, a sudden thaw set in bringing sporadic showers of rain. Saunders told the Marquis that Chard was fit to travel, if not to drive, and then waited for him to speak of leaving. Amberley expressed his pleasure at Chard's good progress and asked for his coat. Then he slipped the customary emerald on to his left hand, shook out his ruffles and walked serenely away to dine with Mistress Vernon. It was destined to be his last tranquil hour for a long time but neither he nor his quietly satisfied valet were privileged to know it.

It began when Rosalind led his Lordship to describe some of the balls he had attended in Paris and then listened with rapt attention whilst he did so. Her expression of dreamy eagerness was not lost on Amberley and after a while he said abruptly, 'What are you thinking?'

She shrugged lightly. 'Oh – that it must feel wonderful to dance.'

'And you wish that you could do it?'

She flushed for it was the sort of admission she preferred not to make. 'A little, perhaps.'

The Marquis pushed his chair back and stood up. 'Then you shall. I'll teach you.'

Rosalind looked startled. 'You – I can't,' she said flatly.

He walked round the table and drew her to her feet. 'I beg your pardon?'

The teasing note produced an uncertain smile. 'I mean I could never dance properly – the way other people do,' she temporised.

'So?' He drew her hand through his arm and led her relentlessly away to the parlour. 'I cannot see that the way you do it matters in the slightest. Come.' He thought for a moment, then took her right hand in his and placed his left lightly round her waist. 'My apologies for the familiarity but I expect it to pay dividends. Now – lift your skirts in your left hand . . . yes, that's it – and it's right foot first. Ready?'

For the next hour, while Broody looked somnolently on and spat the occasional seed, the Marquis led Rosalind up and down the room, counting, instructing and criticising. 'Now . . . one, two, three and point your toe – not like that! Slowly! And turn, two, three – forward, two, three. Yes. Now again – and this time keep your head up and relax. Just move with me and stop worrying. *And* – one, two, three . . .'

And Rosalind dutifully did as she was told, placed her trust in the light, guiding hands and suddenly found that she was enjoying herself.

'That's much better. Now, round me . . . and back, two, three – don't forget to curtsey. Very good! Let's see if you can do it from memory.'

She could and proceeded to demonstrate it with evident delight. His Lordship smiled down into the

72

beautiful face, flushed now with exertion and triumph, and raised the hand he held so that she could pivot gracefully beneath. And then it happened.

As she returned to face him, the violet eyes seemed, for one extraordinary moment, to look full into his and in that second all the baffling emotions of the past week crystalised into a single, breaktaking certainty. The things that he had taken for anger and compassion were neither and the simple truth was that he loved her – and that because of it, everything about her touched him.

The safe shores of friendship crumbled beneath his feet; she was so close that he could smell the scent of her hair and he knew an overwhelming desire to bring her just that one step closer, into his arms. He froze, his fingers tightening on hers, and forced himself to remember that he had given his word and that, even if he had not, it would be an unpardonable abuse of her trust.

Rosalind stopped, her hand poised high in his, and raised enquiring brows. 'What is it? Did I do something wrong?'

For an instant he stared back at her without speaking and then, releasing her hand, stepped abruptly back.

'No – nothing.' His breath returned slowly and he fought to keep his inner turmoil out of his voice. 'You did it beautifully.'

'That's what I thought,' she teased. And then, 'Aren't we going to finish it?'

'What? Oh – no.' He felt quite ridiculously vague except on one point – that he did not dare touch her again until he had himself thoroughly in hand. 'No. It isn't necessary. You are such an apt pupil.'

A tiny frown creased her brow but she merely swept a mocking curtsey and said, 'Thank you, kind sir!' before sinking down on the sofa in a billow of apple-green silk.

A little pale still, the Marquis hesitated for an instant; and then, resolutely putting aside his habit of the last five days, set a seal on Rosalind's confusion by electing to sit opposite her. There were a dozen things he wanted to say but a hundred reasons why, as yet, he could not say them – and since this was assuredly not the time to think of either, he willed himself to concentrate on covering his temporary lapse.

For a time he succeeded tolerably well and had the satisfaction of seeing the faint shadow of anxiety vanish from Rosalind's eyes; but the light, amusing conversation occupied less than half of his mind while the rest of it seemed hopelessly beyond his recall and was dwelling, idiotically, on the curve of her throat and the grace of her hands.

A fraction too late, he realised that she had not replied to his last remark – a trifling reference to his mother and her Richmond home – and, suddenly alert, he wondered what there was in it to produce the inexplicable tension he sensed in her. 'What is it, child?' Try as he would, it was impossible to keep the tenderness wholly from his voice. 'Have I said something to distress you?'

Rosalind started slightly and then shook her head. 'No. It's just that memory plays strange tricks. I haven't thought of Richmond in years and yet . . . yet when you mentioned it just now, I found I could remember it quite clearly. A pretty village clustered about a green – and a steep hill leading up to the gates of the park.' She stopped and gave an uncertain laugh. 'Do you know, I even remember the view from that hill – and I don't think I saw it more than once.'

Amberley was watching her very closely as he said evenly, 'It hasn't changed. I suppose your uncle took you there?'

'Yes.' Her mind was plainly far away and the violet eyes grew dark. 'It was when we lived with him in Sheen. he took us to the park and then we had tea in Richmond. And because I enjoyed it so much, Uncle Rowland promised that we should go again on . . .' She stopped, catching her breath.

'Yes?' prompted the Marquis gently.

There was a long pause and then, 'We were to go again on my birthday – only it wasn't possible.'

'Why not?' He knew that he was on hitherto forbidden ground but he was impelled now by more than a need to understand. He had to know if she trusted him enough to remove the barriers and confide in him. 'Why not?'

The slender fingers were gripped tight in her green silk lap and her face was strained but she answered him. 'There was an – an accident. And I was . . . ill.'

Suddenly he could no longer bear to leave her to tell him alone and without help. Because she never complained, because her blindness, oh, so long ago, it seemed, had ceased to matter, he had begun to lose sight of what it must mean to her. But now her pain was his also; and he could not let her endure it alone.

Rising, he crossed the space between them to sit at her side and take her hands in his. 'My dear, I think I understand. And there is no need to talk of it if you do not wish to.'

'But you want me to.' It was not a question.

'I would like to know how it happened, yes. But only if you are content to talk of it.'

Rosalind drew a long breath and, unconsciously, her fingers clung to his. It seemed to her that the impossible had happened. A minute ago she could not have spoken of it; now she could.

'Very well.'

No premonition of disaster warned Amberley of the axe that was about to fall and if Nemesis laughed he did not hear her. Instead, he went on lightly holding Rosalind's hands and was unspeakably glad that she seemed to have relaxed a little.

'We were playing, Phil and I,' she said quietly, 'and I

75

was chasing him into the wood. I ran up the lane and I remember Phil suddenly shouting to me to stop – only, of course, I didn't. I thought that he was teasing me and, though I could hear the carriage too, I thought it was passing on the road.' She paused, trying to smile. 'So it was quite my own fault, you see. And when the coach came round the bend its driver must have been just as horrified as I was.'

Grim fingers of fear clutched at Amberley's heart and he was suddenly very cold. Ghostly images invaded his mind; of the crumpled leaf-green figure of a child, her face waxy-pale, her eyes closed and her long black hair tumbled in the dust. It isn't possible, he told himself frozenly. Oh my God – it couldn't be. Not that.

'Is that all you remember?' His throat was dry and aching.

She nodded. 'I saw the horses sweeping down on me – they were chestnuts, I remember – and then . . . nothing. I suppose Phil came running. He must have been very frightened – he was only fourteen then and I think that for a long time afterwards he felt responsible.' She paused again, then went on. 'When they found that I couldn't see, they started summoning first one doctor and then another. My uncle brought them from every place you can imagine and each one had a different theory – and, of course, a different remedy. I think I tried them all . . . but nothing worked.'

The Marquis was no longer capable of listening. If he had been pale before, he was now bloodless as a corpse; the very air seemed to sear his skin and, within him, his stomach coiled with revulsion; in horror and guilt; and in bitter, crippling devastation.

Chapter Six

It was a waking nightmare and, coming hard on the heels of the discovery that he loved her, its effect was cataclysmic. He had managed – and God only knew how – to make a reasonably collected exit from the parlour so that he was able to succumb, in private, to the urgent need to be sick; and after that the night was an endless torment in which he did not even try to sleep.

Instead, plagued by twelve-year-old memories that were enshrined in his mind like flies in amber, he lay open-eyed and stared restlessly into the firelit gloom. It had happened on the day that his father, after years of ceaseless persuasion, had at last agreed to buy him a commission, and he, elated, exuberant and still unable to believe his luck, had been consumed of an impatient desire to tell his mother. Even in those days she had preferred the Richmond house to that in Grosvenor Square and so he had leapt eagerly into his chaise and shouted to Pierce to spring the horses.

Over what had happened next he tried to pass lightly and ended by dwelling in excruciating detail; he attempted to understand how he had failed to recognise either Rosalind or the portrait of her younger self as the child he had lifted from the dust that day but cogent thought was lost in a channelled groove of repetition.

I wasn't driving, went the plea to himself.

And then, the inexorable denial of conscience, No – but you might as well have been.

Concussion, the doctor had said and had seemed so sure. No bones broken, no damage save a hard, glancing blow to the head. A headache, then; a few days rest and all would be well. And the uncle, what had been the fellow's name? Weston? Yes – Rowland Weston, had, like himself, been too relieved to question it.

Oh God – why did I tell Pierce to take that short-cut?

They had not wanted him, Weston and the doctor, so he had repeated his apologies and travelled on to Richmond, blithely unaware that he had robbed a child of her sight, her youth. And now that child had become a woman – bright, gallant, unique – and his love.

I wasn't driving.

Fine. Tell that to Rosalind.

He flinched and sat up, driving his face into the dark, cold comfort of his fingers in an attempt to shut out fear. How did you tell the girl you would give your soul to possess that you were responsible for shrinking her world to a place of lightless and solitary monotony? And, having told her, what then? Even if she did *not* draw back in revulsion, it could scarcely be described as an auspicious overture to an offer of marriage.

He was torn between relief and regret that he had not made that offer when first he had thought it – before that second damnable discovery. He had held her hand in his and wanted simply to say, 'I love you. Marry me.' That he had not done so was due to other considerations; adherence to propriety made necessary by the defencelessness of her position and, more importantly, awareness of her inexperience which meant that she had no yardstick by which to judge him. Both of which, as things turned out, were as mere bullets to a cannon-ball. He tried to appreciate the macabre irony of it all but his sense of humour did not seem to be working and the sound that escaped him was not of laughter.

This knowledge of his own culpability was the worst

thing he had ever faced. That he should have so harmed anyone – especially a child – was appalling enough; that the child had been Rosalind put him in hell. But there was no going back and his problem now was the thorny one of whether or not to tell her.

Leaning back, he clasped his hands behind his head and spent the next half-hour convincing himself that there was no point. There was no question now of any close relationship between them – nor could there ever be – so to tell her could serve no useful purpose and might well cause her unnecessary pain. Better, far better, to leave it alone and then he need never put his courage to the test; need never discover that, for this one thing, it was all too probably inadequate. It would be no help, in addition to everything else, to find that one was a coward.

There was only one sensible course and that was to leave before the damage spread any further. As yet she regarded him as no more than a friend – paradoxically, his only consolation in the whole, sorry business – and the least that he could do for her now was to take steps to ensure that it stayed that way.

But if I leave, she will be alone – just as she was before, something in him protested.

And if she is? replied Reason, coldly. Be thankful it's no worse. She got along without you well enough before and she will again.

Indisputably true but somehow no comfort.

When Saunders came bearing his shaving water, he was already up and gazing out of the window, clad in his opulent dressing-gown. He answered the valet's routine greeting automatically and without turning round; then he said abruptly, 'Pack, Jim. We're leaving.'

'Leaving, my Lord?' repeated Saunders, shaken. 'Today?'

The Marquis opened his mouth a deliver a bald

affirmative and then hesitated. Since go he must, he desperately wanted to go quickly, but there was Rosalind to be considered and such a sudden departure must come as a shock to her. He owed it to her to stay just one more day . . . and somehow he must find the strength to both endure it and appear the same as usual.

He said expressionlessly, 'No, not today. Tomorrow – as early as possible. Make what arrangements you can for Chard's comfort and leave out my driving-coat and top-boots.'

Still at a loss, Saunders asked weakly, 'You'll drive yourself then, sir?'

Amberley wheeled suddenly to face him. 'Obviously. Did you expect me to linger here until Chard is well enough to do so?'

If the sarcasm came as a shock to Saunders's system, it was eclipsed by a greater one, for his master's face held an expression that he had never seen before. A white shade tinged the normally humourous mouth and the grey-green eyes were frowning bleakly. He had the look, thought Saunders wonderingly, of a man in purgatory. And the image was so vivid that he made the mistake of answering his Lordship's question. 'No, sir. But I thought you might stay a few days more till the snow clears completely.'

The Marquis lost his last, frail hold on his temper and his voice took on a note of dangerous sweetness as he said, 'Did you so? Then perhaps I should remind you that you are paid neither to think nor to question my decisions. Especially – though it would seem to have escaped your attention – when I am waiting to dress.' He was dimly aware, as he turned away, that never in fifteen years had he spoken to Saunders like that – and rarely to anyone else. But though later he would be ashamed and would apologise, as yet it did not have the power to touch him for his whole attention was tuned to avoiding discussion.

He announced his decision to Rosalind soon after breakfast and for a moment the violet eyes were filled with startled dismay as she said quickly, 'So soon?'

'I am afraid so, yes.'

'But the snow has not gone, has it?'

'Not entirely.' He knew that he sounded abrupt and tried to mend it. 'It will be some days before it vanishes completely and by then the roads will be like quagmires. Just now they are bad but not impassable.'

'Oh.' Rosalind bent her head over her hands. 'You have been out?'

'No. I had Lawson send out a groom early this morning.'

She smiled faintly. 'Like Noah.'

Even mild attempts at humour were beyond the Marquis this morning and he was momentarily at a loss. Then he remembered and said lamely, 'Oh – the raven. Yes.'

This uncharacteristic response caused Rosalind's brows to contract in a tiny frown but she merely said, 'Not quite. Your groom came back – which makes him more like the dove.' She lifted her head, the wide, dark-fringed eyes seeming to gaze straight into Amberley's and her mouth lifted in a wry smile. 'I think I would have preferred a raven.'

His Lordship's breath leaked away and he stared at her helplessly whilst telling himself that this was no more than he should have expected. Then, as he sought desperately for a reply, reinforcements arrived in the shape of Lawson. Mistress Vernon, it seemed, had visitors.

'Lady Warriston and Letty?' echoed Rosalind blankly. 'Good God! What on earth do you suppose they want, Lawson?'

'I really couldn't say, Mistress Rosalind.' The butler contrived to camouflage with reproof what was, in fact, a blatant lie, whilst simultaneously casting the Marquis a glance of eloquent warning. 'Shall I show the ladies in?'

She sighed. 'I suppose so. And you had better ask Mrs Thorne to send up suitable refreshments.' Lawson bowed and withdrew and Rosalind turned back to Amberley with a swift whisper of, 'She is the most *odious* woman!' before her guests were at the door.

At any other time the Marquis would probably have found the next hour hugely entertaining for Lady Warriston was neither subtle nor particularly well-bred and he had her measure inside of five minutes. Wife of the local magistrate to whom he had sent word of the highwayman's corpse, she had learned of the presence at Oakleigh of a real, live Marquis and had only been kept at home so long by the snow. Now she had come primarily to discover as much as she could for the delectation of her neighbours and also for the purpose of contriving that the real, live Marquis should meet her daughter.

In between aiding Rosalind to answer her Ladyship's questions with a semblance of candour that, in fact, said very little, the Marquis toyed with the incomprehensible idiocy that allowed even a fond Mama to suppose that any man was going to look twice at Mistress Laetitia while Rosalind was in the room. Letty put him forcibly in mind of an over-blown rose and would, he thought, grow up as unstylish and with as little elegance of mind as her mother. Then he began to realise that both ladies were treating Rosalind with a strange brand of condescension which suggested that they thought her of no account as a rival for his attention; and from there the reason was not far to seek.

A slow, cold anger began to burn in Amberley's breast and, from that point on, his manner became progressively haughtier and his answers to Lady Warriston's impertinent inquiries much less amicably couched. And when she cut Rosalind out of the conversation by talking of London and bemoaning the fact that he had been in Paris during 'dearest Letty's' season and so missed the pleasure of dancing with her, he resolved to teach them both a small lesson.

Directing an indifferent yet somehow mocking glance at Letty, he said languidly, 'I am afraid I never dance.'

Startled out of her discretion by this blithe disregard for the truth, Rosalind said incautiously, 'But you danced with me!'

'Ah.' He smiled suddenly. 'With *you*, my dear. That is different.' And watched with derisive interest as Letty swelled with indignation and her mother with disbelief.

Before either of them could reply, Broody decided to make himself noticed. 'Wark!' he screeched, spitting a seed at Letty. 'Scabby landlubber! Heave ho, me bullies – splice the mainbrace! Wark!' And began hurling seeds with gay abandon.

Letty squealed and leapt up from her seat covering her ears and Lady Warriston's eyes bulged with disgust. His Lordship's lip quivered and he looked instinctively at Rosalind. Her head was bent, one hand was pressed tightly over her mouth and her shoulders were shaking.

'That bird,' announced her Ladyship throbbingly, 'is vicious!'

'Vicious, vicious, *vicious*!' chanted Broody happily. He was very pleased with himself. 'Damn the Captain – sod the Mate! Wark! Clear for action?' And he added a couple of his choicest phrases.

These proved too much for Rosaliand's self-control; she laughed.

The ladies left soon after that, bristling with affronted disapproval and, no sooner had the door closed behind them, than Rosalind lifted a flushed countenance to the Marquis and said unsteadily, 'That wretched bird – and you too! You should be ashamed of yourselves!'

Absently rewarding Broody by flicking back such seeds as he could find, his Lordship said unrepentantly, 'I know it. But it was no more than they deserved. My

Lady has the mind of a weasel and "dearest Letty" has no mind at all. Do you have to tolerate them very often?'

Rosalind shook her head. 'Hardly ever. They came to pry, didn't they?'

'That was certainly part of it.'

'I know.' She gave a particularly mischievous grin. 'Lady Warriston was hoping to catch Phil – and Letty certainly tried hard enough before his engagement was announced – but I don't think he liked her very much.'

'You *do* surprise me,' was the sardonic reply. 'I wonder why?'

'He s-said she had all the finesse of a Haymarket drab and – and m-much less allure,' announced Rosalind unsteadily. And dissolved again into long, gurgling laughter.

Absently fingering the single, burnished ringlet that lay against her breast, Rosalind sat at her dressing-table and wondered what had occurred to disturb his Lordship's serenity. The day had passed much like the ones before it; he had read to her and they had discussed what he had read; they had tried to teach Broody a new – and more polite – phrase and then gone on to make some music together. But all the time she sensed that, for him, these things had become a refuge; that he was using them to avoid having to talk to her. And all day she had followed his lead and tried to make it easy for him.

The thought of his departure caused a lead weight to settle in her chest and her hands dropped nervelessly into her lap. She had tried not to mind, not to ask him to stay, but it was hard when all there was to look forward to was the old existence that no longer seemed enough. He had given her life; made her think and laugh and feel; but, as he had given it, so he would take it away, for those things ceased to exist when one was alone. And surely, she thought, surely there was more to say than

84

had passed between them this morning? She did not know what; only that it seemed so little.

She stood up, shaking out the folds of her brocaded skirts and admonishing herself for the selfish folly that was making her forget to be grateful for what she had had in a desire for it to continue. Then the door opened and Mrs Reed swept in like a tidal wave.

She fixed Rosalind with a gimlet stare which did not miss the faint aura of wistful uncertainty and said, more sharply than she meant, 'Whatever ails his Lordship to be in such a hurry – and that poor man of his only just fit to travel?'

'Lord Amberley is bound by the state of the roads,' came the cool reply. Rosalind had no intention of exposing her own lack of comprehension if she could help it. 'They will become worse if he delays any longer and since the coachman *is* fit to travel, there is no reason why he should delay.'

To herself, Nurse said crossly, Is there not? And the selfish scoundrel all set to leave you worse off than before! To Rosalind, she remarked obscurely that it was no more than she should have expected since green eyes invariably meant an unsteady disposition.

Her hand on the doorlatch, Rosalind turned back and, wrinkling her brow, said 'Green? He said they were grey.'

Mrs Reed sniffed. 'He can *say* aught he likes. But the plain truth is that he has only to put on a green coat and there they are – green as grass!'

A tiny reflective smile curled Rosalind's mouth. 'And is he handsome?'

There was a scornful pause and then, 'Handsome is as handsome does *I* always say,' announced Nurse wrathfully. 'And to my mind, he's proving a disappointment!'

When dinner was over they retired, as usual, to Rosalind's parlour and sat facing each other, separated by the hearth. The Marquis stared at her as though he would engrave every feature on his memory and a black despair filled his heart and dried up the light flow of insubstantial words on his tongue. For a moment there was silence, then into it Rosalind said diffidently, but as one who could no longer help herself, 'Must you really go?'

His jaw tightened. 'Yes.'

'Is there any particular reason?'

He hesitated, aware that, since she already suspected that something was wrong, any further slips on his part would land him in very deep waters indeed. There appeared to be only one way out and, in a flippant tone that was belied by the grimness in his face, he took it.

'Oh – at least a dozen and all of them exceedingly dull, I assure you. My agent – who by now must be wondering what has become of me – has such a catalogue of matters requiring my attention that I shall be lucky to escape him in less than a week. But escape him I must for I have a number of engagements awaiting me in London and I cannot break them. My only hope is that Henshaw will be so relieved to find me alive and well that he will spare me some of the trivia and forgive both my tardiness and my long stay abroad – for which he has doubtless been preparing a lengthy scold. He has the poorest opinion of absentee-landlords!'

Rosalind digested this apparent snub in silence. Then, raising one sardonic brow, she said unexpectedly, 'My goodness – you *do* sound cheerful!'

The Marquis was somewhat taken aback. 'Why should I not?'

'How should I know?' came the astringent retort. 'Any more than I know why you have spent a good part of the day sounding as though someone has read your death sentence. The only thing I *am* certain of is that neither one is anything to do with the forthcoming delights you've just described.'

A reluctant smile touched the corners of his Lordship's mouth. He should, he supposed, have remembered Rosalind's disconcerting facility for flashes of rare insight; but it was too late now and he would simply have to brazen it out. 'I merely hoped to charm a smile out of you,' he said with devious mildness. 'You looked so serious – and I was coxcomb enough to hope that it was because you like saying goodbye as little as I do myself. As for the rest, I spoke no more than the truth.'

'Oh stop it!' Rosalind stood up and swept round to the back of the sofa in an irritable rustle of brocade. 'If you don't want to tell me what is on your mind or why you have suddenly decided to go, all you need do is say so. It is entirely your own affair, after all. But for heaven's sake, don't answer me with a mouthful of social pleasantries and meaningless excuses that would not deceive a child. I may be blind but I'm not mentally defective!'

There was a catastrophic silence.

Then, white to the lips, the Marquis came slowly to his feet and said quietly, 'I know it – and can only apologise for my maladroitness.' He paused but she neither spoke nor turned to face him and so he went on, 'Since I leave at first light and have no wish to disturb you at so ungodly an hour, I would like to say now that, though no words can fully express the depth of my obligation to you, I hope you will believe that I am very much your servant. Now and always.' Then, with a deep bow, he walked swiftly to the door.

'Don't go!' As if released from a spell, Rosalind turned after him. Her face was as white as his own. 'I'm

87

sorry – I didn't mean it. You are right to be angry but please don't go like this!'

The Marquis stopped as though a chasm had opened at his feet and looked back at the beseeching, violet eyes. Then, without even knowing what he did, he walked back across the room and took her hands.

'I'm not angry. It's alright.'

She shook her head. 'It isn't. Not when you've been so kind and never once . . .'

'Hush.' His fingers tightened on hers as he resisted the desire to take her in his arms. 'You've said you didn't mean it. That's enough.'

For Rosalind, it was one of those moments when the scales of disadvantage weighed heavily. She sensed his scrutiny and, because she could not return it, knew a strong urge to hide her face – preferably against his shoulder. But that was folly, so she managed a crooked smile and said huskily, 'I shall miss you.'

'And I you.' An odd expression lit the grey-green eyes and then, prompted by he knew not what, the Marquis heard himself saying, 'Goodbye is such a very final word and I do not greatly care for it. I think that I would rather say *Au revoir.*'

Rosalind's breath caught raggedly in her throat and the blood returned rapidly to her skin.

'You mean that you – you will come back?'

'Not that, perhaps.' The pleasant voice was curiously remote. 'But I give you my word that we will meet again. One day.' And, bending his palely-gleaming head over her hands, he kissed them each in turn as if to seal his bond.

He was half-way to Amberley before he even began to suspect what had made him offer that rash promise and the explanation, when it finally dawned on him, was so startling that he momentarily let his hands drop and

88

almost put the chaise in the ditch. He recovered in a flash, but his mind continued to dwell on things far removed from his driving and, by the time he swung his team in at his own gates, he had arrived at one inescapable conclusion. If he were not to send himself mad by thinking round and round in circles, he had to talk to someone and, for once, seek advice. And there was really only one possible candidate.

He entered his house like a whirlwind and emitted a *feu de joie* of orders that successfully set it by the ears. Chard was to be put to bed; Saunders was to unpack only the small valise and see the rest of his baggage transferred to the curricle; Henshaw was to be summoned to the library and told that his Lordship would see both him and his papers within the hour. Then the Marquis mortally offended his housekeeper by firmly refusing all offers of sustenance and strode briskly off to the hot-house to give certain explicit instructions to his gardener.

Mr Hensaw awaited his turn with gloomy resignation and had his forebodings swiftly realised. His Lordship was brief and to the point.

'I must apologise for my belated arrival and can only hope that it has not seriously inconvenienced you. The reasons for it, as you have doubtless heard, were entirely beyond my control – but I am afraid that I am now about to compound the fault of my own volition.' He smiled a little and went smoothly on. 'I can give you what remains of today and tomorrow morning – and then I must leave again. So I suggest we deal with the most urgent business first and anything that requires my signature. The rest must either be postponed until I can return or left to your discretion – whichever you prefer to think best. You do not need to be told that I repose the fullest confidence in your capabilities.

'No, my Lord,' agreed the agent dryly. 'And *you* do

89

not need to be told that, though I'm honoured by your trust, it's not what I want of you.'

'Quite,' replied the Marquis pleasantly. 'But be of good cheer. I'm not going to France this time.'

'I am glad to hear it, my Lord. May I ask where you *are* going?'

'Why not?' His Lordship shrugged, faintly amused. 'I'm going to Richmond.'

Chapter Seven

'Denzil, *mon cher* – I thought you in Hertfordshire!' Small, white-haired and eternally elegant, Louise Ballantyne, Dowager Marchioness of Amberley clasped her son's hands and raised her cheeck for his kiss. 'Or is it that you have not yet been, bad one?'

'You malign me,' complained his Lordship calmly. He led her back to the fire and then turned away, stretching out his fingers to the blaze. 'Of course I have been.'

'Ah – but for how long?'

'Approximately twenty-four hours.'

Louise threw up her hands in mock-reproach. '*Vaurien*! Henshaw will have a fit, I know it! And me, I shall have a fit also if he writes to me any more of things I know nothing. All winter long he has done so and it is enough, *enfin*! You are home now and nothing more will I do.' She sat down and fixed a thoughtful green gaze on her son's back. 'However . . . I think perhaps I am a little glad that you did not, after all, go last week for the snow was truly terrible. You would have been stranded *en route*.'

The Marquis dropped one arm to his side and rested the other against the carved mantel. 'I was.'

'*Plait-il?*'

One booted foot moved restlessly along the fender. 'I set out the day after I saw you last but did not reach Amberley till yesterday. I was held up just north of Ware.'

'Of where?' she asked, puzzled. 'It is not grammatical and I do not know unless you tell me. Also – held up by what? *La neige?*'

'No – by highwaymen. And not where, but Ware – in Hertfordshire.' He paused and turned slowly. 'Chard was shot and I was forced to seek shelter for him. Then the snow came.'

For the first time since he had arrived, Louise saw his face in full light and it shocked her but she merely said, '*Mais c'est affreux*! And did you stay at an inn?'

'No. There was none to hand. We stayed at a house – Oakleigh Manor. Until yesterday.'

'And Chard, *le pauvre?*'

'I left him to complete his recovery at Amberley. He will be good as new in a few weeks.' The Marquis sat down, frowning abstractedly at his hands. Then he said abruptly, '*Maman* – I've fallen in love and I don't know what to do for I don't think I can ever tell her.'

'Ah.' The Dowager drew a long breath and her wide, clear gaze became distinctly owlish. 'Why can you not?'

'Because she's blind,' came the blunt reply in a voice that cracked. 'She's been blind for twelve years and it's my fault.'

There was a long silence and Louise sat, straight-backed, staring into the haunted grey-green eyes so like her own. Then, 'I think, *mon fils*, that you had better tell me it all – from the beginning.'

He nodded wearily. 'It's a long story.'

'No matter. We have time. And it's what you came for, *n'est-ce-pas?*'

So the tale was told in a tone that was level and empty of expression but with occasional pauses that were their own betrayal. Carefully, meticulously, his Lordship went through it all, missing nothing; and finally he came to the thought that had struck him so forcibly en route to Amberley the previous day.

'We had grown so close without even noticing it and she was always so natural that I just assumed it was only I who felt more than friendship. And while I thought that, it seemed best to leave her – and was relatively easy to do so. Only now I'm not so sure any more. I can't help wondering if she has not come to . . . care more than she yet knows.'

Not unnaturally, Louise thought that this was more than likely but she considered it quite unnecessary to say so. Instead, she asked lightly, 'Is she pretty.'

'She's beautiful – but that's not it. She's intelligent and brave and vital . . . and something more that I can't explain.' He smiled, almost in the usual way and then said simply, 'I only know that she touches my heart in a way I did not think possible.'

The Dowager's eyes had become very bright. She said gently, 'A week is a very short time, Denzil. And you know, do you not, how important it is that you are sure? Less, I think, for your own sake than for hers. Her blindness, her isolation, her lack of experience – all these things make her vulnerable.'

The Marquis dropped on one knee beside her chair and folded her thin, shapely hands in his own. 'I know – and I was never more sure of anything in my life. And if you could but meet her, you would understand.'

She shook her head. 'It is not necessary. You are neither a child nor a fool – nor are you in the habit of making rash statements. And if you have truly thought, then I am satisfied.'

'*Vraiment?*'

'*Vraiment*,' nodded Louise, smiling a little. 'But this does nothing to solve your problem. It is necessary to be practical – and you may begin by pouring us both a glass of port while I think what is best to be done.' Silently, she watched him do as she asked and her brow creased in thought. Then, 'She must be very lonely, *la petite*. And

93

more so now, perhaps, than before you arrived to show her a little of what she is missing. Me, I do not think she should be left alone.'

'She might as well be walled up,' said his Lordship savagely as he handed her the glass. 'And since her fool of a brother cannot see it for himself, I've a good mind to tell him so!'

'Yes. I think that perhaps you should – though not quite in those exact words,' replied the Dowager slowly. 'Since already you have antagonised him, you will need to be *très diplomatique* if you are not to make things worse. No one likes to have his family duty pointed out to him by a stranger and really, Denzil, it was very stupid of you to upset him in the first place!'

'I know,' sighed his Lordship, ruefully. 'But I promise to try very hard to be charm personified in future.'

'*Bien*. It will do you so much good, *mon cher*,' said Louise flatly. 'You are far too inclined to let the world think what it will and there are times when it is a great *bêtise*. This Lord Philip does not know what you are and I do not think he can be blamed for thinking what it is he thinks. So it is up to you to show him his mistake. You will have to be *very* polite.'

'I am always polite!' said the Marquis, hurt.

The Dowager's eyes twinkled. 'Yes – but you laugh and it is not always well-received. Me, I know for you are laughing now! And that is not the way to persuade Milor' Phillipe to bring his sister to London.'

The grey-green eyes widened a little. 'Bravo, Maman! Now why did I not think of that?'

'Because,' said Louise with aplomb, 'you are not a woman.'

He grinned. 'God be praised! Very well. And if I do so persuade him?'

'Then *la petite* will have the opportunity to gain a little experience and meet other gentlemen as well as yourself.

And when she has had time to do this, you will have to decide what it is you are going to do. *Quant à cela*, I cannot advise you – but this I will say; if she is all you think and *if* she loves you, then she will not allow anything – no matter how dreadful – to come between you. She will only care that you love her. If she lets what you have to tell her matter, it is because she does not care for you enough. And that is something which you must understand and be prepared to accept. *D'accord?*'

There was a long silence and then, '*D'accord*,' he replied with a wry smile. 'And – as always – I am glad that I came.'

At about the time that the Marquis took his leave of his mother to drive up to London, Captain Lord Philip Vernon had just sat down to breakfast in his house in Great Jermyn Street and was sifting idly through his correspondence in between mouthfuls of ham. It did not, at first glance, appear very interesting; the usual selection of bills, including his tailor's modest demand for a totally immodest sum; a number of gilt-edged invitation cards to a variety of functions from a Venetian breakfast to a masked ball; two requests to subscribe to charity and a letter.

Philip eyed this last with mild surprise and, since he had not the remotest idea of who it was from, pushed the rest aside and opened it. When he discovered the signature to be that of Lady Warriston he very nearly changed his mind but some latent instinct for disaster warned against this and, sighing, he began the by no means simple task of deciphering her Ladyship's tightly cramped script.

Half a dozen lines down the page he was rapidly coming to the conclusion that her Ladyship had written under a strong degree of agitation and was as tedious on paper as she was in person; and certainly her protestations of having no wish to interfere but knowing her Christian duty when she saw it were entirely wasted on Philip. But the hub of the matter, when he came to it, changed all that and, caught unawares with a tankard of ale at his lips, Philip choked, spluttered and dissolved into a fit of coughing just as Robert Dacre strolled unceremoniously into the room.

The Honourable Robert regarded him dispassionately and remarked, by way of greeting, that bills always stuck in his gullet too – which was why he never read them over a meal.

'Not a bill,' croaked Philip, rather flushed and gasping for air. 'It's a damned silly letter!'

'Oh.' Robert was not demonstrably interested. 'Well, never mind that now, Ver. I came to see if you'd care to drive out with me. There's a curricle and pair I'd thought to buy.'

'No,' said Philip shortly. 'If I go anywhere today, it will be to Oakleigh to find out what the devil is going on there.' He dropped the letter on the table and gave it a derisive flick. 'Either Emily Warriston has lost her wits or for the past week and more my sister has been cosily closeted with no less a person than the Marquis of Amberley.'

Mr Dacre was suddenly all ears. '*Amberley*? How come?'

His Lordship shrugged impatiently. 'I don't know – some farrago about a highwayman's corpse and six feet of snow. She says, if you please, that she and her daughter called at Oakleigh on Friday and found Rose and his Lordship "on terms of the plainest intimacy" – which, even if it's true, and knowing that precious pair of tabbies, I doubt it, is a dammned impertinence!'

A tiny nagging fear was growing in Robert's brain but he was unable to resist the opportunity to indulge in a little subtle malice. 'Oh quite – and I daresay there's nothing in it for all Amberley's such a shocking flirt.'

'*Is* he?'

'Oh yes. There have been any number of girls who expected him to offer them marriage – all of them disappointed. And one – a Mistress Irwin – was made a complete fool of when he paid her the most marked attentions and then ran off to Paris with – with someone else.' Rather pleased with this skilful blend of fact and fiction, he went on carelessly, 'I suppose he's something of a rake but there's nothing in that. After all, who isn't?'

His Lordship fixed him with a level blue stare. 'I'm not,' he replied coolly. 'And I don't find it any recommendation. Do you?'

'Lord, no!' scoffed Robert airily. 'I've never been much in the petticoat line myself. But it's not generally frowned upon so long as one is discreet – and Amberley is. At least, he's only been out once, as far as I know, and that was years ago.'

'You seem to know a great deal about him.'

'Only what anyone could tell you.'

'Really?' Philip raised an ironic brow. 'Then his Lordship can't be all that discreet, can he? And If I find he's been trifling with Rosalind, he shall have the chance of fighting his second duel. With me.' He paused consideringly. 'And even if he's behaved with perfect propriety, I fancy he still has some explaining to do. Any gentleman should know better than spend a week with an unchaperoned girl and I'd like to know what prevented him from going to an inn – not to mention what made him stop at Oakleigh in the first place. It all seems deuced peculiar to me!'

Robert found himself in a slight quandry. He had three thousand very good reasons for wishing his future brother-in-law to remain on unfriendly terms with the Marquis but he suddenly realised that if he went too far in pursuit of this goal, he might well precipitate the kind of revealing crisis that must at all costs be avoided. He decided to temporise a little.

'Well, Amberley's always been a law unto himself –
but I shouldn't worry about it. I expect it's all harmless
enough. Besides, he only singles out the real diamonds
and your sister is blind, isn't she?' His tone put
Rosalind's sightlessness into the same category as
squints, buck-teeth and pimples.

An expression of faint dislike crept into Philip's
sapphire gaze. 'You haven't met her, have you?'

'No. Why?'

'Because if you had, you would know better,' responded his Lordship inimically. 'And now, if you will
excuse me, I'd like to be at Oakleigh in time for dinner
and I naturally want to call on Isabel before I leave.'

This cavalier dismissal put a spark of resentment into
Robert's eye but he forced himself to accept it with
apparent good-humour. Captain Lord Philip was quite
rich enough to make it worth the effort.

'There's no need for you to see Bella. I can explain it
all to her for you.'

'Thank you. But since I had promised to escort both
Isabel and your mother to Bedford House tonight, I
think the least I can do is to offer my apologies in
person,' said Philip coolly. 'And I should be obliged if
you will treat this matter with the strictest confidence. I
don't wish my sister to become the object of club-room
speculations.'

'Of course not,' replied Robert stiffly. 'But in that case
you'll have to refrain from offering to meet Amberley at
dawn, won't you?' And on this Parthian shot, he took his
leave.

Philip discovered that he was becoming more than a
little tired of Mr Dacre – a fact which owed more to that
single, slighting reference to Rosalind than the three
thousand guinea loan which he was well aware he had
little hope of recovering. But just now he had more
important matters to consider and he promptly forgot his

betrothed's tedious brother in a flurry of preparations for his journey.

An hour later he was on the point of leaving for Viscount Linton's residence in Clarges Street when a travelling-chaise drew up outside his door and its driver tossed the reins into the hands of his groom and jumped lightly down on to the flagway. Lord Philip stood frozen at the top of the steps and stared.

'You!' he said incredulously.

'Ah.' The Marquis of Amberley looked consideringly back at him. 'I have the strangest presentiment that someone's been telling tales. Dearest Letty's weasely mama, I presume?'

In spite of himself, Philip's mouth relaxed a little. 'Yes. I don't think she likes you.'

'No? Well, I must confess it to be entirely mutual.' Amberley paused and then said gently, 'They say the east wind brings on rheumatism and one can't be too careful at my advanced age. Do you think we might go inside?'

Unsure of how to take this, Philip flushed and led the way wordlessly into the house. As at their first meeting, Amberley contrived to set him at a disadvantage and Philip, mildly irritated that he had allowed that description of Lady Warriston to rouse a momentary feeling of kinship, darkly suspected him of doing it on purpose.

In fact he did the Marquis an injustice for Amberley had no such intention. It was merely that the prospect of constructive action enabled him to resume his normal insouciant manner and the amusement in his voice was in no way meant as mockery. He simply assumed that, like his sister, Philip's sense of humour was lively enough to banish constraint and place them on a tolerably amicable footing. That Philip had good reason to mistrust him never crossed his mind and, because of it, the quagmire of misunderstanding was destined to deepen with every step.

He followed Lord Philip into a withdrawing room and

99

eyed him with a gently reflective stare as the tall, blue-clad figure with its powdered head was replaced in his mind's eye by an anxious, dark-haired fourteen-year-old. Philip sustained the uncomfortably penetrating regard for as long as he thought necessary and then said, 'Will you not be seated, my Lord?'

'Thank you.' The Marquis smiled. 'You are remarkably like your sister.'

Philip bowed slightly but his mouth was again set in uncompromising lines and he said nothing.

The Marquis took this failure philosophically and came to the point. 'I have come – amongst other things – to tender my thanks for the hospitality of your house. I am only sorry that I was forced to accept it without your knowledge.'

'Forced?' Philip shot him a sharply questioning glance. 'How so?'

'You don't know? No – you wouldn't, of course. No doubt Lady Warriston had other things she wished to tell you.'

'Quite. Though she did mention something about a corpse on the road.'

'And did she also mention,' asked his Lordship pleasantly, 'that the last mortal act of this corpse was to shoot my coachman? For *that*, you see, was the reason for my presence in your home. It was dark and snowing and my man would quite likely have bled to death had I tried to reach Hadham Cross.'

'I see.' Of course the fellow *would* have to be a damned hero and go about shooting footpads, thought Philip unreasonably. 'But you stayed?'

Conquering his dislike of self-justification, Amberley said briefly, 'That first night I was thankful to do so. Thereafter I had no choice.'

'Because of the snow?'

'Precisely.' Grey-green eyes held blue with unexpected

100

austerity. 'I can all too easily imagine the tenor of Lady Warriston's missive to you but I hope I do not need to tell you that your sister received no disrespect at my hands. I was as fully alive to the impropriety of the situation as you doubtless are yourself.' He paused and gave a sudden and very infectious smile. 'And Lawson was pleased to approve – which I hope will be as big a comfort to you as it is to me!'

Philip resisted the impulse to grin back. He was prepared to accept that if Lawson had been satisfied with Lord Amberley's conduct then it must indeed have been exemplary; but there were still too many other things weighing in the scales against him.

'On the other hand,' continued the Marquis imperturbably, 'I can see that you have every right to be worried. Mistress Vernon's position is – forgive me – as irregular as it is unhappy.'

'I *beg* your pardon?' snapped Philip, startled.

'You sound surprised – but it must surely have occurred to you before,' said Amberley with raised brows. 'A week ago I would merely have said that she should not be living alone save for a parcel of servants; *now* I am of the opinion that . . .' He paused as if selecting his words.

'Oh don't stop there!' said Philip sarcastically. 'I'm fascinated, I assure you.'

Amberley's mouth tightened. 'I rejoice to hear it. I was about to say that I am of the opinion that the problem is a good deal more complex than the mere lack of a chaperone. I perfectly appreciate the circumstances that have prevented you from spending much time at Oakleigh – but have you ever really tried to imagine what her existence there is like?'

'I don't need to!' came the indignant reply. 'I know what it's like – and much better than you! She has every comfort and though naturally I'm aware that it isn't ideal . . .'

101

'No. It's *not* ideal – far from it. And material comfort has absolutely nothing to do with it. Oh – I don't doubt for a moment that you love her – and I know that all her servants do – but love without understanding is a poor thing, my Lord, and your sister is in a cage. I think that it is high time she was set free. Don't you?'

'What I think is that you haven't the faintest idea what you're talking about,' retorted Philip, thoroughly nettled. 'What the devil gives you the right to come here telling me how to look after my own sister when less than ten days ago you had never clapped eyes on her?'

There was a long silence. Then, smiling oddly, Amberley said, 'My apologies. I am doing it rather badly, am I not? Perhaps it will help you to bear with me if I say that I mean well. For I do, you know.'

For the second time in half-an-hour, Philip suffered the irritating sensation of having been put in the wrong. 'I daresay you may do,' he said stiffly, 'but I can't see what difference it makes. There is nothing to discuss.'

The grey-green eyes grew suddenly hard. 'You are mistaken. Your sister is beautiful, intelligent and twenty-two years old and she is wasting her days being civil to Letty Warriston and her like or waiting for the rector's daughter to come and read to her. She is immured in what is little more than a comfortable prison with no one to talk to but a temperamental parrot – and if you think that's good enough you must be damned insensitive!'

Philip came abruptly to his feet, blue eyes blazing and voice tight with anger. 'I think, my Lord Marquis, that you have said more than enough!'

Lithe as a cat, my Lord Marquis also stood up. 'I doubt it very much.'

Philip opened his mouth and then closed it again as if he could not trust himself to speak. Then, drawing a long, unsteady breath, he said frigidly, 'Very well –

finish it. I am sure that you have some startlingly original suggestion you would like to make.'

'You overestimate me,' replied Amberley coolly. 'I merely wondered why you do not bring her to London and introduce her to society.'

Philip gaped at him and then gave a briefly scornful laugh. 'Now I know you're raving! You must be if you think *that* a logical possibility.'

'And why do you think it isn't?'

'Because, Lord Amberley, although it seems to have escaped your attention, my sister is blind.'

'Well?'

'What do you mean – *well*? Isn't it obvious?' demanded Philip irately. 'Away from Oakleigh she couldn't stir a step without someone to guide her – and how the hell do you suppose she would cope with balls and routs and all the rest of it?'

'Better than you think,' came the calm reply. 'And as for her needing to be guided – I don't think you'd find any shortage of volunteers.'

'And that's all I need!' said Philip in exasperation. 'Rose may be two-and-twenty but she has no more idea of how to deal with *that* kind of attention than . . .'

'Then it's time she learned. Or are you going to let her die an old maid simply because you're not prepared to face a little inconvenience?' asked the Marquis, walking to the door. 'If so, she is indeed unfortunate.'

Philip flushed to the roots of his hair. 'Are you saying that I'm selfish?'

'Not necessarily.' Amberley turned slowly to survey him with an air of dispassionate appraisal. 'What I am saying is that you should ask yourself if you are. My own opinion, if it's of any interest to you, is that you want what's best for her but are so completely hide-bound by convention that you'll never achieve it. Or not unless you cultivate a little imagination. Your servant, sir.' And

103

with a swift, elegant bow, he turned on his heel and went out.

Philip was left prey to a multitude of heated and very mixed emotions, foremost amongst which ranked the desire to knock Lord Amberley's teeth down his throat – a desire that was only strengthened by the infuriating suspicion that the Marquis had spoken no more than the truth. Captain Lord Philip swore long and fluently to the empty room and then flung out of the house to pout all his pent-up grievances into the gentle and understanding ear of his bride-to-be.

Isabel Dacre, a diminutive brunette with large, pansy-brown eyes, listened in responsive but increasingly baffled silence and then, when his Lordship finally paused for breath, said quietly, 'I'm sorry – but I'm afraid I don't quite see what is upsetting you so. Not unless you think that what the Marquis said might be true.'

'That's beside the point. He had no right to say it at all!'

'But surely *someone* had to say it? Otherwise it might never have . . .' She stopped, perceiving the lack of wisdom in this remark.

Philip eyed her with smouldering resentment. 'Otherwise it might not have occurred to me? Is that what you were going to say? I thank you! No doubt you'd also like to tell me that I'm stupid or selfish – or both!'

'Oh no,' replied Isabel lightly. 'I'm not so uncivil.'

Philip stared at her, unable to believe that he had heard aright for nothing in his previous experience of Mistress Dacre had ever suggested her capable of such a piece of provocation.

And Isabel smiled serenely back at him, a gleam of mingled amusement and satisfaction in her dark eyes, and wondered what had become of the almost oppressively polite young gentleman she had been betrothed to.

Much of Philip's rage deserted him and he sat down, saying in a more moderate tone, 'I beg your pardon. But I don't like the fellow and he's set me all on edge.'

'Yes. I'd noticed that,' she responded placidly. 'Why don't you like him?'

'Because I watched him win three thousand guineas from your brother at a time when he knew perfectly well that Bob was too drunk to know what he was doing!' said Philip. And then, ruefully, 'Oh Lord! I suppose I shouldn't have said that.'

'Why not?' Although Isabel had turned a little pale, she did not seem shocked. 'Robert is always playing deeper than he should. The only thing I cannot understand is how he managed to pay such a sum for if he had asked Papa the whole house must have known about it.'

Philip coloured a little and made a pretence of arranging the folds of lace at his wrist.

'Oh no.' The brown eyes flew suddenly wide. '*You* lent it to him, didn't you?'

'Well, yes.' His Lordship looked up, rather taken aback at the flatness of her tone. 'Did I do wrong?'

It was Isabel's turn to flush. 'Not wrong, no. It was . . . it was very kind of you. But I . . . oh dear, I would *so* much rather that you had not! You will never get it back, you know and it only encourages him. He will come to you again and again and – oh, I know I shouldn't say so, but he is quite foolishly extravagant and I know of no reason why *you* should be saddled with the cost of it!'

'Do you not?' asked Philip very directly.

'No! You cannot have supposed that I wished you to frank Robert?'

'I didn't suppose it. But I naturally *wondered* if you did. How could I not? He is your brother, after all.'

'Yes. But . . . th-though I'm not aware of the precise terms,' came the halting reply, 'I do realise that you must already have been more than generous or Papa would n-not have . . .' She tailed off uncertainly and then, making a brave effort, met his Lordship's gaze and said simply, 'You know how it is with us.'

105

'Yes,' said Philip with an almost imperceptible note of chagrin. 'And since – if you will pardon my bluntness – that is why you accepted me, I can surely be pardoned for thinking that you expected me to assist Robert.'

This was a bit more than Isabel had bargained for and her composure vanished into a confused morass of half-sentences behind which lay a foolhardy urge to ask why, if his Lordship wanted more than a complaisant wife, he had offered for her. But that was something that even one's feckless Mama would not approve of and, worse, one might not like his Lordship's reply. On the whole, reflected Isabel miserably, it was a lot safer to say nothing, so she relapsed into silence and stared fixedly down at her hands.

Suddenly as embarrassed as she, Philip was regretting his impetuous words but with no idea of how he might take them back. He got to his feet saying jerkily, 'I beg your pardon. I had no right to say that. In fact, the whole topic is grossly improper and it is probably just as well that I have to go. Please present my apologies to your mama and say that I am sorry not to have been able to deliver them in person.'

'Yes, of course,' Isabel replied colourlessly, rising from her seat. 'And pray give my regards to your sister. Shall you bring her back with you, do you think?'

'I don't know – though it seems unlikely. It is a preposterous scheme and I daresay Rosalind will think so too.'

'But you will ask her?'

'I suppose so,' he agreed reluctantly. 'Don't tell me that you think it a good notion?'

'Well, yes. I do,' she replied diffidently. 'I know that I should hate to live alone – and *I* can see. It must be a thousand times worse for her. Perhaps you are right and she will not want to come but I think that she should be given the opportunity to choose. And,' she added winsomely, 'you would not like to think of Lord Amberley visiting her again at Oakleigh – which he might since he obviously feels strongly about it.'

His Lordship's brow darkened again. 'I'll take good care that he doesn't! If Rose stays in the country, then she'll have to have a chaperone. And *that*,' he concluded triumphantly, 'should settle my Lord Marquis once and for all!'

For a long time after he had gone, Isabel remained deep in thought and even a fitting at her mantua-maker failed to occupy more than half of her mind. The path ahead, it seemed, was fraught with pitfalls, for how, even if the opportunity should arise, did one explain that one had been fortunate enough to have duty go hand in hand with inclination? That the wealthy and eligible husband of her parent's choice and the dashing young cavalry officer whose dark good-looks troubled her thoughts were one and the same? There came a point, Isabel realised pessimistically, when the chances of saying so and being believed would be negligible. Not that one *could* say so unless one received some small indication that such tidings would be welcome, and until today his Lordship had behaved with a degree of formality that was almost depressing. And, as if that wasn't enough, there was Robert happily making things worse.

It was not until late afternoon that she saw her elder brother and before she could so much as open her mouth, he dragged her outside to admire his latest acquisition.

'Well?' he demanded gleefully. 'What do you think?'

Isabel surveyed the smart racing-curricle and its pair of gleaming greys with a sinking heart. 'I think it looks very expensive,' she said dampeningly. 'And I also think that you and I had better have a little chat – in my room where we can be private.'

'Oh, don't be such a misery!' snapped her brother. 'And if all you want is to lecture me on the expense, you can save yourself the trouble.'

'That,' said Isabel with unaccustomed firmness, 'is only

part of it. I want to talk to you about the three thousand guineas you borrowed from Lord Philip – and you can either discuss it now in my room or over the dinner-table tonight. The choice is yours.' And she walked away into the house and on up the stairs.

As she had known he would, Robert followed and, shutting the door behind him, leaned sulkily against it and said, 'Well? I suppose Vernon blabbed the whole to you?'

'He told me of it, yes,' she replied composedly. 'And I'm very glad that he did, for it gave me the chance to tell him never to lend you money again.'

Robert jerked himself upright. 'You did *what*?'

'I'm sorry, Robert – but I won't have you sponging off him. So if you were hoping to persuade him to pay for your curricle and pair, you will have to think again.'

'Oh *will* I?' said Robert furiously. 'Well, let me tell you, Mistress Interference, that I'll have no need! It's already paid for!'

He had ample time, before Isabel spoke, to regret this carelessly bestowed piece of information. Then, 'Is it?' she asked sharply. 'How so?'

'It's no business of yours – or of Phil Vernon's come to that.'

Isabel stared at him, chaotic thoughts chasing each other through her brain. 'Robert – you did redeem your debt to the Marquis, didn't you?'

He flushed. 'Ask your precious Philip! He's seen the vowels!'

'Oh.' Weak with relief but still somehow anxious, she said, 'Then how did you pay for the curricle?'

'I've had a run of luck,' replied Robert, just a fraction too quickly. 'It does happen, you know – especially when I'm not playing that devil Amberley.'

Isabel's brow creased thoughtfully. She knew her brother very well indeed and certainly well enough to know when he was lying. Also, there was a great deal about the mysterious Marquis which did not seem to add up for, in her opinion, a man who went out of his way to look after his coachman or improve the lot of a lady he scarcely knew, did not sound a likely candidate for fleecing drunken youths. And if he was not, that left only one alternative that she could think of.

'I don't suppose,' she mused, half to herself, 'that Lord Amberley likes you well enough to return your vowels for nothing?' And then, sickeningly, read the answer in her brother's face. 'Dear God – he did, didn't he? And you let him. I don't suppose you even argued.'

'Of course I didn't argue! Why should I?' Robert knew better than to waste time in fruitless denial. 'It was his idea and he only did it because he didn't want to feature in society as the next best thing to an adventurer.'

'Well in that case he wasted his money,' replied Isabel, quietly contemptuous. 'Only, of couse, the truth is that he didn't care to feature that way, not to society, but to himself.' She leaned back in her chair, hands pressed against her cheeks, and gazed at him with helpless exasperation. 'Oh *Bob* – have you no morals at all? Don't you *care* that, in addition to cheating Lord Philip, you're causing him to dislike a man who has done nothing to deserve it? And now you've spent the money and I can't even tell you to pay it back.'

'I'm glad you've worked that one out,' he retorted brazenly, 'because I wouldn't anyway. And you needn't ask me to tell Vernon the truth because I won't do that either! Amberley deserves everything he gets.'

She stood up and faced him resolutely. 'Then I must do it.'

'No! Bella, you can't – what if Vernon told someone? It would ruin me.' He was frightened now. 'Damn it – I'm your *brother*! You owe me some loyalty.'

'Perhaps. But you don't deserve it, do you?'

109

Robert crossed the room to grasp her wrists. 'Do you want to see me in the Fleet? A word of this and I'll have a pack of damned tradesmen down on me like vultures. And what good will it do? You know I can't pay either Vernon or Amberley – let alone both of them.'

Isabel looked at him out of stark brown eyes. 'I *have* to tell Lord Philip. It's my duty to do so – surely you can see that?'

'No I can't. Your duty is to your family – to me.' He smiled coaxingly at her. 'Bella, *please*. I'll promise you anything you care to name if you'll only keep quiet.'

She shook her head sadly. 'I can't trust you. I wish I could but I can't.'

'Yes, you can,' he insisted. 'I'd have to keep my word, wouldn't I? If I didn't, you'd tell.'

She give a shiver of distaste. Discovery of the full sum of his weakness and dishonesty made her feel physically unwell. There was a long pause and then she said despairingly, 'Oh, very well. But don't ever ask this sort of thing of me again for my silence makes me as despicable as you are yourself!'

'I won't.' Grinning with relief, Robert lifted her hands to his lips, only to have them snatched away.

'And I want you to promise me two things,' she went on relentlessly. 'First that you will never, under any circumstances, try to borrow money from Lord Philip again.'

He shrugged. 'I can't, can I? He wouldn't lend it.' Then, catching her eye, 'Oh alright – I promise.'

'Good. And second, that you will stop making mischief for Lord Amberley. Not just between him and Lord Philip – but generally. I want your word that you won't do or say anything that will add to the trouble you have already caused. In fact, I want you to be as polite to him as it's possible for you to be. Do you understand?'

He scowled and turned away. 'Yes. Alright.'

'Look at me, Robert,' said Isabel quietly; and waited until he did so. 'Now – give me your solemn word.'

For a second he hesitated and then, with a fulminating glance, said grittily, 'Very well. I give you my word I'll leave Amberley to dig his own pit. Is that good enough for you? But if you breathe a word of this to a soul, I swear I'll make sure that you live to regret it!'

And with that, he flung out of the room, slamming the door behind him and leaving his weary sister to placate her conscience as best she could.

Chapter Eight

'Phil – oh, *Phil*!'

Rosalind cast herself against her brother's chest and hid her face in the folds of his cloak, brought perilously close to tears by the unexpectedness of his arrival.

Faintly surprised by this reception, Philip hugged her whilst trying to peer down into her face. 'Rose? Whatever's the matter? Anyone would think I'd been away for a year on active service.'

The dark head moved in a gesture of negation. 'It's just that I didn't expect you,' she explained in muffled accents. 'And I'm so glad that you've come.'

Frowning slightly, his Lordship grasped her shoulders and took a step back. 'You're upset and you don't look yourself,' he accused. 'What's wrong? Is it something to do with that fellow Amberley?'

Rosalind froze and then, without appearing to do so, she slipped from his grip to turn away as a rapid flush stained her skin. 'What do you mean?'

'Exactly what I say,' replied Philip grimly as he unfastened his cloak and tossed it over a chair, 'so you needn't sound so surprised. I know perfectly well that he was here – and for a whole week.'

'Yes. He left four days ago.' *Only* four days, she thought ironically. It did not sound much unless you had had to live through it. 'Who told you? Oh no – let me guess. Emily Warriston?'

'Who else?'

A sardonic grin touched Rosalind's mouth. 'I'll wager that she couldn't wait. Lord Amberley snubbed her beautifully – and Letty too. You would have enjoyed it.'

'Very likely – but that's not what I travelled from London to hear about.'

'Oh?' She sat down gracefully on a sofa. 'What then?'

'Don't play games, Rose. I'm devilish out of temper and not the least in the mood for them. It's been a difficult sort of a day.' His Lordship poured two glasses of wine and handed one to his sister and as he did so his eye lit upon a huge bowl of exotic hot-house blooms. His brow darkened with suspicion. 'Where did those flowers come from? We don't grow anything like that?'

'No. The Marquis sent them from Amberley,' replied Rosalind with evident pleasure. 'Wasn't it kind of him?'

Philip stared at the arrangement critically. 'Mm . . . but there are too many colours, if you ask me.'

'Are there? Well, I don't suppose he chose them for colour. All I know is that they are beautifully scented.'

Feeling himself justly reproved, Philip sat down and said abruptly, 'Yes. I'm sorry. I think you'd better tell me all about my Lord Marquis.'

'I fully intend to – so there is not the least need for you to be so disagreeable. It's simply that, since it is quite a long story, I thought you might prefer not to be bombarded with it the instant you walked through the door,' said Rosalind patiently. 'However, Lord Amberley came here because he had been held up on the road and . . .'

'I know all that,' her brother interrupted. 'What I want you to tell me is how he conducted himself towards you. That Warriston cat says that the two of you were intimate but . . .'

'She would.'

'. . . But *he* says he behaved with perfect propriety,'

continued his single-minded Lordship. 'And though I don't suppose . . .'

'*He*?' queried Rosalind incredulously. 'Lord Amberley? You've *seen* him?'

'Yes. Why should I not? Or did you think he wouldn't wish to face me?'

Very carefully, she set down her glass and ignored most of this speech. 'When and where?'

Lord Philip eyed her irritably. 'This morning. He called on me in Great Jermyn Street.'

'Why?'

'Why do you think?'

'If I knew, I wouldn't ask. He left here for Amberley and he expected to be there at least a week. If he cut short his stay to call on you in London, then it must have been for a very good reason. What did he say?'

'A damned sight too much!' replied Philip feelingly. 'He is without doubt the most arrogant, over-bearing, pompous idiot that it's ever been my misfortune to meet!'

A spark of anger glowed in the violet eyes. 'Arrant nonsense! But it's no more than I should have expected for he said that you didn't like him.'

'Oh *did* he? Well, he's right – I don't and with good reason. But I don't for a moment imagine he told you why.'

'No, he didn't – and I don't want to hear it from you,' said Rosalind tartly when she heard Philip's derisive laugh. 'When I hear the full story, I'd like it to *be* the full story and not the biased view which is all I'll get from you!'

'Ha!' scoffed Philip. 'I'll bet he told you it was all some tragic misunderstanding.'

'Well, if you think that,' she retorted, 'he'd have spoken no more than the truth because you must have a ludicrously inaccurate idea of his character. There is nothing tragic about Lord Amberley and if you will take

114

a word of advice, you won't accept him at face value. He has an unusual sense of humour.'

'Warped is the word I'd have used.'

'Quite probably – but you are by nature over-hasty.' She smiled suddenly and said coaxingly, 'Try not to be prejudiced, Phil – at least until you've given yourself time to know him better.'

'Like you, you mean?' There was a measure of disapproval in the sapphire gaze. 'He appears to stand high in your esteem.'

'Yes. He does.' She paused and then added simply, 'I've never met anyone like him before.'

An appalling prospect suddenly occurred to Lord Philip and it was with dire foreboding that he asked, 'Did he flirt with you?'

Rosalind looked blank. 'Did he what?'

'Flirt with you – treat you with familiarity, pay you a lot of silly compliments and so on.'

She began to laugh. 'Well, he *did* say that even though I can't see my face I must have been told how beautiful it is but that was less of a compliment than a challenge. As for "so on" – I'm not at all sure. But I shouldn't think that he can have done or I expect I would have noticed. And the only time he was what you would both describe as familiar, was when he taught me to dance. But that was unavoidable and he did apologise for it.'

'When he *what?*' snapped his Lordship, thoroughly startled.

Rosalind grinned. 'Taught me to dance. I thought you would be surprised. And to tell the truth,' she went on reflectively, 'I was rather surprised myself – not because he offered to teach me but because I didn't think that it was possible. In fact, there seem to be a number of things I've been mistaken about.'

'Such as?'

'Oh – walking in the snow and throwing snowballs. Silly things like that.'

Totally unable to picture the elegant Marquis playing in the snow like a schoolboy, Philip drew a long breath and said, 'He's beginning to sound like two different people. Either that, or one of us is a fool. And since you are undoubtedly going to tell me that *I* am the one, you had better start convincing me.'

'Well I'll try.' The dimple peeped and was gone. 'But you mustn't interrupt.'

'Who me?' he asked, grinning reluctantly back at her. 'I wouldn't dare!'

So Rosalind talked and Philip made the rather surprising discovery that he had not the least desire to interrupt for, though the picture she drew of the Marquis was a wholly astonishing one, there could be no doubt that Amberley had achieved more for her in a week than Philip himself had done in twelve years. It was an uncomfortable thought.

'It's difficult for you to understand, perhaps,' she concluded faintly wistful, 'but he treated me as a person. Everyone else puts my blindness first; he never did. And when *I* was inclined to do so, he wouldn't let me. Do you see?'

Philip frowned down at his hands and his mouth was grim. 'Yes. I think I'm beginning to. Tell me, Rose – he said you were in a cage. Has it seemed like that to you?'

She flushed a little. 'Sometimes.'

'And now?'

'Now more than ever.' She said it coolly, for how did you explain that, now the long tolerance was over, you had gone back to the beginning again and were living with your sightlessness in helpless, frustrating rage? 'But it's no one's fault, Phil, so there is no need for you to feel responsible.'

'My Lord Marquis wasn't so generous,' he replied

116

slowly. 'And though I'll not deny that he made me blazingly angry at the time, it's starting to look as if he was right. It doesn't absolve him of – of other things – and I doubt that I'll ever actually like him, but I suppose I must be grateful that he has opened my eyes to what he described as my "insensitivity".' He paused for a moment and looked steadily across at her. 'His Lordship is of the opinion that you would be happier in Great Jermyn Street with me. Would you?'

Rosalind's breath drained slowly away and she was suddenly very pale. The idea dazzled, beckoned and terrified all at once, but fright seemed to have the upper hand; only, just as she opened her mouth to say 'I can't', it was as if the Marquis stood at her side, replying with laughter in his voice, 'Can't? Why not?' – and the words died in her throat. Instead, she said weakly, 'I don't know. I'd like to . . . but I'm afraid. It – it's a big step to take.'

Philip nodded. 'I know and so I told Amberley. But he behaved as though it were no more than a walk around the garden. He doesn't seem to have any understanding of the difficulties it would present to you.'

'Oh yes he does,' said Rosalind quietly. 'He understands very well indeed – which is why he pretends he doesn't. It's a clever and extremely effective technique.' And then she fell silent and two important implications began to dawn upon her.

Lord Amberley, it seemed, wanted her to go to London; and if she went, then she could hope to meet him again just as he had promised. And was it not perhaps a sort of test? A question of whether she had enough courage to leave the things she knew for the strange world outside? Rosalind began, suddenly, to feel very peculiar indeed and she drew a deep, bracing breath. 'I shall probably make an utter fool of myself,' she said shakily, 'but if I don't try, I shall never know. And that would be a pity.'

With his new-born insight, Philip recognised the effort

she was making and, like any soldier, gallantry was a thing he could appreciate. 'Do I,' he asked smiling, 'take that as an acceptance?'

'Yes – I think so. In fact, I'm sure of it. Later on I may even be glad as well.' She achieved a wry smile. 'But how Broody's going to take it, I just can't think.

As it turned out, Broody took it rather well – largely because, since no one in the household felt equal to the task of caring for him in Rosalind's absence, he made the journey with them. Oakleigh waved him off with active enthusiasm whilst indulging in the optimistic hope that he would not come back; and Broody set out on his travels in an unusually amicable frame of mind occasioned by the inborn knowledge that this was what parrots were made for.

He liked the chaise and its motion excited him. Swaying rhythmically on his perch, he peered coyly through the bars of his cage at Lord Philip and then spat an experimental seed. Philip cast him a withering glance and brushed the seed from his cravat.

'Wark! screeched Broody happily and walked sideways along the perch with his head on one side. 'Damn the Captain!' And, carefully selecting another seed, spat again.

'Did we *have* to travel with this wretched bird?' asked his Lordship, picking the seed out of his powdered hair.

Rosalind grinned. 'Yes. He behaves very badly when I am not by and it wouldn't be fair to inflict him on Nell and your valet.'

'Lawks!' said Broody and scored a bulls-eye on his Lordship's nose.

'He's behaving very badly now,' observed Philip irritably. 'He keeps spitting seed at me.' And watched without apparent pleasure as his sister succumbed to helpless laughter. 'It isn't funny!'

118

'Y-yes it is,' sobbed Rosalind unsteadily. 'I should have t-told you about that. It's a game.'

'A game? Oh wonderful! And what am I supposed to do – spit back?'

'Yes,' said Rosalind, dissolving afresh.

'And who,' asked Philip ominously, 'was responsible for teaching him this little habit? Or no – don't tell me.' He leaned back in his corner, chin on chest. 'I have the feeling it's going to be a very long journey – and when I get to London I've a mind to send my Lord Amberley a small present.'

'Oh?' quivered his sister appreciatively.

'Yes.' Philip fixed Broody with a stare of pleasurable anticipation. 'I think that I shall give him a parrot.'

Rosalind's first day in London was spent in the determined attempt to become familiar with the geography of her brother's house and so well did she suceed that, by evening, she could confidently travel between her bedchamber, the parlour and the dining-room and climb up and down the stairs without help. Returning home to dine, Philip found her ensconced before the fire in his favourite chair, still clad in an afternoon gown of blue dimity. With diabolic cunning, he asked if she intended changing for dinner only to be told that, having already climbed more stairs that day than a *muezzin*, she had no wish to add to her score unnecessarily. 'So I'm afraid you will to put up with me as I am,' she concluded cheerfully.

Philip subsided on to a sofa he had never liked and wondered gloomily if this sort of thing was why some men preferred not to marry.

The following morning brought Rosalind her first two visitors and, since Lord Philip had already retired to his club, she was forced to receive them unassisted. Surprisingly, she found it a good deal easier than she had expected and even enjoyed it. Mistress Isabel proved to

119

be much as Philip had described her but with an air of gentle warmth, while her mama was an irresistible blend of placid good-humour and outspoken vagueness.

Neither lady paid any undue attention to their hostess's blindness and when Lady Linton rose to go, she smiled absently upon her and said, 'Dear child – I shall so enjoy chaperoning you! For with so much beauty – and not to mention the money – you are *bound* to be a success. I don't suppose,' she asked hopefully, 'that you would like to marry Robert?' And then, without waiting for Rosalind to reply, 'But of course you wouldn't. I am quite sure you have too much sense – and Lord Philip too, I expect. No one with sense would take Robert. I wouldn't myself. Now . . . what was I going to say? Ah yes! We have an engagement for tomorrow evening and hoped that you might be persuaded to join us. I can't quite remember what it is but Isabel will no doubt tell you and I must leave her to do so for I shall be late for my fitting with Phanie. And that would *never* do, for her gowns are quite ravishing and she is perfectly aware that I can't pay for them!' And, on this obscure utterance, her Ladyship drifted away into the hall, entirely forgetting to make her goodbyes.

Isabel gazed after her with rueful fondness and then said, 'I am sorry, Mistress Vernon. Mama is a dear – but just a little eccentric.'

Rosalind laughed. 'Please don't apologise – I found her charming. But who on earth is Robert?'

'My brother.' There was a marked lack of enthusiasm in Isabel's tone and, realising it, she proceeded to change the subject. 'The engagement that Mama spoke of is my Lady Crewe's assembly. Do say that you will come!'

'I – I don't know. Phil mentioned it last night but everything is moving so very fast and I'm not at all sure that I am ready for it,' confessed Rosalind, carefully understating a condition that closely resembled pure panic. 'And then there is your mama to be considered. Phil told me that he asked her to chaperone me but I am persuaded that she will find it very tiresome.'

'No she won't,' announced Isabel candidly. 'Mama never does anything she dislikes so she won't accompany you anywhere she would not have gone anyway. And her notion of chaperonage consists of handing one over to her hostess and then vanishing into the card-room from which she only emerges in time to call for the carriage.'

'Oh.' Rosalind was faintly stunned. 'Is that usual?'

'For Mama it is. But don't worry. Your brother has promised to escort us and I know a number of agreeable girls who will be present. And, if you will permit me to say it,' she added shyly, 'you are so very pretty that the gentlemen will probably be falling over themselves to gain an introduction. Please come, Mistress Vernon!'

Rosalind was inclined to regard the latter part of this speech dubiously but it was somehow impossible to disappoint Mistress Dacre and so she threw caution to the winds and said lightly, 'Well, I suppose one has to start somewhere and you are so kind that I can scarcely refuse. Thank you – I will come.'

Isabel smiled. 'I am so glad.'

'But only on condition that you will call me Rosalind – for the truth is that I would very much like to ask you to look at my evening gowns and tell me whether or not they are hopelessly unfashionable. And I really can't do that if we are to be formal.'

'Thank you. I shall be delighted,' replied Isabel, flushing with pleasure. 'And if – if you should wish to visit a mantua-maker, I would be happy to take you to Phanie. For Mama is quite right – her gowns are much the prettiest.'

'And shockingly expensive?' teased Rosalind.

'Well, yes. They are a *little* dear.'

The violet eyes gleamed wickedly. 'Splendid,' said Rosalind with relish. 'If I am going to do this thing at all, I may as well do it properly. And, as your mama pointed out, I am well able to afford it!'

Chapter Nine

Exquisitely gowned in cream silk, heavily broidered with gold, Rosalind sat on a cabriole-legged chair at the edge of Lady Crewe's ballroom and grew more tense with every minute.

It was noisy; a cacophony of differently pitched voices and laughter, footsteps and scraping chairs, all set against the continuo of my Lady's hired orchestra. It was so crowded that, having arrived safely at her seat, she did not think she would dare leave it again with even the strongest arm to guide her, and the rooms were stuffy. Scents of ambergris, cassia, heliotrope, musk and lavender battled with those of cosmetics, hair-powder and perspiration. Rosalind knew very little of brothels or Turkish seraglios – but she did not think that those places could smell any worse than did this noble company.

And then there were the introductions. Several young gentlemen had made a point of greeting Lord Philip and were duly presented to his sister only to find a constraint either in the discovery that Mistress Vernon was blind or in his Lordship's hawklike surveillance. And, at the end of an hour, Rosalind had the greatest difficulty in remembering one of them from another.

Two of Isabel's 'very agreeable girls' had been so embarrassed by her disability that they had not known what to say while the third had asked so many patronising and impertinent questions that Rosalind had finally lost her temper and delivered a crushing snub. This had served the purpose of ridding her of Mistress Hawley but had called forth a low-voiced but nonetheless annoyed reproof from Lord Philip. Rosalind raised sardonic brows and informed him that neither for him nor anyone else was she prepared to be treated like the freak at a village fair, after which they maintained a state of frigid neutrality thoroughly unnerving to Mistress Isabel.

From within the doorway a pair of darkly mocking eyes surveyed the trio with lazy interest before centering more particularly on Rosalind and then their owner began to thread his leisurely way across the room. Newly arrived and already bored, his Grace of Rockliffe had decided that the situaton was intriguing enough to warrant his attention; and, of course, it would not do for London to think him unaware of its latest beauty.

He came to rest beside Lord Philip and made an elaborate leg. 'My Lord . . . Mistress Dacre.' He cast a glance of mild enquiry at Rosalind then looked back at Philip. 'It is quite abominably crowded is it not? But then, it always is. My Lady Crewe is a notable hostess.'

A gleam of appreciation dawned in Rosalind's eyes at the sweetly veiled criticism implicit in the gentleman's suave tones and she waited, with interest, to hear her brother's reply.

Philip, who had never before been singled out by his fastidious Grace, was startled and a little wary. 'Yes, indeed,' he said lamely. 'Just so.'

Rosalind stifled a giggle and Isabel, who knew Rockliffe quite well, having been at school with his youngest sister, stepped nobly into the breach and fulfilled the ambition which had brought him to their side.

'Your Grace, I believe you do not know Lord Philip's

sister, Mistress Vernon? She is but newly come to Town,' she said quietly. 'Rosalind – his Grace, the Duke of Rockliffe.'

Smiling, Rosalind extended her hand and felt it taken in a coolly insubstantial clasp.

'Your servant, Mistress Vernon,' said the Duke softly. 'I begin to know why I came.'

'Oh?' The dimple quivered into being. 'And why was that, sir?'

'Why – to beg your hand . . . for the gavotte,' came the smoothly audacious reply. And, raising her fingers to his lips, Rockliffe lightly kissed them.

Quite apart from the obvious problem, this was going too far and too fast for Philip. H cleared his throat. 'I am afraid my sister does not dance,' he began stiffly. 'You see . . .'

'Philip.' Rosalind spoke his name with flat implacability. 'I am sure Isabel must be longing to dance.'

Amusement lurked in Rockliffe's heavy-lidded eyes and Isabel directed a level brown stare at him before turning to Philip and responding dutifully to her cue. 'Indeed, I should like to dance – and I am sure that we may trust his Grace to entertain Rosalind.' If there was anything deliberate in her choice of words only the Duke noticed it and, ignoring the faint curl of his lip, Isabel went on, 'Rosalind, you will not mind?'

'Not at all. I think I should be glad.'

Lord Philip frowned. He had nothing against Rockliffe except a very reasonable dislike of having his hand forced. 'Yes, but . . .'

'Dear Philip,' sighed Rosalind, smiling brilliantly. 'Do go away – or we shall quarrel. Again.'

And Philip, left with nothing to do but give way gracefully, offered his arm to Mistress Dacre and experienced a strong desire to wring his sister's neck.

'Lord Philip takes his reponsibilities seriously,' remarked the Duke as he watched them go.

'Yes.' Rosalind held her head up to preserve herself from any suspicion of cowardice. 'I should perhaps explain that I am blind.'

The dark eyes widened suddenly but there was no change in the drawling tone as he replied, 'Are you? That is a pity – for it means you are probably unaware that yours is the most stylish gown in the room. Er . . . allow me to mention the fact that there is a vacant chair on your left.'

Rosalind's mouth quivered. 'Then will you not be seated, sir?'

'I thank you, madam – I shall be honoured.' He bowed and, having occupied the chair, withdrew a gold snuffbox from one capacious pocket. Flicking it open with practised dexterity, he proceeded to help himself from it with his usual languid air while his eyes, curiously alert beneath their sleepy lids, never left Rosalind's face. 'I now know why you do not dance but must confess myself at a loss to know why you are not . . . er . . . besieged. Never say I am your first London acquaintance?'

'No, your Grace. You are not.' Mischievous amusement rippled through the musical voice. 'On the other hand, you *are* the first who is in any way different from all the others.'

Rockliffe was somewhat taken aback. 'I rejoice to hear it! One does one's poor best, Mistress Vernon and it is comforting to be assured that one does not . . . labour in vain.'

She smiled demurely. 'I am sure it must be.'

'It is reprehensively vulgar of me,' he continued blandly, 'but I would dearly love to know who . . . "all the others" . . . might be.'

The violet eyes grew speculative. 'Would you? *How* dearly?'

'Enough,' replied the Duke with his peculiar glinting

126

smile, 'for you to name your own terms. Or do you think I cannot meet them?'

Rosalind laughed. 'Oh no, sir – I am sure that you can! It is simply that I should like you to describe the gentlemen I shall name in such a way that I may hope to remember which is which. I have the feeling, you see, that you have a discerning eye.'

'Naturally. Which is why I am sitting here with you.'

There was a brief pause and then, 'Your Grace – are you by any chance flirting with me?'

Rockliffe appeared to consider the matter. 'I believe,' he said at length, 'that I am *attempting* to do so. Have you any objection?'

'Not in the least,' she assured him politely. 'I merely wondered. Please go on.'

And his Grace was finally obliged to relinquish his languid sophistication as he gave way to rare laughter.

Lord Philip eyed them dubiously as he led Isabel down the set.

'What the devil do you suppose she's saying to him?' he asked despairingly. 'Everyone is staring.'

'Yes.' Isabel spread her skirts and pointed one slender foot. 'In envy, I expect.'

As the movement of the dance drew them apart at this moment, he had to wait a while before demanding an explanation; and then Isabel merely smiled and pivoted gracefully round him saying nothing.

'Well?' his Lordship insisted.

She sighed. 'All the gentlemen are jealous for obvious reasons and the ladies because the Duke isn't in the habit of sitting with unknown provincials and engaging in conversation. And he *never* laughs aloud – he's too busy being bored.'

'Oh.' Philip digested this. 'That's alright then.'

'Yes.' Isabel gazed distraitly across the room. 'What did you say the Marquis of Amberley looks like?'

'Tall and fair-haired,' replied Lord Philip absently, minding his steps. 'Why?'

'Because I think he's just come in with Mr Ingram.'

Philip jerked his head round and trod on her foot. 'Oh hell!' he said.

All tensions forgotten, Rosalind was enjoying herself – finding Rockliffe's caustic wit much more to her taste than the civil inanities she had endured earlier and his indolent manner irresistibly amusing. Then, quite without warning and in striking contrast to his Grace's drawling tones, she heard a light, crisp voice, close at hand and unmistakably familiar.

'Oh no, Jack! You must allow me *some* secrets, you know.'

And from that moment the Duke could have been a hundred miles away.

The shock of surprise drove the blood from her skin while something inside her gave a great lurch and effectively stopped her breath. She was completely unaware that Rockliffe had ceased speaking and was regarding her with an air of detached anticipation or that, half-a-dozen steps away, the Marquis of Amberley stood rooted to the spot, staring at her.

Equally oblivious, it was the Honourable Jack Ingram who walked blithely through the invisible barriers saying, 'Well, Rock? Do we qualify for a friendly greeting or are you ignoring us in the hope that we shall go away?'

Rockliffe sighed. 'Hardly. Some things are too much to hope for.' His gaze travelled to the Marquis and narrowed a little. Then, after a fleeting glance at Rosalind, he raised one thin, black brow and said mockingly, 'My dear fellow – you look as if you had seen a ghost.'

Pulling himself together, his Lordship looked into the lazily amused eyes and walked slowly forward. He knew that the Duke had already made some rather astute assumptions but it did not cause him undue concern. Rockliffe was inclined to perceptive curiosity but he was not a gossip.

'Imagination, Rock,' he said easily. 'I was merely dazzled by that opulent cravat pin of yours. I suppose it *is* a diamond?' And then, without waiting for a reply, he turned to gaze down at Rosalind. 'How do you do, Mistress Vernon? I scarcely dared hope to see you again so soon.'

Rosalind's colour fluctuated deliciously and she smiled shyly. 'Phil acts quickly – once he is convinced he should act at all,' she said. 'I have been here for three days.'

'Then you won't have met Mr Ingram.' Amberley presented his friend in a vague attempt to prevent any further disclosures. 'Jack – this is Mistress Vernon whose brother, Lord Philip, I think you know.'

Blinking a little, Jack bowed over Rosalind's hand and said, 'Your servant, Mistress Vernon. And are you enjoying your first taste of society?'

'Well, I *wasn't*,' came the candid reply, 'but I must admit that it has improved tremendously over the last half-hour.'

'I thank you,' murmured Rockliffe, provocatively meeting Amberley's eye.

'Mountebank!' retorted Jack amicably.

Rosalind laughed. 'Possibly – but his Grace is quite right, you know. He has been keeping me very well entertained.'

'My point, I think?' suggested the Duke gently.

The Marquis, who was deriving no pleasure from the discovery that Rosalind was on the friendliest of terms with his Grace, chose this moment to remember his carefully-considered decision to remain aloof. He subjected the room to a swift, keen scrutiny and then said lightly, 'Ah – I see Lady Wendover beckoning to me and must pay my respects. If you will excuse me, Mistress

129

Vernon . . . gentlemen?' And with a slight, graceful bow, he was gone.

Mr Ingram stared after him and then looked blankly at the Duke. 'Now why,' he demanded flatly, 'did he do that? Charlotte Wendover only wants him to dance with one of those platter-faced girls of hers – and Den must know it!'

'Yes.' His Grace smiled enigmatically. 'You would think so, would you not?'

Shortly after that Lord Philip and Mistress Dacre returned from the dance-floor and the Duke moved skilfully on, leaving Jack to exchange half-hearted banalities with his Lordship. Rosalind hardly noticed any of it. Somewhere inside her was a cold incomprehension caused by Amberley's conduct. He had greeted her with the same formality he might have offered to any chance-met acquaintance, and then left her with what his friends apparently conceived a mere excuse – and it hurt. She felt rebuffed and abandoned to a degree that she sternly told herself was out of all proportion to the event; but it was no use and her only positive emotion was a strong desire to go home.

It was not to be. The Duke of Rockliffe's pleasure in her company had not gone unremarked and, as soon as he removed himself, there were suddenly numerous gentlemen eager to obtain an introduction. Even Mistress Hawley, who had spent a whole month in a vain attempt to engage Rockliffe's interest, came back reinforced with two of her friends and charged with a wrathful determination to repay Mistress Vernon's ill-advised snub.

Plunged into a sea of strange voices, all seemingly intent on warring for her attention, Rosalind struggled desperately to stay calm and reply to them as best she could. They were all around her, bombarding her from every side with their questions, their compliments, their contrived witticisms, until her already weakened defences began to crumble and, with her nerves vibrating like violin strings, it was all she could do to stop herself screaming. The voices sounded nightmarishly similar and, even given the opportunity to accustom herself to each separately, she doubted her ability to identify one from another. Only one was recognisable as it jibed and sneered and cut at her; the thin tones of Maria Hawley – and harder to bear than all the rest.

'Where is my brother?' she asked at last, unable to understand why Philip was not making any attempt to protect her. And' had to repeat the question three times before she got an answer.

'Oh – his Lordship is caught fast in the talons of Colonel Harding,' said one of the gentlemen carelessly. 'Being regaled with the old fire-eater's memoirs, I shouldn't wonder. Terrible bore, old Harding, y'know – and the very devil to get away from.'

'But of course you don't know the Colonel, do you?' asked Mistress Hawley brightly. 'In fact, you don't really know anyone yet. Except Rockliffe.'

'No,' agreed Rosalind baldly. And only just prevented herself adding, 'And I wish to heaven that I didn't know *you*!'

Under cover of a laborious conversation with the elder Mistress Wendover, the Marquis of Amberley shifted his position so that he could the better observe Mistress Vernon. He did not like what he saw and a hint of grimness touched his mouth as he wondered what Lord Philip was about not to put a stop to the situation. White with strain, Rosalind turned this way and that, trying to face her persecutors – all of whom must be singularly stupid, thought Amberley savagely, if they could not see how much they were frightening her. And then she came abruptly to her feet and his Lordship hesitated no longer but, with a curt excuse to Mistress Wendover, strode briskly across the room.

Almost immediately he was detained by a light hand on

his arm and he swung round to meet Rockliffe's veiled gaze. 'Well?'

Without removing his hand from the wide velvet cuff, his Grace stared absently at the ruby on his finger and said remotely, 'Denzil, my loved one – you look ripe for murder and it doesn't take a genius to guess why. Either dissemble a little . . . or let *me* go.'

For a second, the Marquis could not trust himself to speak. Then he said unevenly, 'No. But I thank you for your advice and will repay it with a little of my own. Stay out of it, Rock.' And, shaking off the restraining hand, he walked on.

'So . . . you cannot dance,' Mistress Hawley was saying pityingly. 'What a shame! But perhaps you should try. After all, one never knows *what* one may achieve with a little perseverance – and I am sure that any of these gentlemen would be happy to oblige you.'

A murmur of enthusiastic assent rippled through the assembled ranks.

'No!' There was a note of rising panic in Rosalind's voice. 'I can't dance with any of you and don't wish to be – to be *obliged*!'

'Quite right,' approved Amberley lightly as he threaded a watchful passage through the group to her side. 'And certainly not by any of these gentlemen. What you need is a man of experience – such as myself.'

With a startled gasp, Rosalind turned towards him, hands outstretched. 'Oh – it's you!'

The Marquis received her hands in his and held them reassuringly. What he wanted to do was to take her right away from these criminally foolish people but he knew it to be unthinkable – not because of the gossip it would cause, but because he suspected that, once alone with her, he would not stop at holding her hands. And, since it was equally impossible to simply tell her tormentors to go to the devil, he opted for a third course that was no less shocking but at least had the merit of appearing less singular to Rosalind.

He said, 'Yes. It is I – come to beg you to make an exception in my case and attempt this minuet.'

She shook her head and he felt her hands shaking. 'I can't,' she said, low-voiced and pleading. 'You know I can't.'

'On the contrary, I know that you can – with me,' he demurred calmly. 'Come.' And, without giving her time to reply, he led her back through the uneasily silent group which parted like the Red Sea under the single contemptuous glance that was all he gave it.

'I can't!' whispered Rosalind again as they moved out of earshot. 'It's insane – and I only want to get out of here!'

'I know. But you can't – any more than you can disappoint me,' he told her with apparent ease as he drew her to a halt and turned her to face him. 'Give me your hand and pretend this is your parlour at Oakleigh – and smile. It will be alright, I promise you. Ready?'

Rosalind's insides twisted with cramp pains and she drew a long, unsteady breath. 'Oh God – if I must then! But you are quite mad, you know. Mad and . . . and inhuman if you don't know that the last thing I want to do just now is dance!'

'Mm. In fact, I'm little short of a monster,' responded his Lordship cheerfully as the music started. 'You curtsey, my dear.'

Rosalind did as she was bidden. 'And what's more,' she went on crossly as she arose and turned to move at his side, 'you have absolutely no right to bully me like this – not after the shabby way you ignored me earlier.'

Amberley placed his arm lightly around her waist and heard a distinct gasp of shock from behind them.

'Very true. I beg your pardon.'

Obedient to the pressure of his fingers, she stepped

gracefully across him and held out her skirts. 'So you should! For if you didn't mean to speak to me, you shouldn't have persuaded Phil to bring me to London. And you must know that I only came because . . .' She paused to concentrate more fully on her steps.

'Yes?' prompted the Marquis with ill-concealed eagerness. 'You only came because . . ?'

'Because I thought you wanted me to.'

'I did.' With resolute cowardice he avoided meeting Lord Philip's eye as they danced past him.

'Really?' Rosalind asked sardonically.

'Yes – really!' Rueful amusement quivered in the pleasant voice and he resisted the childish impulse to point out that, with Rockliffe in attendance, she had not appeared to need him. 'Stop ripping up at me! I thought you wanted to be rescued?'

And since this was indisputably true and since there was also something very soothing in the strength of his guiding arm, Rosalind relinquished her grievances and elected not to reply.

From the edge of the floor, Philip followed his sister's progress with hideous fascination. 'I don't believe it,' he said weakly, half to himself. 'I know she said he taught her to dance . . . but I can't say I ever thought that they would be crazy enough to do it here – in public!'

'Damned scoundrel's got his arm round her!' observed Colonel Harding loudly, peering disapprovingly through his glass. 'Modern manners – disgraceful!'

Philip flushed, uttered a muffled curse and eyed the Marquis with mounting wrath. Then Isabel emerged at his side and he hissed furiously, 'I thought you were with her! Why didn't you stop her making such a spectacle of herself?'

'I couldn't!' snapped Mistress Dacre, stung by the injustice of it. 'Any more than I could stop Maria Hawley and those others from upsetting her!'

134

'Well *I* can – and I will!' He took a hasty step towards the dancers.

'No you won't.' Isabel clung determinedly to his sleeve. 'You'll cause a scene and make things worse. Leave it to Lord Amberley. From the little I've seen of him, he's more than capable of taking care of her.'

The blue eyes blazed dangerously. 'Better than I?'

'Much better,' said Isabel unkindly. 'And if you think he's not perfectly aware of the stir he's causing, you can't have looked at him properly.'

In point of fact the Marquis, whilst trying to devote himself exclusively to Rosalind, was acutely conscious of every curious glance, indrawn breath or murmured word and a faint, tell-tale flush stained his cheek. He had never cared very much for the mass of public opinion but this kind of exhibitionism was little to his taste and, as the couples around them gradually fell silent and started drifting from the floor to watch from its perimeter, he began to wonder if he had not made a severe miscalculation.

A glance into Rosalind's face brought a modicum of comfort and revived his sense of humour. Their roles were now so ludicrously reversed and it was he who was tense while she, unaware that they were being stared at from all quarters, appeared comparatively relaxed. Just at that moment, he thought ironically, she was better off than he.

As he watched the last couples desert the floor to leave them in sole possession of it, the usual glint of laughter began to dawn in his eyes and, bending his head, he murmured, 'I don't know about you – but I have only one small regret.'

Rosalind swayed elegantly under his arm. 'Oh? And what is that?'

'That Letty Warriston isn't here to see us,' he replied wickedly. And had the satisfaction of hearing her deliciously husky laugh.

Standing beside his Grace of Rockliffe, Jack Ingram gazed incredulously at the Marquis's fair head tilted intimately close to Mistress Vernon's dark one and at the velvet-clad arm encircling her slender waist.

'Christ!' he breathed. 'What the devil does Den think he's doing?'

'I really couldn't say,' replied the Duke, evincing faint signs of regret. 'But I wish I'd thought of it.'

Jack grimaced. 'You would!'

'Yes.' The dark eyes held a gleam of pure enjoyment that contrasted oddly with the weary tone. 'But the point which really interests me is not what Denzil is doing, but how and where he found the opportunity to practise it.'

'*Practise it?*' echoed Mr Ingram, thunderstruck. 'Don't be ridiculous!'

A mocking smile touched the corners of Rockliffe's mouth as he gazed across at Amberley. 'Dear Jack,' he sighed. 'Always so naive.'

Remarkably, since they were all craning their necks to see what everyone was looking at, the orchestra brought the dance to a timely and triumphant conclusion while the Marquis responded to Rosalind's curtsey with a flourishing bow. Then, in the deathly hush that followed, he directed a briefly challenging glance along the flanked rows of their bemused audience and raised Rosalind's hand to his lips.

'My child,' he teased, 'you are a credit to your teacher. I congratulate you – both.'

And, as if in response to a signal, the silence around them dissolved into a buzz of pleasurably shocked chatter.

Chapter Ten

It was really no surprise to anyone that, as a result of Lady Crewe's assembly, Rosalind became a nine-day-wonder; but what *was* surprising was that her spectacularly public defiance of convention did not appear to do her any social harm. Lord Philip found this very hard to accept and, for a whole week, lived in the horrid expectation of seeing his sister ignored or snubbed – or, worse still, hearing her name coupled with Amberley's. But none of these disasters occurred and, instead, flowers, invitation cards and a constant stream of callers poured into the house in Great Jermyn Street so that the door-knocker was never still; and not one person openly alluded to the possibility of a relationship, past, present or future, between Mistress Vernon and the Marquis. Philip relaxed.

Gradually, he came to realise that this happy state of affairs was owed to the exertions of three people; quietly reliable Isabel, mischievously theatrical Rockliffe and, of course, Amberley – who had what Philip was fast coming to regard as an excessively irritating knack of always appearing to be right. Between them, these three had ensured that everyone knew Rosalind to be blind and effectively stopped any gossip with a few discreet words in the appropriate quarters. And substantially contributing to the general reluctance to link Mistress Vernon's name with that of the Marquis, was the simple fact that Rockliffe's interest in her was demonstrably the greater – for, in the days that followed, it was he who was usually to be found at her side and not Amberley. It was just confusing enough to silence the doubters and, when added to the palliative that Rosalind was known, though, by what means, Philip could not tell, to be well-dowered, it meant that she could not lightly be dismissed.

The only negative aspect of the affair was the deepening of Lord Philip's hostility towards the Marquis and this manifested itself immediately Amberley restored Rosalind to her brother's side at the end of their dance. Philip was unable to resist addressing a low-voiced tirade at the guilty pair and his temper was not improved when Rosalind received with irrepressible laughter the intelligence that everyone else had left the floor to watch. The Marquis said very little and this Philip attributed to an arrogant dislike of having his conduct criticised. It naturally never occurred to him that Amberley was in perfect agreement with him – up to a point – but was carefully restraining himself from replying in kind with a pithy denunciation of his Lordship's care of his sister. With heated indignation on one side but only cool reticence on the other, it cannot be said that they quarrelled; but the atmosphere between them was most definitely strained and misunderstanding became mutual.

Although she knew exactly what the trouble was, Rosalind very wisely refrained from discussing it with her brother – aware that any attempt on her part to persuade him that the Marquis was neither devious nor arbitrary would automatically end in failure. Philip was never deliberately contrary but he was possessed of a stubborn streak that inevitably made him dig in his heels if pressed against his inclination; he and Amberley had got off on the wrong foot at their very first meeting and it was plain that Philip thought he had good reason to dislike him. And even if, as Rosalind suspected, he was mistaken, the only sure way to put matters right was for him to discover it for himself. Philip would not be told, but he could – and must – be shown.

That her views were shared by Mistress Dacre came as a pleasant surprise and, as a result of it, Rosalind found herself liking Philip's engagement a good deal better than she had anticipated. Behind Isabel's quiet, unassuming manner lay a strength of character that enabled her to wield a subtle influence that was remarkably effective because no one seemed to notice it. Isabel would never raise her voice or repeatedly urge her point or make a play with wet eyelashes; she would never need to. And Rosalind found it admirable.

Most astonishing of all was the fact that the Lintons should have produced such a daughter, for her Ladyship's vague charm in no way concealed that she was essentially both frivolous and impractical – while, equally feckless, Lord Linton covered his basically weak character with bluff good-humour or blustering irritability, depending on the circumstance. As for the Honourable Robert, it was Rosalind's considered opinion that he had unfortunately inherited the worst traits of both his parents and was selfish, spineless and totally lacking in self-control.

She reached this conclusion on the occasion of a family dinner in Clarges Street when Robert abandoned all pretensions to good manners and slammed petulantly out of the house for no better reason than a vaunted desire to sit beside Rosalind instead of the youthful and extremely shy cousin assigned to him by his Mama. This display left the Viscount in a state of ineffectual fury, his Lady visibly unmoved and his daughter embarrassed. Lord Philip was both shocked and uncomfortable but carefully avoided showing either and Rosalind was frankly relieved. She had very little patience with spoiled young men prone to tantrums and rather feared that, given the opportunity, she might say so.

Robert, never one to know when to let well alone, rejoined the party later in the evening at Devonshire House and promptly set about isolating Rosalind in order to persuade her that no one understood him. He failed.

'You had much better address all this to your mother,' said Rosalind with a kind of flat patience. 'Although I'm inclined to think an apology might be more to the point. You were very rude, you know.'

Robert flushed slightly but, because Rosalind was both rich and pretty, he put a curb on his tongue and said ruefully, 'I was, wasn't I? And, of course, I know I must make my peace with Mama. But she should have known how it would be for I only agreed to be present because I knew you would be there.'

Rosalind raised a sardonic brow. 'Really? I thought you were just reluctant to waste your time on a mere cousin.'

He laughed self-consciously. 'Partly, perhaps. I'm afraid Jane and I don't get on very well. She bores me.'

'And I don't? How nice! You can't imagine how flattered I am.'

This shaft missed its mark altogether.

'Then I'm forgiven?' he asked with a hint of practised, boyish charm.

The dark head tilted fractionally away from him. 'Perhaps,' said Rosalind absently. 'I'll think about it.'

'A dangerous admission, my dear,' said a soft voice from behind her. 'Think if you must – but never confess to it.'

Robert started and then frowned with annoyance as Rosalind turned, smiling, to the newcomer.

'The advice of experience, your Grace?' she asked.

'Certainly.' Rockcliffe took her hand and raised it lightly to his lips. 'With me, you know, it generally is.'

Robert was not amused. 'Another dangerous admission, surely?' he suggested waspishly.

'Not at all – merely a statement of fact.' A mocking gleam lurked in the Duke's dark eyes. 'And the difference, you might say, between buying Fitzroy's breakdowns and . . . er . . . *not* buying them.'

'What do you mean by that?' snapped Robert. 'Those greys are well-matched and beautiful steppers – everyone says so!'

'True. And in the park they will do very well indeed,' Rockcliffe replied. 'But not, I think, on the road to Newmarket for they are not a racing pair. No stamina.'

'I think I should tell your Grace,' said Robert grittily, 'that *I* bought those horses!'

The smile grew and instantly Robert realised his error.

'Dear me! Did you indeed?' said his Grace, patently unsurprised. And then, encouragingly, 'But you will know better next time, won't you?'

Rosalind shuddered inwardly and waited for the storm to break. Strangely, it did not do so.

Instead, in a voice shaking with rage, Robert said, 'I am engaged to race Seaforth on Friday. Perhaps, when I've beaten him, you'd like to match me with a pair of your own?'

'Nothing is impossible,' taunted his Grace wearily. 'Though some things are, let us say – unlikely. But you may ask me again . . . if, of course, you beat Seaforth. And in the meantime, I see Mistress Hawley is striving to attract your attention.'

'Or yours,' retorted Robert, wishing he dared slap that cynical face.

'Oh no,' came the gentle reply. 'I am not so favoured. Do not, I beg, allow us to detain you.'

Which left Mr Dacre with nothing to do but take a typically ungracious leave.

'He is extremely tedious,' remarked the Duke, watching him go. 'You should be very pleased with me.'

'Well I am,' Rosalind owned, 'but I think perhaps you were a *little* unkind. After all, I don't suppose a pair of match greys are precisely cheap – even ones with no stamina.'

'No,' admitted his Grace thoughtfully, 'they were not cheap – and neither was the curricle I saw them pulling up Salt Hill yesterday.'

Three weeks' acquaintance with the Duke had taught Rosalind quite a lot and formality had been abandoned at some stage during their second meeting. She said, 'So you *did* know what you were saying. I thought as much.'

'Oh yes. I am never tactless by accident. But what I do not know is how the Honourable Robert paid for his turn-out.'

'I am surprised you didn't ask him,' responded Rosalind dryly. And then, 'Does it matter?'

Rockcliffe lifted his glass and gazed pensively across the room. 'It might. Are you thinking it's not any concern of mine?'

She grinned. 'Yes.'

'Mm . . . well, I hope you are right,' he said cryptically and, restoring the glass to his pocket, proceeded to take snuff from an onyx box. 'Tell me – how lies the land between Amberley and your brother these days?'

'The same as ever,' she replied gloomily. 'Furrowed and thorny. Or so I imagine.'

'Imagine? Is it possible you don't know?'

'No, I don't.' The dimple peeped and she said innocently, 'I hoped that *you* might tell *me*. Mr Ingram says you are omniscient.'

Amusement tugged at Rockcliffe's mouth but he subdued it and said plaintively, 'I used to think so, certainly – but I rather fear I must be slipping.'

'And that,' remarked Rosalind cheerfully, 'means that you still haven't discovered how Lord Amberley and I came to be acquainted. What a shame! I wonder why he won't tell you?'

'Like the peace of God, the working of Amberley's mind passeth all understanding,' drawled the Duke. 'Why don't you ask him?'

'I might if I were granted the opportunity. But I don't think we've exchanged above half a dozen sentences since the Crewe assembly – and that was weeks ago. Do you think he's afraid of Philip?'

Caught unawares, his Grace was betrayed into a choke of laughter.

'No, my child, I don't,' he said positively. 'And neither do you. But it's an enchanting thought.'

'No – just a last resort.' Rosalind sighed. 'Do you know if he intends to come here tonight?'

'He is here already,' Rockcliffe informed her negligently. 'In fact, for the past five minutes I've been wondering just what he and the blushing Mistress Isabel are finding to discuss so privately. And I think . . .' He paused wickedly. 'I rather think that Lord Philip is wondering exactly the same thing.'

This was perfectly true but, had Philip been privileged to know it, Isabel's blushes owed nothing to any gallantry on Lord Amberley's part; it was simply that, after three weeks of summoning her courage, she had embarked on the self-imposed task of attempting to remedy her brother's omissions by thanking the Marquis for his generous forbearance. And she was finding it difficult.

As soon as he realised what she was saying, Amberley stemmed the tide of her stumbling recital with a movement of one tapering hand and said, 'Mistress Dacre – there is no need for you to thank me. What I did was done, not for the convenience of your brother, but to suit my own peculiar code of ethics. I don't know where you came by this information and I wish very much that you had *not* done so – but, greatly though I appreciate your thought, I would much prefer not to discuss it.'

143

Already a little pink, Isabel flushed afresh.

'Yes. I – I guessed you would say that,' she replied, her voice very low. 'And I *do* respect your feelings. But I wanted you to know that – that we're not all as ungrateful as Robert!'

The Marquis experienced a twinge of remorse. 'I *do* know it and must beg your pardon if I seemed churlish. Did I?'

Isabel looked up into ruefully gleaming grey-green eyes and was lost. 'Not at all. I don't think you could,' she said naively. 'And naturally I shan't speak of it again – of Robert, I mean.'

'Naturally,' Amberley agreed with strenuous gravity. 'And do you think I may rely similarly on Lord Philip's discretion?'

'I'm sorry?' she asked blankly.

There was a slight pause and then, 'Perhaps I am at fault. I assumed that his Lordship was the source of your knowledge.'

'Oh no! Lord Philip doesn't know – he thinks that . . .' And there she stopped, staring at the Marquis in frozen dismay.

'So Lord Philip thinks I took the money, does he?' he mused, half to himself. 'Well, well . . . that explains a lot.'

'You must be wondering why I haven't told him,' began Isabel wretchedly. 'But indeed I . . .'

'My dear, odd though it may seem, I am very glad that you haven't – and I applaud your restraint, for I feel sure it can't have been easy,' said his Lordship lightly. He smiled suddenly. 'But I'm forever in your debt. It's extremely comforting to know that Lord Philip's dislike of me isn't as personal as I'd begun to think it!'

Throughout his conversation with Mistress Dacre, Amberley had been acutely conscious of the fact that, not only was his Grace of Rockliffe the sole recipient of

144

Rosalind's attention, but that they wore the air of old friends. It was like salt in a wound and, when Isabel was claimed by her partner for the minuet, the Marquis shrugged all his resolutions aside and strode purposefully across the room. There was quite definitely a limit, he thought irritably, to the amount of experience Rosalind needed in order to form a rod of assize; and he was damned if he was going to watch that devil Rock steal a march on him.

'Good evening, Mistress Vernon,' he said pleasantly. 'It suddenly occurred to me that you must be missing your parrot.'

'Broody?' Rosalind frowned, a little puzzled. 'Why do you ask?'

'Because,' replied the Marquis, grinning down at the Duke, 'I can see that you've adopted a popinjay in his place.'

Provocative grey-green eyes met deceptively lazy black ones and locked, as Rosalind gave a gurgle of laughter.

'This fellow,' announced Rockliffe calmly, 'is a person of no discrimination. He is also untruthful, unreliable and no gentleman.'

'And his Grace,' countered Amberley smoothly, 'is just about to desert you for the card-room.'

Rosalind turned her head to smile enquiringly at Rockliffe.

'Are you?' she asked.

'It seems unlikely,' he replied. And then, raising one quizzical brow to the Marquis, 'Am I?'

'Yes.' Still looking his friend in the eye, Lord Amberley committed unhesitating perjury. 'Jack demands your presence and I promised that he should have it.'

His Grace sighed and came unhurriedly to his feet. 'I scent a ruse – and a deplorably unoriginal one at that. But I suppose I must be certain before I call out that pretty small-sword of yours.' He turned to Rosalind. 'It's common piracy, of course – but what can one do?'

'Careful, Rock!' Amberley's voice brimmed with mischief. 'As the challenged party, I'd have the choice of weapons – and I'd choose pistols, you know.'

'Yes.' The Duke eyed him with anguished resignation. 'Yes. You probably would. *So* unsubtle!' He took Rosalind's hand and held it for a good deal longer than was necessary. '*Au revoir, mademoiselle*. One does one's poor best, you understand – but there are some things that even *I* cannot remedy. I leave him to you – regretfully.' And, with an elaborate bow, he kissed her fingers and cast Amberley a glance of perfectly amicable mockery before strolling away in the direction of the card-room.

The Marquis moved towards his vacated chair. 'May I sit down?'

Rosalind suddenly discovered that she felt distinctly nettled.

'Of course. If you think it's worth your while.'

'I beg your pardon?'

'Well, I didn't think you would be staying,' she explained in a dulcet tone.

His Lordship sat. 'Why should I not?'

'*I* don't know – but you usually manage to think of something, don't you? Unlike his Grace,' she said kindly, 'I find your ingenuity quite startling.'

Laughter stirred in Amberley's eyes. 'No you don't. You think I'm the snake who lured you away from Oakleigh only to ignore you.'

The dimple quivered and was gone. 'And aren't you?'

'Very probably – though not in the way that you mean it,' came the unhelpful reply. 'And, in all conscience, you have to admit that you haven't exactly needed me to swell the throng. The town is awash with your admirers.'

'That,' said Rosalind severely, 'is not the point. I

146

could have half the gentlemen in England at my feet but it wouldn't alter the fact that I've only three real friends; Isabel, his Grace of Rockcliffe – and yourself.'

The Marquis found little pleasure in the knowledge that she regarded him as a friend and none at all in ranking equally with the Duke. He said, 'Do you see much of Rock?' And then could have bitten his tongue out.

If Rosalind noticed his slip, she gave no sign of it. 'Well, everything is relative, of course,' she said composedly, 'but I suppose you might say so. He calls on us from time to time and last week he took me for a drive. Oh – and he has invited Phil and Isabel and I to share his box at the Opera on Saturday. I'm looking forward to that.'

'I see.' Clever Rock – I wish I'd thought of that one. 'And how does Lord Philip view all this?'

Long silky lashes veiled the violet eyes. 'Long-sufferingly,' she replied deviously. 'It's to be "*Iphigénie en Aulide*" and he doesn't care for Gluck.'

Just at that moment, Gluck was not all Lord Philip did not care for. After twenty minutes spent trying to corner his uncommonly elusive fiancée, he did so only to discover that she was behaving unusually like her mother.

'At last!' he said, manoevring her into an alcove. 'Now – what the devil was that fellow saying to you?'

Mistress Dacre regarded him owlishly. 'What fellow? Monsieur de Fontenac?'

'No – Monsieur le Marquis!'

Light broke upon Isabel. 'Oh – *Amberley*!'

Philip's temper began to rise. 'Yes – Amberley! What was he saying to you?'

'Saying to me?' she repeated vaguely. 'Why, nothing very remarkable. He – he asked if we were going to the Queensbury rout. Or no – that might have been Mr Consett.' She paused doubtfully, a tiny frown creasing

147

her brow. Then it cleared and she said happily, 'But no – I was right the first time. It was Mr Consett who talked about Mrs Clive.'

If Lord Philip had been in the habit of grinding his teeth he might have done so then. As it was, goaded, he said, 'Well, perhaps you'll explain just what there was in that to make you blush like a poppy?'

'Surely, my Lord,' she asked, making expert use of her fan, 'you don't expect me to repeat it to you?'

'Yes. I do.'

The brown eyes widened and filled with shocked reproof. 'But I couldn't possibly! I hesitate to say it, but you must know as well as I do that . . . that some of Mr Consett's tales are rather – *warm!*'

There was a glacial silence. Then, 'In which case,' retorted Philip with relish, 'you shouldn't have been listening to them. Do I take it that Lord Amberley's conversation was also . . . *rather warm?*'

Isabel lifted a limpid gaze to meet his Lordship's sardonic blue one. 'Oh no,' she replied sweetly. 'Lord Amberley is all courtesy – and extremely charming. I like him.'

Something he took for anger passed like a red-hot wire through Philip's chest and his mouth set in a grim line. 'Do you?' he asked frigidly. 'Then it seems I am answered, doesn't it?'

Chapter Eleven

March passed, cold and blusteringly equinoctial, and gave way to rainbow-hued April – and still the Lord Marquis pursued, in a desultory fashion, his policy of vigilant *laisser-faire*. And then, quite without warning, something occurred to change his mind.

It began at the Cocoa-Tree where he and the Honourable Jack Ingram passed a pleasant hour at picquet before being joined by the Duke of Rockcliffe who, it appeared, had won two thousand guineas at *écarté*, lost them again at hazard and subsequently decided that gaming was a tedious pastime.

Sighing, Jack pushed the cards aside and ordered a bottle of canary. 'If, by that, you mean that you wish you'd stuck to *écarté*,' he said good-naturedly, 'I entirely agree with you.'

'And if by *that*,' replied his Grace, casually drawing up a chair, 'you mean to infer that I am interrupting your game, you are perfectly right. I am. I have a firm belief that one's friends have a duty to share one's misfortunes.'

The Marquis grinned. 'You hear that, Jack? He needs cheering up. Tell him a bawdy story.'

Mr Ingram was busy counting up points. '*You* tell him one . . . Devil take it! You beat me.' He threw down the pencil and leaned back in his chair in mock disgust. Then, 'Or better still, let him tell *us* one. Come on, Rock – what's the latest gossip?'

149

The Duke sighed. 'Nothing,' he said regretfully, 'in the least bit scandalous. Depressing, isn't it?'

'It must be,' agreed Amberley sympathetically. 'And mentally taxing too, I shouldn't wonder. What *will* you find to talk about?'

Rockcliffe surveyed him from beneath mocking lids and then replied with a single, pleasantly-delivered word of explicit vulgarity.

His Lordship laughed. 'You've met Mistress Vernon's parrot.'

'Yes.' The Duke raised his glass to the light and examined it meditatively. 'A singularly ill-mannered bird. I am not enamoured of it. It . . . er . . . spits.'

'It *what?*' demanded Jack.

'Spits,' obliged Amberley. 'And does it spit at you, Rock?'

'It spits at everyone,' came the pained reply. And then, pensively, 'One cannot but wonder if it did not spit at young Caversham in the very moment he knelt at the divine Rosalind's feet.'

Just for an instant, the candlelight danced oddly before Amberley's eyes and the cheerful sounds of the room became muffled, like things heard from under water. Then the world righted itself and he heard Mr Ingram say, 'Do you mean that Harry Caversham has offered for her at last? Well . . . the Lord be praised! I thought he'd never get round to it.'

'And was he accepted?' asked the Marquis, carefully remote.

Rockcliffe considered the sudden absence of amusement in his friend's voice and the strained look in his eyes. They did not surprise him but, even though he felt a certain sympathy, he could not resist one tiny jibe.

'My dear Denzil – I thought you disapproved of gossip?'

A white shade bracketed Amberley's mouth but he said nothing.

Jack glanced idly at him and drew a sharp breath, his gaze widening suddenly. Then he turned back to the Duke and said easily, 'Well, *I* don't – so tell me. *Has* she accepted him?'

A faint smile gleamed in the saturnine gaze. 'Dear Jack,' his Grace murmured. 'Always so *good*.' He sighed. 'No, my loved ones. To the best of my knowledge, she has *not* accepted him and he is now drowning his sorrows in the other room.'

The icy constriction in his Lordship's chest began to ease a little and some of the colour returned to his face. He said expressionlessly, 'You had this from Harry himself?'

Rockcliffe replied with an almost imperceptible inclination of his head and sought in his pocket for his snuff-box. 'The lady, I gather, was perfectly kind and charming . . . but excruciatingly final. A pity – perhaps. Young Caversham is a pleasant youth and a very eligible parti . . . and a great improvement on previous offers.' He smiled blandly at Amberley and, flicking open the silver box with one long finger, held it out to him. 'De Lamerie – circa 1740, I suspect. Quite pretty – though a trifle heavily chased. But possibly you do not admire the use of the rococo in so small an object?'

Ignoring both snuff and box, the Marquis said abruptly, 'What previous offers?'

Without any undue haste, Rockcliffe passed the box to Mr Ingram and then helped himself from it with a languid air. 'I believe there have been two,' he said at length. 'And though Lord Philip did not, for obvious reasons, disclose the names of the unfortunate gentlemen from whom they came, one might, I think, hazard a tolerably reasonable guess. Fortune-hunters both; one a known libertine and the other addicted to dice.'

'Longley,' announced Jack. 'and . . . Ludo Sterne?'

'My thoughts precisely. How nice,' said his Grace

simply, 'to have them so beautifully endorsed. You will have guessed, by the way, that these two were also rejected – but by his Lordship, who did not consider them worthy to approach his sister. One cannot but applaud his good-sense.'

Frowning down at the emerald on his left hand, the Marquis said, 'You say Vernon told you this himself? Why?'

Rockcliffe shrugged. His private suspicion was that Lord Philip entertained hopes of seeing his sister a Duchess but this was a thought he preferred not to share – yet. He said, 'Why indeed? He may be feeling the weight of his responsibilities . . . or, like myself, he may enjoy hearing his decisions endorsed. Even I cannot be expected to know everything. And my interest is now centered on which of the flower-and-verse offering multitude will be next to declare himself.'

Jack grinned. 'Well don't shatter my illusions by saying you don't have a theory!'

'I do, of course,' the Duke admitted slowly. 'But I fear it is unlikely to prove popular. I am inclined to nominate Robert Dacre.'

'Hell!' breathed Mr Ingram. 'Well I can see why he might offer – but not why she would accept.'

'Quite.' Rockcliffe looked across at Amberley and raised one enquiring brow. 'No comment, Denzil?'

'None.' The Marquis rose from his seat with lithe fluidity. 'Except to say that I am going home and to bid you both goodnight.' And with a slight nod and a briefly mechanical smile, he walked away.

Jack watched him go, a concerned frown shadowing his pleasant face. He said, 'He's in love with her, isn't he? With Rosalind Vernon? I had no idea. But I suppose you knew?'

'Yes.' The Duke smiled faintly. 'I've known since the first time I met her. But I'm not quite the crass oaf you imagine. For some reason, Denzil is holding himself aloof and it seemed to me to be time he ceased to do so – hence what I said.'

Mr Ingram eyed him uncertainly. 'And she?' he asked. 'Has it occurred to you to wonder if she returns his regard?'

'Naturally.' His Grace picked up the cards and, shaking back his ruffles, began dealing them with deft expertise. 'But you really can't expect me to divulge quite all my secrets, you know.' He spread his cards and smiled urbanely. 'Will you declare?'

Not for the first time, in the last two months, the Marquis of Amberley passed a night pacing his library floor. The first shock of Rockcliffe's disclosures had gone, leaving behind a bleak sense of temporary respite – for while the thought of Robert Dacre, though galling, was easily dismissed, Harry Caversham was a different matter. An engaging young man, universally popular and heir to an earldom, he was – as Rockcliffe had said – a very eligible parti. Not that Rosalind would care for that – but Lord Philip would; and Harry was a crony of his.

Yet Rosalind had rejected him and that, surely, should be a small comfort? Something that was not quite a smile twisted his Lordship's mouth for the joyless truth was that it made no difference at all to his basic problem. All these weeks he had been running very fast in order to stand still and he was no nearer now to his goal than he had ever been; the hour, so long awaited, was upon him and it found him unprepared. All the poise and assurance he had taken for granted throughout his adult life evaporated like mist in the sun beneath the growing dread he had of confession. He could not make the decision to say what must be said; and he despised himself for it.

The situation, then, was as fixed as the pole-star and as blatant. In addition to the requisite courage, one needed some small hope that one's feeling might be returned; and, since one could not, in honour, pay court without being sure one could offer marriage, nor offer marriage without first laying bare one's dark burden of guilt, there was no chance for such hope to be realised. The wheel, it seemed, had turned a full circle.

'Oh God!' said the Marquis aloud to the empty room. 'What in hell's name is the matter with me? If I can't do better than this, I *deserve* to be bloody miserable!'

Unthinking, his feet had carried him to the large knee-hole desk that occupied one of the window embrasures and, on impulse, he pulled open one of the drawers and withdrew a large sheet of parchment. For a long time he stared down without really seeing it. He did not need to see it for he knew what it was; the collected verses of James Graham, first Marquis of Montrose, all laboriously copied in Amberley's own sloping hand from a torn and faded folio. They had been meant for Rosalind – something he had thought she would like to have. Only he had not given them to her, held back by the knowledge that someone would have to read them to her and conscious that he wanted that someone to be himself. So here they still were.

Slowly, his eyes focused on the page and, quite at random, he began to read. The stanza was by no means new to him and so it was not that which caused the grey-green gaze to sharpen suddenly or to go back and re-read.

> '*He either fears his fate too much*
> *Or his deserts are small,*
> *That puts it not unto the touch*
> *To win or lose it all.*'

No blazing comets or strange and potent omens, then; just a quiet message for the man who cared to look for it.

And the Marquis not only looked but understood – and when he laid the paper back on his desk, he was smiling.

Isabel looked a little wistfully at the elegant scroll tied up with violets and silver ribbon that the butler placed in Rosalind's hands and then, with dawning amusement, at the expression of resignation on its recipient's face.

'Oh – Rose!' she laughed. 'You might at least wait until you hear what it says – and it's quite the prettiest one you've had.'

'Is it?' Mistress Vernon was not noticeably enthusiastic. Her fingers delicately explored the flowers and she bent her head to smell them. 'Violets, aren't they?'

Isabel allowed the footman to take her cloak and agreed that they were.

'Oh God,' said Rosalind forebodingly. 'It's going to be another ode to my eyes – I know it. Why *do* they do it?'

Mistress Dacre abandoned all thoughts of sorting out the fruits of their morning's shopping and ushered Rosalind into the parlour away from prying ears.

'Well, I suppose it *is* a little tactless. But . . .'

'*Tactless?*' echoed Rosalind. 'It's asinine! But I could put up with that if only they weren't all so incredibly silly. *O Goddess mine, whose purple eyes/Doth mine unwary heart capsize,*' she parodied disgustedly. 'I ask you – what man of sense could write such stuff without realising that, at best, it will only make me laugh?'

Isabel sat down and arranged her wide skirts with a thoughtful air. 'None, perhaps. But I should think that – that if one cared for a gentleman, one wouldn't laugh. No matter *how* bad his poetry.'

The violet eyes widened a little. 'No . . . I suppose not. I'll admit that that aspect of it had never occurred to me. But does Phil send *you* this sort of . . . or no. It's not his style, is it?'

'No.' Isabel looked down at her hands. 'I doubt if it would ever occur to him.'

'Do you wish it would?'

The bluntly phrased question caught Isabel unawares and she flushed painfully and lost herself in a tangle of evasive half-sentences.

'Don't be shy,' said Rosalind. 'I promise not to quote you so you are perfectly safe. *Would* you like Phil to address sonnets to your left eyebrow?'

A wavering smile touched the corners of Isabel's mouth. Then, 'Yes,' she said simply. 'I should like it very much indeed. But the chances of his doing so are about as great as those of – of Rockcliffe addressing such a one to you!'

Recognising a gallant attempt at levity, Rosalind responded by holding out the violet-adorned scroll. 'Speak not too soon!' she grinned. 'This might be the one.'

Isabel took it and, sliding off the ribbon, opened it out. Her eyes scanned it rapidly and then she looked expectantly across at Rosalind.

'It's not from Rockcliffe. It's from Lord Amberley.'

'*Amberley?*' The shock of it took Rosalind's breath away and she said uncertainly, 'You are joking, surely? He wouldn't . . . *would he?*'

Isabel laughed. 'No. It's *from* Amberley and it *is* poetry. But he didn't write it.'

'Oh,' said Rosalind lamely. 'Then who did?'

'Someone called James Graham. His Lordship seemed to have copied it out and it's very, very long.'

'Oh!' said Rosalind again but differently. 'How kind of him to remember! But I wish he'd . . .'

'Yes?' prompted Isabel. 'You wish he'd what?'

'Oh – nothing. It's just that I'd have liked him to read it to me himself . . . but it doesn't matter. Will you do it for me?'

'Of course. I've only been waiting for your permission,' said Isabel candidly. And, clearing her throat, she looked down at the lines of verse and began:

156

> *'My dear and only love I pray*
> *This noble world of thee . . .'*

And stopped again. The brown gaze settled in awed fascination on Rosalind's face. 'Goodness! I think he *should* have come himself!'

Rosalind grinned. 'He didn't write it, remember. Go on.'

So Isabel went on and soon began to realise that those first lines were somewhat misleading for, if this was a love-poem, it was unlike any she had ever read. And then she arrived at the fifth verse and was in doubt again.

> *'But if thou will be constant then,*
> *And faithful of thy word,*
> *I'll make thee glorious by my pen*
> *And famous by my sword.*
> *I'll serve thee in such noble ways*
> *Was never heard before;*
> *I'll crown and deck thee all with bays*
> *And love thee evermore.'*

She paused and then said lightly, 'I think that's probably the most beautiful declaration I've ever heard.'

'Yes.' An odd smile lit Rosalind's eyes. 'But that isn't why Lord Amberley sent it.'

'Is it not?' Isabel leaned back in her chair and surveyed her future sister with an air of mild discovery not unmixed with impish retaliation. 'And do you wish it was?' she asked.

It was that night after dinner that Lord Philip seized the opportunity of their first evening at home inside a week and embarked on what he intended to be a frank and thorough exploration of his sister's attitude to matrimony.

'Lord Rayne,' he said without preamble, 'has asked my permission to pay his addresses to you.'

Rosalind's mind was far away but she heard the words and replied to them with an ease that caused scarcely a ripple in the flow of her thoughts. 'No.'

'No?' echoed Philip. 'What do you mean – *no*?'

She stirred reluctantly. 'I mean that I won't marry him. But I don't mind telling him so myself if you would prefer it.'

The blatant disinterest in her tone roused his Lordship to indignation.

'Well that's fortunate because you will have to! And is it too much to ask what's wrong with Rayne?'

'Nothing,' replied Rosalind patiently, 'that I can think of. But I don't want to marry him.'

'But *why*? Damn it, Rose – you can't go on refusing perfectly good offers for no better reason than that! I don't mind so much about Rayne but, for the life of me, I can't understand why you won't take Harry. He's . . .'

'Phil, we've been through all this before,' sighed Rosalind. 'Lord Harry is a very pleasant young man and I like him; but not well enough to live with him for the rest of my life.'

'Then who,' demanded Philip bitterly, '*are* you going to marry? Rockliffe?'

A slow smile curled Rosalind's mouth. 'You're taking a lot for granted. He hasn't asked me.'

'But if he did?'

The smile grew infinitely wicked. 'Wait and see.'

Lord Philip eyed her with gloomy exasperation as she sat idly turning a roll of parchment between slender hands. 'What have you got there?' he asked irritably. 'Another love-lorn lyric?'

There was a brief pause and then she said placidly, 'No. Isabel read some of it to me earlier this afternoon and I thought you might be persuaded to finish it.'

158

'I doubt it,' he replied sourly. 'What is it anyway?'

'Some verses written by Montrose. Lord Amberley sent them. And don't jump to conclusions,' she advised sardonically. 'His Lordship read Wishart to me at Oakleigh and he sent the verses because he thought they would interest me. And if you can bring yourself to set aside your idiotic prejudices for a moment, it's possible that they would interest you too.' She held out the scroll to him. 'Well?'

For a moment, his Lordship hesitated and then he reached out and took it with a reluctant grin. 'Very well – you win. Temporarily. Where shall I begin?'

If anyone had told Philip that he would enjoy reading poetry to his sister and then discussing it with her, he would have berated them as a fool; but the fact remained that he did enjoy it and, at the end of an hour, his mood was so much improved that Rosalind was emboldened to ask a question.

'Phil – why are you marrying Isabel?'

The sapphire gaze rested on her in surprise. 'You know why. It's a suitable match and Uncle Rowland wished it.'

'And is that the only reason?'

He shrugged. 'Yes. What other would there be?'

Rosalind's eyes grew troubled. 'So it's a marriage of convenience? One of those fashionable alliances where you are scrupulously polite to each other over the breakfast table and go your separate ways the rest of the time?'

Philip laughed. 'And how much do you know of such marriages?'

'Enough to name you several instances,' came the disconcerting reply. '*You* form a liaison with some similarly-disposed married lady and Isabel, when she's dutifully presented you with an heir, is free to choose any rake in London as her lover. Is that what you want?'

He flushed, 'She'd better not!'

'Meaning that you can do as you please but she must do as you say?'

'No! I never said that – or meant it! And you shouldn't speak of such things,' responded Philip, hard-pressed.

'Why not? After all, if I married Lord Rayne, it would be exactly the same for me, wouldn't it? As I understand it, one is not required to be faithful – just discreet. Is it not so?'

'Devil take it – *no*! And if Isabel thinks I'm going to let her carry on like that she very much mistakes the matter,' announced his single-minded Lordship without stopping to wonder why the mere thought of it roused him to wrath. 'I won't have it!'

A faint glimmer of satisfaction gathered in Rosalind's eyes. 'I see. Then I suggest,' she said pleasantly, 'that you tell her so.'

Chapter Twelve

Having finally made the decision to put his fortunes to the touch, Amberley discovered there were unforeseen difficulties in its implementation and at the end of a week he had contrived to meet Rosalind only three times and then always in company. The first had been on the occasion of the Davenant soirée when he had quite skilfully, or so he had thought, removed her from Jack Ingram's side and been foolishly heartened by a fleeting lapse in her usual friendly composure. For the space of a heartbeat she had seemed absurdly pleased and yet shy; and when he had kissed her hand – a thing she must surely be accustomed to by now – her fingers had not been entirely steady and she had undoubtedly coloured a little. But these signs of encouragement had been so short-lived that, in less than an hour, he was wondering if he had not imagined them; for though she had thanked him with obvious sincerity for the poetry and been eager to discuss it with him, she had done so with easy un-affectedness and he was left with the depressing impression that he had so far failed to make any signal advance.

At the Grantham's ball he had not even achieved a moment of semi-privacy – a fact that made him quite unreasonably annoyed and was directly responsible for goading him into his first visit to Great Jermyn Street. Unfortunately, this was similarly unproductive for he was not the only visitor and, instead of carrying Rosalind off for a drive in the park, he had been forced to watch Robert Dacre making sheep's eyes at her whilst he himself endured a half-hour of stilted conversation with Lord Philip – who had plainly not been pleased to see him.

The Lord Marquis had retired to Grosvenor Square in a mood that no one in his household recognised and spent almost an hour contemplating the hitherto un-suspected advantages of abduction.

It is possible, though perhaps unlikely, that Amberley would have derived some small comfort from the knowledge that Nemesis did not tread solely in his footsteps; that she was also dogging those of the Hon-ourable Mr Dacre and driving him at last to desperate remedies.

For Robert was facing ruin. Incapable of reducing his extravagant rate of expenditure, prohibited from approaching Philip, refused by his similarly embarrassed parents and by unpaid friends who were reluctant now to throw good money after bad, he was left with a mountain of debts and no way of paying them. Even the money lenders turned him away, knowing that, as he had no prospects of inheriting anything but an already grossly encumbered estate, he could only represent a loss. And by the time his tailor had disobligingly, and none too politely, indicated that until his account was settled he would advance no further credit, Robert was becoming very frightened indeed.

Dreadful visions of angry tradesmen demanding payment invaded his waking thoughts and his sleep was haunted by nightmares in which he was clapped up in the stinking squalor of Newgate or the Fleet and from which he awoke shaking and clammy with sweat. All day long he skulked in one or other of his clubs, too afraid now to indulge in the pastime of cards or dice, but even more afraid of an outside world that seemed to be

162

peopled with his creditors. Each day brought more bills; from his bootmaker, his saddler, his peruquier and his now openly importunate tailor; and every day Robert grew a little more desperate as he wondered how long he had before the axe fell. And on top of it all, he owed a thousand guineas to the Duke of Rockliffe.

It had been, he now realised, the crowning folly to challenge Rockliffe to that race; but when he had beaten Lord Seaforth, even though it had been due to a lame off-leader, he had not been able to resist it – and the more so when he became aware that the Duke did not wish to oblige him. So Robert had publicly harrassed him until his Grace had finally given way and the stake had been fixed and the course determined. Robert had been jubilant; and then the race was run and Rockliffe had beaten him by a margin that was little short of humiliating and left him with a new debt. A debt of honour.

A thousand guineas; just a thousand. Nothing to Rockliffe but everything to Robert and meaning that, in addition to avoiding his trades-people, he had now to dodge the Duke as well. Two days after the race they had come face to face in the foyer at White's and for a moment those cynical dark eyes had rested on him in smiling mockery before he had made his escape. But that single look stayed with Robert for a long time afterwards and told him many things he should have seen before; such as the fact that Rockliffe knew he could not pay even a paltry thousand and had used his knowledge quite deliberately – not out of any personal vindictiveness, but because he, Robert, had given him the opportunity on a plate. And Rockliffe was Amberley's friend.

In Robert's feverish mind all his troubles could be traced back to the Marquis – most notably the fact that, because of him, it was impossible to approach Lord Philip. Robert considered taking his woes to Isabel in the

163

hope that she might waive his promise just this once, but was forced to conclude that it was unlikely. Isabel was not prone to changes of heart and she had, moreover, become deplorably friendly with the Marquis. One could no more trust her than one could trust Philip to keep quiet if one approached him without her knowledge. The situation was hopeless and Robert could think of only three ways out; theft, flight or marriage to a lady of means.

Each of these being equipped with its own drawback, he felt no decided preference for any of them; but, since his chances of planning and executing the perfect robbery were undeniably remote, he naturally opted for the lady of means and duly set himself out to engage her interest, aware all the time of a pressing need for haste. And when he received a politely-worded reminder from his Grace of Rockliffe, he set off that evening for a ridotto in Vauxhall Gardens in a mood of last-ditch determination, dangerously tempered with recklessness.

The party, hosted by Lord Philip and including, amongst others, Mistress Dacre and Mistress Vernon, travelled to the Gardens by boat, then strolled down lantern-lit walks to the gaily-hued booth which his Lordship had reserved. And here, much to Robert's disgust, the party largely stayed. It was not until close on midnight when, having consumed Lord Philip's carefully chosen supper, everyone finally decided to saunter around the arbors or watch the Grand Firework Display, that Robert's chance came at last and he seized it with an eagerness born of anxiety.

It cannot be said that Rosalind was pleased to find herself walking *à deux* with Robert Dacre but, since she had no reason to be wary of him, she was perfectly resigned to making the best of it. The best, of course, could be no more than boredom and the worst, irritation – but it seemed a small price to pay for allowing Isabel and Philip a little time to themselves.

She was just wondering how long it would take her dear, dim-witted brother to begin to suspect that his much-vaunted marriage of convenience had gone sadly awry and how much longer after that before he could be brought to admit it, even to himself, when she was jerked rudely back into the present by Robert's hand grasping hers.

'Say yes!' he pleaded urgently. 'Please say yes! You will, won't you?'

Having no idea of what he had been saying, Rosalind was unable to comply with this request. She was also, she discovered, unable to withdraw her hand from his hot clasp and this annoyed her.

'I beg your pardon. I am afraid I wasn't attending,' she said coolly. 'What is it?'

Robert stifled a curse and simultaneously experienced a strong desire to shake her. Then, glancing round him, he espied a secluded bench almost completely screened by the trailing fronds of a willow and, pulling Rosalind towards it, he did what he realised he should have done in the first place.

'Sit down,' he said curtly. And then, belatedly, 'Please.'

Rosalind sat, though not from choice and felt him imprison her other hand as well; but before she could open her mouth to demand its release, he was speaking again.

'You must – you *shall* listen to me! I will not be put off!'

'No,' agreed Rosalind dryly. 'Even *I* can see that. But for heaven's sake let go of my hands and stop enacting me a drama – just say what you have to say.'

Far from setting her free, Robert's hands tightened convulsively. His face was white with anger but he managed to keep his voice level. 'Very well. I have been asking you to marry me.'

The violet eyes widened a little and then became quite blank. 'My goodness – *have* you? Why?'

Having already exhausted his meagre supply of lover-like ardour, Robert had as little ability as he had desire to give a

165

repeat performance. But the devil was driving and so he did his best.

'I love you! You are so beautiful – so completely and utterly perfect – I can't live without you!' And that, at least was true.

'Nonsense,' said Rosalind composedly. 'And though I'm very sorry to have to say it, I don't think you've ever loved anyone in your whole life.'

The words hit him like an icy douche and successfully reminded him that this was his one and only chance to win free from the pit into which he was being sucked. He gazed helplessly around their charmingly romantic setting, silently damning the fact that Rosalind was immune to it and said sulkily, 'You don't believe me. What else can I say?'

'Well, you might try telling me the truth.'

'But this *is* the truth – I *need* you!' Just for an instant conviction throbbed in his voice. 'If you won't marry me I might as well put a pistol to my head!'

She frowned. 'Robert, I don't wish to be unkind but I can't and won't tolerate that sort of folly. You know as well as I do that you've no such intention – which is just as well since *I've* no intention of marrying you.'

Robert discovered that he felt slightly sick. The last shreds of his temper deserted him and, with them, his veneer of beseeching persuasion. 'Why not?' he said nastily. 'You've got to marry someone, after all and it isn't every man who'd want a blind wife.'

Rosalind flinched and then, with a sudden, unexpected movement, tore her hands free and stood up. 'I think,' she announced bitingly, 'that you have said more than enough, don't you?'

'Well, it's your fault,' he retorted. 'You should have believed me.'

'No. I may be blind but voices are my speciality – and yours has been lying to me.' She pulled the folds of her

166

scarlet domino more closely over her gown. 'And now we'd better re-join the others before I'm tempted to tell you a few home-truths. Shall we go?'

Robert remained seated, his hands opening and closing mechanically. 'Find your own way.'

'As you are perfectly aware,' she said stonily, 'I can't.'

He smiled. It was not a pleasant smile and his voice matched it as he said, 'Then you'll have to stay here with me, won't you?'

Rosalind was suddenly visited by an overwhelming gust of wrath and she replied unsteadily, 'I'd rather be shut in a cage full of snakes.' And with more spirit than wisdom, she stalked off in the direction in which she thought – and hoped – they had come.

It was odd how the ground, which had seemed quite smooth while she had an arm to guide her was suddenly pitted and uneven. She stumbled a little, heard Robert laugh and moderated her pace; she would not give him the satisfaction of seeing her fall. Indeed she must *not* fall, for the ground was as distant now as it had been twelve years ago when she had taken her first dark steps. *No, Uncle Rowland, please – I'll fall. I can't see the floor . . . it's so far away. I can't walk – I'll fall.*

Vivid recollection of that feeling – a feeling that she had believed overcome long ago – made her nerves jump sickeningly. Sustaining rage fell away to be replaced by the first tingle of fear and only pride prevented her calling to Robert for help; pride and the thought that he might well refuse. Then her outstretched hand encountered the roughness of bark and she stopped abruptly, uncertain of whether to turn aside from it or hope to use the trees and shrubs to guide her along the path. She chose the latter and moved cautiously on towards the muted sound of the orchestra.

For a minute, perhaps two, it seemed to work and then something tugged sharply at her and she heard the dry sound of tearing silk. She stopped again, tried to disentangle herself and pricked her fingers on the thorns which had snared her. Somewhere away to her right she heard Robert laugh again and was disconcerted, less by the sound, than by its location; then she realised that he must have moved and, gritting her teeth, tried to concentrate on freeing her domino from the sharp prickles. But they did not wish to release her and her hands, strangely unsteady, only served to make matters worse whilst being stabbed and scratched. Stupidly, the incident contrived to heighten the fear she had been attempting to suppress and her heart began to beat unpleasantly fast. Then, just as she was about to give up and slip the domino from her shoulders to leave it behind, she heard footsteps close by.

'Robert?' she asked uncertainly.

'Wha's this?' said an unknown and oddly slurred voice. 'Beauty in dishtress, by God! Well, well . . . just you be shtill, m'dear. Soon have you free.'

'Oh thank you,' said Rosalind with real gratitude. And then, 'Do I know you, sir?'

She heard a long, wheezing laugh and then a pair of hot, clumsy hands settled heavily on her shoulders.

'Don't need to,' came the reply on a gust of wine-laden breath. 'I know *you*. You're Venus . . . or . . . Di-Diana. One of 'em, anyway. You just give me a kiss, my pretty – and then I'll . . .'

'No!' Too late Rosalind realised what was happening. 'Let me go!'

But he did not let her go and suddenly all her apprehensions fused into a single, escalating terror and she was struggling wildly against unseen hands that stroked and pawed and tried to hold her; against sour breath and avid, searching lips that pressed themselves to her neck, her cheeks, her hair as they sought her mouth. A great retching sob rose in her throat. She

168

struck out desperately with one arm and felt it connect with something; there was a groan of pain, then the grip on her relaxed and, wrenching her domino free of the thorns, she turned and fled heedlessly back the way she had come.

This, then, was the nightmare; her own, special nightmare that she had so often had in the early days after the accident. She was running, running, alone in a place she did not know and it was dark; she was no longer frightened of falling – only of that terrible all-enveloping blackness and the unspeakable horrors that inhabited it.

Mama, help me! I can't bear to live in the dark. I'm afraid of it.

Something snatched at her hair. It was only a twig but she stopped dead like a cornered animal, her pulse racing and her breath coming in uneven gasps. Then she heard a rustle of movement behind her and she swung round to face it, alert but helpless and almost despairing.

'What's the matter, my dear?' asked Robert maliciously. 'Can't you find your way?'

Rosalind fought down an hysterical laugh. 'You know I c- can't,' she said, her voice seeming to come from a long way off. 'And now you've p-proved your point, will you please t-take be back?'

'Say you'll marry me,' he replied, 'and I'll do anything you like.' And he took her hand.

'Don't touch me!' She wrenched it away from him. 'And stop playing games – it isn't f-funny any more. Just take me back to Philip.'

Robert merely laughed and slid an arm round her waist; and because his voice and touch were both things of the darkness, Rosalind was engulfed once more in a rising tide of panic. She pushed him away – and ran.

Dear God – this isn't happening. Why am I running? Where am I running?

And then there were cool hands closing hard on her forearms and a faint scent of ambergris.

'No! Let me go – don't *touch* me!' She twisted violently

and then was suddenly still as, through the fear, came inexplicable knowledge. 'It's you! Oh – thank God,' she sobbed. 'It *is* you, isn't it?'

The Marquis of Amberley stared down into wide, frightened eyes, enormous in her paper-white face and answered without thinking. 'Yes, my darling. Hush . . . you're quite safe.' And wrapped her close in his arms as she subsided abruptly against his chest.

Chapter Thirteen

Over Rosalind's head, the Marquis directed a level, flint-like gaze at the Honourable Robert Dacre.

'Of course, it *would* be you,' said Robert sarcastically as he moved forward a little way.

'Yes.' Very gently, his Lordship detached Rosalind's fingers from his coat. 'It's alright. Just wait here for a moment.'

She clutched at his hand. 'You won't go away?'

'No. I won't go away.' And he stepped unhurriedly past her to confront Mr Dacre; but silently, almost as though he was waiting for something.

'*No, I won't go away,*' mimicked Robert savagely. 'How touching! And no wonder she won't take an offer of marriage from anyone else – she's been hoping for one from you ever since the two of you were so cosily marooned at Oakleigh. For I doubt you ever told her that a man doesn't take his whore as his . . .'

And that was as far as he got before the Marquis hit him.

'You talk too much,' said Amberley in a voice that Rosalind had not known he possessed. 'And if you ever say that again . . . I'll kill you.' Then, with one contemptuous glance at the sprawling, earth-bound figure, he turned back to Rosalind and, pulling off his coat, draped it snugly around her. 'Come, my dear. I'm going to take you home.'

He did not speak again but Rosalind did not care. It was enough to feel the comforting strength of his arm and to know herself safe and protected again. She walked exhaustedly at his side, her head leaning on his shoulder, and did not care where he took her.

Amberley's thoughts were less pleasant and, if Rosalind had been able to see his face, she might have been roused from her lethargy for his expression was one of grim harshness. As yet he knew nothing of what had happened to her – only that he had found her dishevelled and terrified, like a child lost in the dark; and it filled him with a cold, murderous rage, so strong and unfamiliar that he did not know if it was directed against Robert or Philip. All he *was* certain of was that he felt a primitive need to do a good deal more than just knock a man down.

They reached the gate where his Lordship summoned a hackney with a snap of his fingers and then handed Rosalind into it. 'Great Jermyn Street,' he told the driver crisply.

'Gawd!' said the jarvey, impressed. 'All the way, milord?'

'Of course all the way!' snapped the Marquis, preparing to mount the steps. 'It's hardly the Antipodes – or did you suppose we wanted to travel part of the distance by camel?' And without waiting for an answer, he took his place beside Rosalind.

Mistress Vernon closed her eyes, leaned her head against the tired-looking squabs and gave way to weak, unsteady laughter.

Amberley stared at her. 'What are you laughing at?'

'At the thought of you riding a camel,' she replied slowly, her voice husky with fatigue. 'It's not much, I know – but it's better than crying. Am I very untidy?'

'Very,' he agreed, forcing himself to express a lightness he did not feel. 'But it doesn't matter. You look charming – you always do.'

And that, surprisingly enough, was true. Her face was still greeny-pale, her eyes wide and dark and the thick, blue-black hair, having lost most of its pins, was falling heavily down her back; her domino was in ruins, fragments of leaf and twig adorned her foaming white gown and, over all, his coat lay round her shoulders, far too large and its green clashing horribly with the scarlet silk. And still she was beautiful. His gaze travelled to her loosely-clasped hands and he stiffened, reaching out to examine them more closely. 'How did you come by these scratches?'

'It was a rose-bush, I think. My domino got caught and I made a very poor job of trying to free it.' She paused and then, a little less evenly, said, 'What did Robert mean – about you and I and Oakleigh?'

'Nothing – except to make mischief. It is of no consequence and I want you to forget that you heard it.'

'But . . .'

'*No*. It need not concern you,' he said, unexpectedly stern. 'I assure you that he will not repeat it.'

'No,' agreed Rosalind, shivering a little at the memory, not of the threat he had made, but the unmistakable tone in which he had made it. 'I don't suppose he will.'

The Marquis frowned down at the small, scratched hands that lay in his own and then he said abruptly, 'What happened, Rosalind?'

It was the first time he had used her name but she did not find it odd. She smiled and shook her head. 'It doesn't matter. It was nothing . . . and I expect I over-reacted.'

'I doubt it. But nevertheless I want to hear about it – and from the beginning, if you please. I take it that you didn't go to Vauxhall alone with Robert Dacre?'

'Hardly! I wouldn't go to the end of the street with him,' replied Rosalind, stung. And, keeping it as brief as possible, she explained.

The Marquis listened in silence. She spoke only of what had taken place and, he suspected, with a certain degree of under-statement. Of her feelings, she made no mention at all – nor did she need to. He had seen what they had been with his own eyes and, even if he had not, it was not difficult to imagine what the experience must have been like for a gently-bred, sightless girl, alone for the first time in her life in a strange and hostile environment. The mere thought of it made him feel physically unwell.

'And then you came,' concluded Rosalind, matter-of-factly. 'And I am very glad that you did.'

'So am I,' came the grim reply. 'Though the word glad in no way expresses my feelings on the matter.'

She turned her face towards him and said uncertainly, 'You sound angry. Are you?'

The grey-green eyes were hard as slate but the pleasant voice softened a little. 'Yes – very angry. But not with you. Don't worry. I expect I shall get over it.'

His voice was reassuring but Rosalind was not convinced and a tiny troubled frown creased her brow. She said flatly, 'You blame Philip but you're not going to discuss it with me. I wish that I . . .'

'Yes?' he prompted.

She gave an odd little laugh. 'Oh – nothing. Or, at least, nothing new. It's just that I wish . . . I wish I could see your face.'

The pit of Amberley's stomach fell away as if the carriage had bounded over a deep rut but the very faint wistfulness in her tone had its effect and he did not hesitate.

'Then, since I can't show it to you, perhaps this will help.' And, lifting the hands that still lay in his, he laid her palms lightly against his face and released them.

The effect on Rosalind was as immediate as it was cataclysmic. The breath seemed to catch in her throat and her fingers trembled, tingling, against his skin. Then, slowly, delicately, she traced the line of his cheekbones and the flat planes beneath, the angle of his

174

jaw and the firm moulding of lips and chin; and, with a sudden, bitter-sweet joy as his face became visible in her mind, wondered why she had never thought of this for herself.

The Marquis remained quite still under her exploring fingers and watched with infinite tenderness as her pallor was replaced by a tinge of colour and her eyes became lit with the glow of discovery. And then he ceased to think at all.

His arms slid round her, drawing her close, then closer still so that her hands fell to his shoulders and that ineffable, heart-stopping face was tilted back on its slender neck, only inches from his own. The long, silky lashes veiled her eyes and there was about her an aura of expectancy, as if, like him, she had waited long for this moment; and then the waiting was over and his mouth found hers.

Naturally, willingly, her arms crept round his neck and her body melted against his like a sweet and fragrant dream; as sweet and fragrant as the lips that parted gently under his or the soft, rippling hair that cascaded over his hands. Her every pulse and heartbeat were one with his own and, cradled possessively in the haven of his arms, Rosalind felt that reality no longer existed outside the touch of his hands and the lingering warmth of his mouth.

He kissed her eyelids, her throat and her hair, twining his fingers in its living silkiness; and then the carriage drew to a halt.

Very slowly, Amberley raised his head and looked down at her. Then, with a species of remote ruefulness, he said, 'My heart, if I could do it without lying, I'd beg your pardon. It seems that I'm no better than your mythological cavalier of the rose-bush.'

A tender and strangely beautiful smile lit Rosalind's face. 'Are you not?' she asked simply. 'How odd. I had thought this was quite different.

There was a long pause and then the Marquis smiled back at her, smoothing away a stray lock of hair from her brow. 'Yes. Quite different,' he agreed quietly. He caught sight of the jarvey hovering outside the carriage window and waved him aside. 'But there are . . . there are many things which must be said; things that should have been said before I – before we . . .' He stopped and gave the ghost of a laugh. 'If I call tomorrow, will you receive me?'

'Don't you know that I will?' The husky voice was enticingly radiant. 'But why must it wait until tomorrow?'

'Sufficient unto the day is the evil thereof,' he quoted with a hint of bitterness. 'And I think that you have had enough excitement for one day. Be grateful – ten minutes ago I had a firm intention of escorting you in and waiting for your esteemed brother for the purpose of asking him to explain just what his notion of looking after you actually entails. He would not have liked it – and neither, I think, would you.'

'And tomorrow?'

'Oh – tomorrow I may contrive to be tolerably civil . . . should the need arise. But I can't promise to say nothing – not even for you.' He grinned crookedly. 'Hardly Sir Galahad, I know, but some things are too much to ask. Does that sink me utterly below reproach and decide you to forbid my admittance?'

'No.' She laid a hand very gently against his cheek. 'As you say – some things are too much to ask.'

A large mark that would shortly become a bruise stood out against the whiteness of Robert's face and a daub of mud adorned one sleeve of his rose-brocade coat as, still shaking with mingled rage and fright, he stared defiantly back at Lord Philip and his guests.

'I asked you,' repeated Philip in a low, tight voice,

176

'where my sister is. And I don't intend to wait all night for an answer. Well?'

'Gone home,' muttered Robert. And then, relieved to discover that, though exceedingly painful, his jaw was not dislocated after all, he added spitefully, 'Or that's where he *said* he'd take her.'

Isabel rose to stand beside his Lordship. 'He?' she asked sharply. 'What are you talking about?'

Robert's gaze flickered over the faces in front of him and said, with careful distinction, 'Amberley. She's gone off with the Marquis of Amberley.'

There was a catastrophic silence. Then, in the buzz of shocked chatter that succeeded it, Robert found his arm seized in a crushing grip as Lord Philip hustled him out of the booth and away across the grass.

'I don't know,' began Philip with furious scorn, 'what it is that drives you to behave like a woman – and a stupid, vindictive one at that – but now you are deprived of your audience, perhaps you'll be good enough to explain that remark. Quickly and in plain English.'

Robert eyed him with nervously sullen resentment. 'How much plainer does it have to be? I was about to bring her back here and then he came and asked her to go with him. And when I tried to prevent it, he knocked me down.' It was a poor effort, he knew, but the millstones that were grinding inside his head made it difficult to think. 'What more is there to say?'

'Quite a lot,' came the curt reply. 'My sister is neither a fool nor a piece of Haymarket ware. And, whatever else he is, I doubt Amberley is the man to treat her as such – or to use his fists without a reason.'

'Then you're a bloody fool!' retorted Robert, his control snapping. 'A title don't make a gentleman – and Denzil Mallory Ballantyne is capable of doing anything that takes his fancy!'

'*What did you say?*'

177

Something in Philip's voice made Robert's heart skip a beat and he said lamely, 'That he's capable of . . .'

'Not that – the name. What did you say his name was?'

'Ballantyne,' replied Robert, mystified and a little dazed. 'Denzil Mallory Ballantyne. Ridiculous, isn't it?'

Philip ignored the question and his oddly glittering blue stare seemed to go right through Mr Dacre.

'So that's it,' he breathed. 'That's it . . . and I should have known. God damn it, *I should have known!*' And, turning on his heel, he strode back to his guests.

He entered his house to the strains of *It was a Lover and his Lass* and marched unhesitatingly into the parlour to find Rosalind sitting at the harpsichord clad in a blue silk peignoir with her hair hanging down her back. Philip closed the doors with a snap and leant against them breathing rather hard.

'I suppose I should be grateful to find you here. But what a pity Lord Amberley could not stay; I should have enjoyed exchanging a few words with him.'

With a hey and a ho and hey nonny no, tinkled the harpsichord merrily.

'No, you wouldn't,' replied Rosalind with a sweet, vague smile, apparently oblivious of his anger. 'He hit Robert Dacre, you know . . . and I think he'd quite like to hit you too.'

His Lordship's lip curled derisively. 'He's welcome to try – but *I* am not Robert Dacre so it's conceivable he may have a little trouble.'

She did not reply but the harpsichord jeered at him. *When birds do sing hey ding-a-ding-a-ding* . . .

'Why,' demanded Philip as evenly as he could, 'did you leave Vauxhall with Amberley? And why did he hit Robert?'

Rosalind tilted her head over the keys. 'Haven't *you* ever wanted to hit Robert?'

178

'Yes. But that's not the point. I asked you why Amberley *did*?'

'Didn't Robert tell you?' *Between the acres of the rye . . .*

Perilously close to losing his temper, his Lordship swept down on his sister to pull her away from the keyboard. And in doing so he caught sight of her hands. 'What the devil have you been doing to yourself? And you can stop playing tricks, Rose – I want the truth.'

The truth was that Rosalind was in a slight quandry. She wanted to make sure that Philip harboured no misconceptions about the Marquis but affection for Isabel made her reluctant to expose the full extent of Robert's perfidy. So she temporised with the slightly mendacious information that she and Mr Dacre had become separated, followed it with an account of her troubles beside the rose-bush and concluded by explaining that, before Robert had re-appeared, the Marquis had found her and offered to bring her home.

Philip frowned. 'So what made Amberley knock him down?'

Rosalind sighed and took refuge in maidenly modesty. 'Robert said something extremely rude and deliberately provoking,' she replied primly. 'But Lord Amberley said I was to forget it and so I have.'

'And a few other things too, I think?' came the sarcastic response. 'It's the most unlikely story I ever heard. And, thanks to Robert, by tomorrow morning half of London will know that you came home alone with Amberley.'

Rosalind bent her head over her hands. 'I don't think,' she said cautiously, 'that it will matter.'

'Don't be ridiculous – of course it matters! What should stop it?'

A slow exquisite flush stained Rosalind's skin and, when she raised her face, it held an expression that Philip had never seen but instantly recognised. She looked quite transparently happy, and with a sort of shy simplicity, she said, 'Lord Amberley will. He is coming here tomorrow and I think – I hope . . . that he is going to ask me to marry him.'

Philip's breath left his body with the suddenness of a physical blow and he sat down without even realising it. Then, 'No,' he said flatly.

A little of Rosalind's joy evaporated. 'No? What do you mean?'

There was a white shade around his Lordship's mouth. 'I mean that you're not the first to think that – and I doubt you'll be the last. My dear, I'm sorry if it hurts you, but it seems the man has a reputation for this kind of thing. He won't ask you . . . and, even if he did, I couldn't allow it. I'd as soon see you married to Ludovic Sterne – sooner. He may be a gamester but at least he has some conception of what the word honour means.'

'*Stop it*!' Rosalind came abruptly to her feet and the blood drained from her skin. 'I know that you've never liked him but you have no right to say such things and I won't listen to them! I'm . . .'

'Oh yes you will!' said Philip grimly, reaching out to grasp her hand. 'Though you may not believe it, this gives me as little pleasure as it does you – but the time has come to stop burying your head in the sand. And I'm damned if I'm going to let you eat your heart out for him without knowing exactly what he is. Sit down.'

'I *know* what he is! He's kind and thoughtful and – and he understands!'

'He's a rake and a liar,' retorted Philip brutally. '*Sit down!*'

And because her knees no longer felt very reliable, Rosalind sat. 'Very well,' she said shakily. 'Convince me – if you can.'

'Oh I can – unfortunately. You've wondered why there has always been ill-feeling between us, haven't

180

you? Well, it's quite simple. On the night I first met him, the noble Marquis was engaged in winning three thousand guineas from Robert Dacre at dice. Perhaps you don't find that very bad; but how does it seem when I add the facts that Robert is a callow boy in comparison to Amberley – and that, as his Lordship was perfectly well aware, he was too drunk to know what he was doing?'

'It seems that Robert was well-served,' replied Rosalind stonily. 'Unless you are trying to say that the Marquis *forced* him to drink too much?'

Philip made a gesture of impatience. 'No. what I'm trying to say is that a gentleman with any pretensions to honour doesn't care to win large sums of money under those kind of circumstances. Amberley should have left the table or passed his bank to another but he didn't. He only stopped milking Robert when Rockliffe made him.'

'I don't believe it. His Grace is Lord Amberley's friend.'

'What has that to do with it? And if you're about to suggest that Amberley nobly declined to accept his winnings, you can forget it. Robert paid him with my money and I saw the returned vowels.'

Rosalind gripped her hands together so that the knuckles glowed white. 'Is that all?'

'Isn't it enough?'

'No. Not for me. You see, I think that I know him rather better than that.'

'You don't know him at all!' exclaimed Philip bitterly. He got up and walked restlessly across to the fireplace. Then, raising his arms to lean heavily on the mantel, he said curtly, 'Very well. I'd hoped I need not tell you but it seems I've no choice. How much do you remember of the day that you had your accident?'

The unexpectedness of it threw Rosalind off balance. 'A – a little. Why do you ask?'

'And have you ever spoken of it to Amberley?'

'Yes. But I don't understand why . . .'

'You will.' Philip's hands dropped to his sides and he turned slowly to face her. 'The man whose coach knocked you down that day was called Denzil Ballantyne. I don't suppose you ever knew it . . . but I did. He told me his name when he sent me to fetch Uncle Rowland and it isn't the kind of name – or occasion – that one easily forgets.'

'No,' agreed Rosalind, dutiful but blank. 'But I still don't know why you are telling me this now.'

'Don't you?' Philip looked down at her with unutterable weariness. 'It's because Denzil Ballantyne and the Marquis of Amberley are one and the same.'

Rosalind heard the words and realised suddenly that she had known he was going to say them; but for a long time they echoed meaninglessly in the long corridor of her mind. And then, when they reached her, she dug her nails into the palms of her hands and said frozenly, 'No. He can't be.'

'My dear – he can. And you must face it.'

To herself, Rosalind said, Not this; not now. I can't stand it. And then, aloud, 'But he can't know. If he knew, he would have told me. And it needn't matter. The accident wasn't his fault. He wasn't driving, was he?'

Philip remained silent. He stared at her white-lipped face and hated himself.

'If it doesn't matter to me, it need not matter to you!' she whispered pleadingly. 'Oh – why don't you *say* something?'

He dropped on one knee beside her chair and took her hands. They were cold as wax. 'Rose – try to understand. Of course his part in your accident matters, but less than the fact that he has tried to hide it. And he *must* know; if you spoke to him about it, he couldn't *not*! You say he will ask you to marry him . . . well, supposing he did?

Would you ever be sure he hadn't done so out of pity or guilt? And, knowing that he had deceived you once, could you ever completely trust him? My dear, I want something better for you than that.'

The violet eyes were bleak and drowning but she lifted her chin and said stubbornly, 'I won't believe it unless he tells me so. It isn't as you think and tomorrow you'll discover how wrong you've been – that he isn't capable of any of it. It will be alright. All I have to do is wait.'

Chapter Fourteen

The Marquis was still at breakfast when he was informed that Lord Philip Vernon had arrived to see him and was waiting in the library. For a long moment, Amberley said nothing but stared meditatively at his butler; and then, without any visible change in his expression, 'Oh hell!'

'My Lord?' queried Barrow, unaccustomed to this kind of reception.

The Marquis got up. 'I said "Oh hell",' he repeated kindly. 'And it probably will be. There is no need for you to return to the library – I will see his Lordship now. And Barrow . . ?'

'Yes, my Lord?'

'I don't wish to be disturbed unless I ring – in which case you will come yourself. Understand?'

Barrow bowed. He had, of course, heard tales of drawing-room brawls but he had never expected to receive such an order in this house. He drew a lugubrious sigh and wondered where it was all going to end.

Lord Philip, sombre in black velvet, was standing at a window frowning down into the square but he turned as the doors opened and looked across the room into Amberley's eyes. The Marquis met that stern gaze with one equally direct but expressionless and then, closing the doors behind him, walked unhurriedly forward. 'Good morning. I hope I have not kept you waiting for very long?'

The calm courtesy of this overture made Philip suddenly aware of his perennial problems in dealing with Amberley and he reminded himself of the folly of losing his temper.

'Not at all,' he replied curtly. 'I imagine that you know why I am here?'

An odd smile flickered in the grey-green eyes. 'Well, no. In fact, I don't. It is about last night, of course – but as yet I am not quite sure whether you have come to thank me or to . . . quarrel with me. But I am forgetting my manners; will you not sit down?'.

'Thank you, no. And the answer is that it is neither – I hope. No doubt you acted with the best of intentions when you took my sister home,' a decidedly dubious note crept in here, 'but I should naturally have preferred it if you have seen fit to restore her to me.'

'Did you happen to see in exactly what state she arrived home?' asked the Marquis interestedly.

Philip stiffened. 'I – well, no.'

'I see. And I daresay you received some explanations from Robert Dacre?'

'Yes.'

'An explanation which I doubt Mistress Vernon confirmed.' It was not a question.

Philip found himself recalling in precise terms the unsatisfactory nature common to both conflicting accounts. 'I really don't see where this is getting us,' he said defiantly.

There was a pause and then Amberley shrugged. 'Nowhere, perhaps. But I've never liked fighting on strange ground. Very well – what is it you wished to say to me?'

And Philip, who had been up half the night rehearsing in detail what he intended to say, suddenly experienced the demoralising sensation that something was missing. He clasped his hands tightly behind his back and said briefly, 'I believe you planned to wait on my sister this morning. I have come to save you the trouble.'

This was unexpected and Amberley's eyes widened a little. He said slowly, 'I don't think I understand you. What I have to say to Mistress Vernon is – forgive me – a matter which is between her and myself and not something I propose to discuss with you.'

'Is it not?' demanded his Lordship. 'But perhaps the fact that Rosalind is in my care has escaped your attention.'

'Not *mine*,' responded the Marquis with dry significance. 'But perhaps you are making up for lost time?'

The hold that Philip had over his temper suffered a noticable relapse. 'What the devil do you mean by that?'

'I mean that your care should have been evident last night. Robert Dacre is not a fit companion for any girl – let alone one with your sister's difficulties. And especially in a location such as Vauxhall. I don't know how much she told you of what happened – though I suspect consideration for Mistress Dacre caused it to be rather less than she told me and *that* was little enough – but when I found her she was alone, dishevelled and very frightened. I will not bore you or abuse her confidence by relating details but this I will say; the prime cause of her distress was Robert Dacre and, if I had known then what I know now, I would have done considerably more than just knock him down. I do you the credit to think that, had you been in my place, you would have felt exactly the same . . . but in case I am wrong, I would like to point out that I will not tolerate any further instances of a similar nature. I trust I make myself quite clear?'

'Perfectly!' A tinge of angry colour began to burn high in Philip's cheeks. 'And I will do the same. For whatever service you rendered my sister last night, I give you her thanks – but beg leave to inform you that, since there is

186

no future in any further communication between you, I should prefer there to be none. In short, My Lord Marquis, if you call in Great Jermyn Street, my butler will have instructions not to admit you.'

Amberley went white and for an instant his eyes flared dangerously. Then, with a perceptible effort, he said evenly, 'May I ask why?'

'Certainly. Rosalind has already suffered enough at your hands and I am merely employing my right to protect her from your thoughtless and light-minded attentions.'

'*My what?*' The normally pleasant voice cut like the lash of a whip.

Just for a minute, Philip entertained the enlivening hope that he was about to be served in the same manner as the unfortunate Mr Dacre. Then it passed and he said, 'Are they not, then?'

'No. They are not.' The Marquis discovered that his hands were not quite steady. 'And Mistress Vernon knows it.'

'Mistress Vernon knows a number of things that might surprise you,' came the sardonic reply. 'But are you asking me to believe that you mean marriage?'

'I'm not asking you to believe anything – yet.'

His Lordship gave a brief, unamused laugh. 'Quite. And that answers my question, doesn't it?'

'No – damn it, it doesn't!' snapped the Marquis, driven at last to abandon his controlled reserve. 'And I've had more than enough of your insulting insinuations. God knows where you obtained these peculiar notions of my character but it's time, for the good of your sister, that you said goodbye to it; and if it will help you do so, I'm willing to request your permission to pay my addresses to her in form. Does that make you happy?'

The stunned amazement in Lord Philip's eyes was replaced by a look of blazing anger.

'*Happy?*' he echoes scornfully. 'You must be insane. I'd sooner see her dead at my feet than married to you!'

187

Amberley blinked as though unable to believe he had heard aright. 'But *why*? You can't surely be simpleton enough to despise me solely on account of what you think I did to Robert Dacre – so what in hell's name is it?'

'It's quite simple,' replied Philip. 'I want my sister to wed a man with some notion of honour and decency – not a liar, a libertine and a coward!'

Green sparks flashed in a face that had no more colour to lose and the Marquis took a swift step forward, his hands clenched tight at this sides. Then he checked himself and, breathing hard, said with perilous softness, 'You must be well aware that, as both a guest in my house and the brother of the lady I hope to make my wife, I cannot answer you as I should wish. But . . .'

'Don't' begged Philip politely, 'allow that to stand in your way.'

Amberley eyed him with icy contempt. 'Try not to be a bigger fool than God made you. There is nothing you can say that will make me deliver the challenge it seems you so badly want. And I see no point in continuing this conversation; for, though you have successfully made plain your opposition, you must know as well as I do that Rosalind will make her own decision; and I don't somehow think that she agrees with you.'

Something in that last sentence coupled with the cool assurance in the crisp tone sent Philip's temperature soaring to boiling point and if he could have thought of any pretext, however slight, for calling Amberley out, he would not have hesitated. But, since he could not, he said in a voice that shook, 'Don't count on it, Ballantyne; life is full of small disappointments.'

Stark grey-green eyes met glitteringly hostile blue ones and the silence, heavy, profound and alarmingly total, seemed to stretch on to infinity. After the first eviscerating jerk that marked recognition of Philip's words, their significance came slowly, like something seen from a long way off, and the Marquis turned gradually colder, his stomach coiling with cramp and his nerves throbbing like plucked wires. Then, with absurd concentration, he laid his hands on the polished wood of his desk and said remotely, 'I see. How long have you known?'

'Since last night,' replied Philip, unsurprised but sick with disgust at having his expectations so swiftly verified. He supposed he should be glad that the fellow had not troubled to dissemble but he wasn't; he merely felt ill. 'No doubt it's amused you that it took me so long.'

Amberley continued to stare down at his hands, their bloodless grace outlined against the dark wood. 'No. In fact, it didn't. I don't believe I thought of it.' He drew a long, unsteady breath. 'And . . . your sister? You've told her?'

'Of course. Someone had to, didn't they?'

'Yes.' Very slowly the Marquis stood upright. A shaft of sunlight rested on his face, throwing its lines and planes into harsh relief. He looked suddenly very tired. 'Are you saying that she doesn't wish to receive me?'

Philip wished that he could bring himself to tell the blatant and deliberate lie that would probably solve all his problems – but he could not quite do it. Instead, he said sarcastically, 'What did you expect?'

'I . . . Nothing. But I hoped that perhaps she would allow me the chance to explain.'

'How? With more lies? *God!*' said Lord Philip with wrathful incredulity, 'It must be wonderful to be as sure of oneself as you are – to be able to believe yourself so irresistible that twelve years of blindness and four months of rank deceit don't matter! You once called me insensitive but I don't think you have the remotest conception of what she's been through; of the endless bloody treatments that made her sick or crippled her with pain; of the fear and nightmares and the sheer, gruelling hard work that has made her what you see. And now you want to marry her – though God alone knows why. Don't you think,' he finished acidly, 'that you have done enough?'

Something not quite a smile touched Amberley's mouth and his eyes were grey and bleak. Then he made a small gesture of capitulation, more hopeless than resigned, and said quietly, 'More than enough, it seems. But I promised to call today and therefore I shall do so; so . . . to tender my apologies. You will permit that, I presume?'

'Hardly,' came the cold reply. 'Rosalind has no need of either you or your apologies and if you cause her any more distress by trying to force your way into her presence, I'll take pleasure in kicking you down the steps. If you'll only stop ruining her chances, she'll be happily married by midsummer.'

The Marquis was suddenly very still. 'Who?' was all he said.

Philip picked up his elegant tricorne from where it lay on a gessoed side-table and gripped it in fingers that were stiff and tight.

'The Duke of Rockliffe,' he replied mockingly. 'I'm surprised you hadn't guessed.'

It was almost a full hour before, out of the shattered fragments of Amberley's self-command, came sufficient resolution to overcome his indifference and make him resume the painful business of thought and movement. Even then he did not touch on the question of Rosalind's reaction; it lay like a raw, gaping wound on his mind – expected and understood, but too ugly to be looked at. So he thought, instead, of that other legacy that Lord Philip had left behind him. And finally he roused himself to investigate it.

His Grace of Rockliffe was still at breakfast when the Marquis strode unceremoniously in to rest his fingers on the table-edge and fix him with a grimly white-faced stare.

Rockliffe looked back with an air of gentle bewilderment and said plaintively, 'My dear Denzil – I am naturally delighted to see you at any hour but I really must beg you to sit down. I have the greatest aversion to being intimidated at breakfast – it is most unrestful.'

Amberley ignored this speech and remained where he was. 'Is it true that you are on the point of offering for Rosalind Vernon?' he asked in a voice curiously unlike his own.

A gleam of interest crept into the saturnine eyes. 'And if it is?'

'Don't play games, Rock – I'm not in the mood.'

'Ah.' Enlightenment burst on his Grace and, abruptly dropping his affectations, he said hopefully, 'Fight me for her, Den?'

The Marquis gave a bitter laugh and collapsed neatly into a chair. 'No. Neither you nor anyone else.'

Rockliffe sighed. 'What a pity. May one ask why?'

'Because it wouldn't help.' Amberley plainly had scant interest in the point. 'You haven't answered my question.'

His Grace helped himself to another cup of coffee and poured one for his guest.

'The answer,' he said languidly, 'is no. She is entirely charming, of course, and I've rarely seen a girl so beautiful. She even has the added lure of money. But I've no ambition to wed her.'

'Because she is blind?' asked the Marquis dryly.

'No. Because I am not . . . er . . . in love with her.' Rockliffe's tone was equally dry but a faint tinge of colour stained his lean cheek. 'You should be glad.'

Amberley leant on the table, pressing the heels of his hands against his eyes. 'Oh God. I *am* glad. And I beg your pardon.'

'Unnecessary, my dear.' The heavy-lidded gaze dwelt on him thoughtfully. 'So where had you this extraordinary tale?'

'From her brother.' He looked up. 'He was quite definite about it.'

'Was he so? I really cannot imagine why. I have given him no cause to think it.'

The Marquis gestured impatiently. 'What he thinks does not interest me. I had rather know what Mistress Rosalind thinks.'

'Who can tell what any woman thinks – or, indeed, *if* they do,' drawled the Duke. And then, meeting Amberley's eye, 'But be calm, my loved one. I have neither trifled with the lady's affections nor raised false hopes in her breast – and I doubt very much that I could have done so even had I tried. I am a diversion – nothing more.'

'You're very sure.'

'I know the game,' explained Rockliffe, half-smiling. 'And the onlooker always sees most of it. In short, I could have staked my reputation on the premise that, if she married anyone, it would be yourself. Would I have been wrong?'

For a moment Amberley stared at him and then he turned away, saying abruptly, 'Yes. You would. She won't have me. And there's nothing I can do about it – even if I was calm enough to do anything. Which, of course, I'm not.'

'I see.' A faint frown creased his Grace's brow. 'There is, I imagine, a reason?'

'Yes.' The Marquis gazed unseeingly into the street. 'There has always been a reason . . . and the irony of it is that if I'd spoken last night she would probably have accepted me. Today she won't even receive me. But don't ask me to explain. Perhaps later I may do so – but not yet. I think,' he concluded with careful lightness, 'that I've had enough for one day. And what I really need is something else to think of.'

'Such as what?'

Amberley turned and gave a metallic smile. 'Oh – nothing much. A town to take; an arsenal to blow up; a night ride behind enemy lines. Just some little thing to occupy my mind. I'm very flexible.'

The Duke surveyed him consideringly and then got up, tossing his napkin on to the table. 'I'm afraid I cannot provide you with a battle. But how do you feel about a race to Newmarket – my blacks against your greys?'

The brittle look was replaced with a hint of appreciative warmth. 'I should probably enjoy it. But I'm sure you have other plans for today.'

Rockliffe shrugged. 'Nothing I should not be happy to cancel. And please rid your mind of the mawkish suspicion that I suggest it out of sympathy – I don't. It is merely,' he explained reflectively, 'that I should like my revenge for our last race. *Voilà tout*. Shall we go?'

Partly from a desire to avoid her brother and partly so that she could be free to think, Rosalind took the precaution of instructing her maid to inform her the instant Lord Amberley arrived and then elected to wait upstairs in her boudoir. Her mind was in chaos; a tangle of soaring hope and churning fear that made her long for him to come but dread what he might say. And, though she recognised the injustice of it, she felt that she almost hated Philip for turning what should have been a time of joy into this limbo of doubt.

For a while she paced restlesly to and fro; then, realising the futility of this, she sat near the window where she would hear a carriage if it stopped at the door, arranged the folds of amethyst tiffany neatly around her and settled herself down to wait with what patience she could muster.

There seemed to be only one thing left that was not open to argument and that was the fact that, beyond pride or reason, she loved the Marquis; that she loved him so much that nothing else signified – neither the accident, nor his failure to speak of it, nor anything else. He need not even tell her why he had remained silent if only he would say he cared for her. And that, of course, was the rub – for even last night when he had held her in his arms, he had not spoken of love.

'But neither did I,' Rosalind's heart protested. 'And I knew. I've known ever since Isabel made me see it on the day he sent the poems. Only it didn't seem necessary to put it into words when it was there, warm and living, between us. And surely he couldn't have kissed me like that if he hadn't meant it?' She flushed a little at the memory of her own response and then smiled at the thought that she ought to feel shocked – but didn't.

But the uncertainty persisted and was reinforced, against her will, by the one thing that Philip had said which she could not forget.

'. . . *How will you ever be sure he didn't do so from pity or guilt?*'

'I can't and won't believe it,' she thought resolutely. 'He couldn't be so foolish and he isn't sorry for me – not a scrap. He never has been. As for guilt – why should he feel that? He wasn't driving and he must know it wasn't his fault. Oh *damn* Philip! Why did he have to put the idea into my head? I won't think about it!'

Yet, as the hours dragged slowly by bringing no sign of the Marquis, she did think about it and with increasing frequency. And gradually the sweet memories she had cherished, the rosy dreams she had nurtured for so short a time, withered and crumbled until they were dust at her feet. Like the princess in her high, stone tower, she waited in vain for her lover to come – until at last the chiming clock told that there was nothing left to wait for.

'The golden laws of love shall be
Upon this pillar hung;
A faithful heart, a single eye,
A true and constant tongue.
Let no man for more love pretent
Than he has hearts in store,
True love begun shall never end
Love one and love no more.'

Chapter Fifteen

By early evening and after a day of unparalleled tedium with only Broody for company, Lord Philip decided it safe to asume that Amberley had heeded his warning and set off to pour his troubles into the sympathetic ear of his betrothed.

He found Mistress Dacre on the point of going upstairs to change her dress for dinner but had no difficulty in persuading her to accompany him instead to a small parlour at the back of the house where they could be private. There was, as usual, no sign of Lord or Lady Linton and Philip who, if the truth was known, had no desire to see either of them frowned irritably and thought that it was remarkably typical of this ramshackle household.

He began with a slightly garbled account of what appeared to have taken place in Vauxhall Gardens – to which Isabel listened with confusion verging on suspicion. She had, in fact, already tried to coax this information out of Robert but he had proved surlily reticent and refused to do more than admit that he owed his bruised and swollen jaw to the Marquis of Amberley. Isabel put two and two together, arrived at some shrewd but unpleasing conclusions and wondered, shuddering, if she ought, in fairness, to share them with his Lordship.

But Philip did not give her the chance. Like water rushing through a floodgate, he went swiftly on to pour out his shocking discovery about the Marquis, the horrid details of his interview with Rosalind, the pungent logic behind his own attitudes. And that was as far as he got for, unable to stay silent any longer, Isabel steeled herself to interrupt him.

'But you can't assume that!' she said blankly. 'If he loves her he must feel awful about it. And perhaps Rosalind is right and he doesn't know. Afer all, *you* only discovered it last night.'

'He knows,' responded Philip grimly. 'I saw him this morning and he didn't trouble to deny it.'

'Oh.' She eyed him curiously. 'But did he tell you why he's said nothing?'

'He didn't need to. It's perfectly obvious, isn't it?'

'Not to me; though I suppose he might have been afraid.'

'Afraid? *Amberley*?' Philip forgot that he had called the Marquis a coward and gave a brief laugh. 'Never!'

Isabel thought it over and said seriously, 'Not in the normal way, perhaps. But if he blames himself, then he may well think that Rosalind would too.' She paused and then asked wistfully, 'If – if *you* were in that position, how easy would you find it to tell the truth?'

Philip shrugged. 'Oh God – I don't know! But it's all supposition anyway – and if it isn't, why didn't he say so to me this morning?'

She smiled a little. 'Would you have believed him?'

'No. But he knew damned well what I was thinking and if he had an explanation, he should have offered it. *I* would have done. Anything rather than let someone believe me wilfully dishonest.'

Isabel stared unseeingly at her hands. She had very little hope of being attended to but, because she liked the Marquis and felt that she owed him some defence, she was determined to try. 'Yes. But you set more store by the world's opinion than does Lord Amberley. He . . . I think you will find that he lives by a code of his own – and, in many ways, it is a good deal more strict than – than . . .'

'Than mine?' snapped his Lordship, nettled. '*Merci du compliment*! Perhaps you'll be good enough to explain *how*?'

She flushed. 'I'm sorry. I didn't mean that precisely. But I think – l-largely because of Robert – you do the Marquis a grave injustice. He does what he thinks is right; and he's the only person I've ever met who categorically refuses to speak of anything that reflects unfavourably on anyone else. He'd rather that people maligned *him* – and that must take a special sort of courage, don't you think?'

Lord Philip did not, and nor, he discovered, did he care for the gentle admiration in Isabel's tone or the concern in her eyes. With a sudden sense of shock, he realised that he had never known her display either one on his own account and the thought did more than rankle; it hurt.

'Not courage,' he replied blightingly, 'just arrogance. And he has plenty of that and to spare. I'm only surprised that he took me at my word and stayed away today.'

The brown gaze sharpened a little. 'Did you tell him that Rosalind did not want to see him?'

'Not exactly.' He coloured, not particularly proud of this admission. 'I merely . . . implied it.'

'And is it true?'

'No. But it should have been – for if I have my way, she'll take Rockliffe!'

Isabel regarded him with a sort of awed fascination. 'And did you tell Lord Amberley *that*?'

'Why should I not?'

Mistress Dacre opened her mouth as if she could have told him and then closed it again. For a moment or two she toyed with the falls of lace at her elbow and then she said diffidently, 'Forgive me for asking – but do you really expect Rockliffe to make Rosalind an offer?'

'Not if she continues making herself the talk of the town with Amberley,' replied his Lordship wrathfully. 'But he might if he received the slightest encouragement.'

'I see. And, if he did, you would approve?'

'Yes.' Sensing disapproval, he bridled afresh. 'She likes him – and he's worth a dozen of Amberley. Or don't you think so?'

'Well, no. In fact, I don't.' Isabel hesitated and then went on apologetically, 'The truth is that I can see very little difference between them save that of manner . . . and that the Duke can sometimes be – not exactly malicious, but a little overly mischievous. So I think, if I had to make a choice between them, that I must choose the Marquis.'

An unpleasant weight settled on Philip's chest and he turned rather pale. He said, 'Indeed? I perceive that his Lordship stands high in your esteem. I only wish I knew why.'

There was a long silence while Isabel gazed back at him using her most owlish stare to cover the mass of hopeful conjecture that seethed in her brain. Then her mouth curved in a slow, deliberate smile and she said simply, 'I've told you. *He nevere yet no vileyne ne sayde in all his lyf* . . . And he has such a charming smile.'

'I see.' Philip came abruptly to his feet and simultaneously recognised the sensation that had been plaguing him. He managed a hard, brittle smile and said, in a voice from which he could not quite banish the hurt, 'Then it is, perhaps, a pity that your father contracted you to me. I must be something of a disappointment.' And before she could reply, before he let himself say anything more, he made her a small, jerky bow and left.

From Clarges Street Philip went directly to White's where,

199

for the first time that he could remember, he set out to get purposely drunk. And, by the time Amberley arrived at the club, he had succeeded well enough for a single glimpse of the Marquis to bring his profound sense of ill-usage surging to the surface and make him long to plant his fist squarely in that fine-boned face.

Chin on chest, Philip considered his woes; a sister who would not speak to him, a parrot that either spat at or cursed him and bride-to-be who had clearly fallen under the spell of Another. It was more, he decided gloomily, than a man should be asked to bear; and, looking at the cause of all his troubles, a mere punch no longer seemed enough.

It was at this point that Fate, pink-clad and lisping, deigned to take a hand in the game. Viscount Ansford, an inveterate gossip who greatly resented the gentle way Amberley had of nipping his best stories in the bud, watched the Marquis cross the room and was prompted to utter a spiteful remark.

'Upon my thoul!' he tittered to the gentleman sitting beside him. 'I hardly exthpected to thee Amberley here tonight. They thay he eloped from Vauxthall with the fair Rothalind latht night – and I thupposed them half-way to the border by now!'

With a strangled oath and a force that overturned his chair, Philip came to his feet and dived at the dainty Viscount who, until that moment, had not seen him. His fingers hooked themselves into the foaming lace cravat, twisting savagely and, in an equally savage voice, he said, 'You little lying worm – take it back before I choke you!'

The Viscount, unfortunately, was in no position to say anything – either in renunciation or otherwise – and, though every head in the room turned to watch, no one appeared to find him worth saving. No one, that is, except for the Marquis of Amberley who strode swiftly forward and obtained his release by means of a hard, well-placed blow to Lord Philip's wrist.

'*You!*' Philip's eyes blazed and, because his right hand was still a useless mass of pins and needles, he clenched his left and took a wild swing at Amberley's nose.

Stepping back, the Marquis caught his wrist in an inflexible grip and said under his breath, 'No, you bloody fool! Think what you're doing! I know you'd like to break my jaw but you can't do it here – you'll ruin her.'

Philip was not so drunk that he could not understand what Amberley was saying, but he was by no means sober and his brain was aflame with a hurt anger that no longer had very much to do with Rosalind. He wrenched his arm free and said softly but with tolerable clarity, 'Not me – you. And I thought it's what you wanted.'

The Marquis flinched but replied with unimpaired composure, 'You're drunk. And Lord Ansford made a mistake – did you not, my Lord?'

'Y-yeth,' agreed the decorative Viscount, glad to be offered a way out. 'A mithtake. I beg your Lorship'th pardon.'

'Make it again,' said Philip slowly, 'and I'll cut your tongue out. And as for you, my Lord Marquis – you will meet me.'

There was a sudden, mind-cracking silence and then, very gently, Amberley said, 'Why?'

It was a good move but Philip was ready for it. And because when he looked at the Marquis all he could see was a pair of admiring pansy-brown eyes, he was able to deliver his excuse in a tone that, for one person at least, robbed it of any element of comedy. 'Because it was you who taught that damned bird of Rosalind's to spit and it's been spitting at me all day. There's no peace in the house – thanks to you. And I'm sick of it.'

The tension around them dissolved into a ripple of amusement.

'What bird?' asked a baffled voice; and received a polyphonic reply of 'Mistress Veron's parrot,' or 'Broody', from those who knew.

Someone said, 'Give it up, Phil – you can't challenge a man over a parrot!'

'You can't know Broody,' laughed another. 'He could start a war!'

'Well?' Philip's vivid, too-steady gaze never wavered from Amberley's face. '*Will* you fight me – over a parrot?'

For a second or two, the Marquis stared measuringly back at him out of eyes that were as hard as granite and then, though he had never felt less amused in his life, he achieved a smiling shrug and said carelessly, 'Why not? Though I'd like to point out that, if you hadn't bought a bird of such boundless vulgarity, I should not have needed to teach it little tricks. You see – I grew weary of being sworn at.'

This raised another general laugh and Lord Caversham said feelingly, 'Don't I know it!'

Jack Ingram finally succeeded in making his unobtrusive way to Amberley's side. His eyes were anxious but he said pleasantly, 'Don't you think that the joke has gone far enough? You can hardly intend to fight over a parrot!'

'Spoilsport!' grinned Harry Caversham, blithely unaware of the dangerous undercurrents so apparent to Mr Ingram. 'I'll stand for you, Phil. That feathered limb of Satan has used me as a target far too often!'

'Thank you.' Philip smiled mockingly at his adversary. 'And your friends, my Lord Marquis?'

Amberley glanced enquiringly at Mr Ingram. 'Jack?'

'Not me,' came the flat reply. 'I'll have nothing to do with anything so damned silly.'

The Marquis smiled faintly and then looked back at Philip. 'Rockliffe will act for me,' he said with deceptive insouciance. 'And now I come to think of it, there is a

certain poetry in restricting our little meeting to Broody's
more . . . intimate . . . acquaintances. You might even
bring him to watch.'

Twenty minutes later when Mr Ingram followed the
Marquis out into the street, he found him leaning with
closed eyes against a stone pilaster and was suddenly
worried.

'Denzil – are you alright?'

'Yes.' Slowly the grey-green eyes opened and focused.
'How long do you think before they start realising that
it's not the farce it appears?'

'Not long,' came the forthright reply. 'Tomorrow
morning, perhaps.'

'That's what I thought.' With a visible effort,
Amberley stepped away from the wall and squared his
shoulders. 'Rock's engaged with a party at the Cocoa-
Tree. Are you coming?'

'Yes.' Already half-regretting his refusal to act as a
second, Jack fell into step beside his friend and said
curtly, 'You could have said no. Why didn't you?'

He had not really expected an answer and was therefore surprised when the Marquis said expressionlessly,
'Because his Lordship won't rest until he's given the
opportunity to let a little of my blood. It doesn't matter
why.'

'But he was drunk!'

'Quite. So he'd have pressed it.'

Enlightenment dawned on Mr Ingram. 'And you
didn't know what he might say next so you made a joke
of it. Wonderful!' he said sardonically. 'What if he kills
you?'

'He won't.' The light voice was totally indifferent.
'Don't judge him too harshly, Jack. He thinks he has
reason.'

Mr Ingram eyed him with shrewd resignation. 'You

203

mean he's been listening to Robert Dacre. Do you mind if I say "I told you so"?'

'Not at all. But that's only a small part of it.' The Marquis paused on the steps of the Cocoa-Tree and smiled vaguely. 'If that were all, there wouldn't be a problem.'

The tidings that he was to act as second in a duel prompted the Duke to exhibit faint signs of enthusiasm which even revelation of its cause failed to entirely subdue.

'How original,' he said with simple admiration. 'I really must remember to offer Lord Philip my compliments for I doubt anyone ever fought over a parrot before. Only think . . . you will be making history.'

A withering remark sprang to Mr Ingram's lips but before he could utter it he caught sight of the expresion in Rockliffe's veiled gaze and realised that it was unnecessary.

'Just so,' murmured his Grace suavely. And then, to Amberley, 'I shall, of course, be delighted to indulge you with an hour's practise if you feel your wrist to be in need of exercise.'

'Thank you.' A shadow of amusement crept into the Marquis's eyes. 'But there will be no need. We fight with pistols.'

There was a moment's incredulous silence and then his Grace asked carefully, 'By whose choice?'

'By mine.'

Rockliffe closed his eyes and achieved a delicate shudder. 'Barbarian!'

Mr Ingram gave a reluctant laugh. 'Disappointed, Rock?'

'Scandalised.' Allowing himself to recover, the Duke directed a gleaming glance at the Marquis. 'But perhaps our young cavalry officer is something of a swordsman?'

'Don't be a fool!' The amusement was wiped from Jack's face. 'There is no need to be offensive.'

The Marquis rested his chin on his clasped hands. 'Careful, Jack,' he warned lightly. 'Rock is motivated by two aims – the first being to measure swords with someone. And if he can't provoke me, I daresay he'll be content with you.'

Mr Ingram eyed the Duke irritably. 'Isn't one fight enough for you? And if and when I feel the need to lose a little blood, I'd as soon let the leech do it.'

Rockcliffe looked across at Amberley and sighed. 'Foiled again. And my second goal?'

'To hear all the gruesome details.'

The dark gaze glinted with lazy laughter. 'And?'

'Oh *hell*!' The Marquis leaned back in his chair and dropped his hand flat on the table. 'Alright. I'm fighting because it didn't seem that I had any choice – except in the proffered reason; hence the bloody parrot. And I'm choosing pistols because they are quicker and . . . less personal than a yard of steel. I don't want to make a meal of it; I simply want to get it over and done – preferably tomorrow. The early morning will doubtless be out of the question since Lord Philip was showing every sign of making it a heavy night – but you must know of some secluded spot where we could meet at around noon. Well?'

His Grace sighed. 'I do, of course. I perceive that you now wish me to set off . . . er . . . hot-foot for White's in pursuit of Harry Caversham?'

'Yes. That is exactly what I want.'

'I see.' Rockliffe came reluctantly to his feet. 'How very fatiguing it all is . . . and doubtless a punishment for my little victory of this afternoon. I do hope,' he said wearily, 'that your shooting of tomorrow will be a thought better than your driving of today. Or perhaps you wish me to carry out what is, in fact, my principal duty as a second – that of seeking a reconciliation?'

The Marquis looked up at him with reflective irony. 'You can try,' he said dryly, 'but I imagine that even *your* unique resources are likely to prove unequal to the task.

Lord Philip, you see, is convinced that he will be performing a public service.'

Although he did not obtain a reconciliation, his Grace of Rockliffe proved his worth not only by arranging the duel for noon of the following day but also by providing as a location the garden of a house in Kensington which he himself owned.

The day was a fine one and the Duke did his principal the honour of personally driving him to the meeting-place. For a time, he maintained a flow of gentle conversation that had nothing to do with the flat mahogany box that reposed on the seat between then; and then, with an apparent irrelevance that was the very essence of cunning, he said, 'Why the hurry, Denzil?'

Amberley, immaculate in slate-coloured velvet and seemingly a good deal less tense than he had been on the previous evening, smiled a little and replied with rare candour.

'I'm still trying to minimise the possible consequences. The only safe-guard of this affair is its apparent lunacy – but that can't last because I doubt that either Vernon or I could keep up the pretence of its being nothing but a friendly jest. And then the fat *would* be in the fire.'

'And Mistress Vernon's reputation with it. Yes. It is rather difficult to understand why Lord Philip challenged you,' said Rockliffe thoughtfully. 'He is not a fool . . . and neither is he in the habit of drinking too much. Does he want to kill you?'

The Marquis shook his head. 'No. He may think he does – and in the heat of the moment whilst pitting his sword and skill against mine, it's just possible he may have tried. But not in the cold light of day at twenty paces. For that you have to be either a murderer or very sure of your motives . . . and Lord Philip is neither.'

'No,' agreed his Grace dryly, swinging his pair into a

wide but rather overgrown drive. 'He is merely stubborn with a deplorable tendancy to jump to conclusions. But the Dacre child should prove a match for him . . . and that should be interesting to watch.' The curricle drew to a halt in front of a shabby stable-block and the Duke surveyed it with mild distaste. 'Dear me! The place appears to be falling apart. My apologies – I really had no idea.'

Amberley raised one quizzical brow. 'I thought it belonged to you?'

'It does. But I have only been here once before – what you might call a courtesy call, immediately following the death of my lamented father.' He smiled blandly. 'It was then – and for some time afterwards – the residence of the opulent and very accomodating actress whose . . . er . . . performances proved too much for him. Or so my mother thought.'

Grinning, the Marquis jumped lightly down on to the cobbles. 'And what did you think?'

'That it was all too likely,' came the languid reply. 'In my opinion, she had too much of everything. Ah – this should be the doctor's gig.'

It was and it was followed almost immediately by a second curricle bearing Philip and Lord Harry Caversham. The Duke withdrew a chronometer from the pocket of his vest, flicked open the silver casing and smiled. It was five minutes to twelve.

After descending briskly from his seat, Philip remained quite still, staring at the Marquis; the grey-green eyes looked gravely back at him and then Amberley bowed, silent and formal. That Philip hesitated to do likewise was due to the strange and rather sick sense of unreality that had clung to him ever since he had awoken – but hesitate he did and then the moment was lost as, having exchanged amicable greetings with Lord Harry, the Duke led his guests

207

through a peeling door, once painted green, and into a large walled garden.

There was a sweet smell of new-cut grass and Philip heard Rockliffe explaining that he had taken the precaution of having the ground scythed, since no gentleman could be expected to settle an affair of honour in a hayfield. Harry laughed and Amberley made what seemed to be a joke about pistols. Philip did not listen; he had given up wondering what madness had possessed him to issue this challenge and was foolishly annoyed that he had not responded to his adversary's bow. Then he remembered that in ten minutes' time he might be dead – and after that nothing seemed to matter very much.

Rockliffe and Harry were inspecting the pistols. They belonged to the Marquis and were elegant things, their butts silver-mounted and inlaid with mother-of-pearl and their graceful ten-inch barrels delicately engraved with flowers and leaves.

'Beautiful!' breathed Harry enviously.

And lethal, thought Philip, walking absently away to stare at a clump of wild iris. I should have written Isabel a letter. Just in case . . . And then Harry was calling to him that they were ready.

The pistol was cold in his hand and for a moment he stared curiously at it, as if wondering what it was doing there. Then he looked across at his foe, deliberately reminding himself of the grievances that had brought him here and wishing that he could believe them as securely now as he had last night. He had never before shot a man in cold blood; he wondered if Amberley had.

The Marquis was a little pale but as coolly composed as ever and even moderately relaxed. Philip watched him expertly checking the loaded pistol and resetting its trigger at half-cock; his hands were steady and his face showed nothing but concentration for the task in hand.

Then he looked up into Philip's eyes with a sort of wry understanding that he seemed to be inviting Philip to share; and he smiled.

Rockliffe's soft voice was instructing them and Philip took his place, held his weapon so that its barrel pointed down at the bruised, scented grass and concentrated on listening to the familiar words. He had never fought a duel in his life but everyone knew the procedure and in the army they had often joked about it. Philip wished it seemed funny now.

'When I give the signal,' the Duke was saying, 'you will walk ten paces, turn and fire at will. Are you ready, gentlemen?'

'Perfectly,' replied the Marquis calmly.

'Yes,' said Lord Philip and in the same instant felt the spell around him dissolve. 'Quite ready.'

Rockliffe stepped back to stand beside Lord Harry.

'Very well, gentlemen. *One . . . two . . . three . . .*'

Philip and Amberley paced steadily away from each other in time with his Grace's measured count.

'*Eight . . . nine . . . ten.*'

They wheeled smartly to face each other, levelling their pistols. Then the Marquis jerked up his hand and deloped and an instant later Lord Philip's bullet sliced through his left arm just above the elbow. With a gasp of pain, Amberley dropped his own weapon to clamp his fingers hard over the wound from which blood was already pouring down over his hand and on to the bright grass. Then he glanced up to encounter the Duke's astounded gaze and said, with what might have been weak laughter, 'Damn you, Rock – where's that confounded leech of yours? Or are you going to let me bleed to death?'

But the doctor was already hurrying across the turf and, smiling a little, Rockliffe strolled lazily after him.

'My dear Denzil – you would be well-served if I did,' he remarked resignedly. 'I suppose you *had* to delope?'

The Marquis stifled a curse as the doctor helped him out of his coat and then he dropped to his knees. 'You are just peeved because I didn't tell you,' he replied breathlessly. 'But you must have expected it.'

'Yes.' His Grace sighed. 'You know . . . there are times when I wonder if you aren't too noble for this world of ours.' Amberley looked up and, with a grimace of mingled pain and irritation, demonstrated his nobility with one of Broody's choicest phrases.

All this time Philip had been staring at the results of his marksmanship in utter disbelief. He heard Harry say blankly, 'My God, Phil – I didn't think you'd actually *shoot* him!' And realised that *he* had not thought it either – any more than he had expected the Marquis to fire in the air.

White to the lips, he strode across to Amberley's side and stared helplessly at the doctor's attempts to stem the crimson tide trickling steadily down one tapering hand. And then he met the Marquis's slightly furrowed gaze and heard him say cheerfully, 'I don't know whether to commiserate with you for failing to make a good job of it or congratulate you on hitting me at all – but I'm inclined to the latter. You shoot remarkably straight . . . for a grenadier.'

Philip flushed a little and then, just as he was about to utter a stiff reply, he made a discovery that was wholly astonishing. There was no mockery or anger in the grey-green eyes and the grin bracketing Amberley's mouth was there to cover the fact that he was in pain. It was more than just unexpected as it produced a stupidly illogical feeling of liking that flooded Philip's brain with shocked incomprehension and set him at a loss.

He said haltingly, 'Too straight, perhaps. I – you won't believe it, I suppose – but I never wanted to kill you.'

'No.' The Marquis smiled hazily. 'I know you didn't. If I'd thought that, I don't suppose I should have deloped.'

'Would you not?' asked the Duke sweetly. 'Well, well!'

'Leave it, Rock,' came the laconic reply.

Philip cast a doubtful glance at his Grace and then looked back at Amberley. 'Why *did* you delope?' he asked bluntly.

The Marquis winced as the doctor began to bind his arm and said unevenly, 'It's usually considered an acknowledgement of fault.'

'I know. But I don't think that's why you did it.'

A tinge of colour stole into the bloodless cheek. 'No.'

'Then why?' persisted Philip. 'It's important that I understand.'

'Very true,' agreed Rockliffe smoothly. 'And, since Denzil is too shy to tell you himself . . .'

'No – damn it!' The Marquis struggled to get to his feet only to be pushed back by the Duke's hand. 'You don't *know* why . . .'

'Gently, my dear,' said his Grace soothingly. 'I have known you since we were both eighteen so I think I have a reasonably shrewd idea of how your mind works. And, if I am wrong, you can always correct me, can you not?'

Amberley closed his lips together and said nothing. Indeed, there was nothing he *could* say that was likely to stop his obliquely-purposeful friend now.

Rockliffe turned his heavy-lidded gaze to Lord Philip. 'It may come as a surprise to you,' he drawled, 'but my Lord Marquis is possessed of a certain crude ability with firearms and could, I believe, have put a bullet through any part of you he chose. Possibly he would attribute it to the fact that he was not a grenadier – but a hussar.'

Philip shot a surprised look at the Marquis. 'Were you?'

'Yes,' replied Amberley tonelessly. He did not look up but confined his attention to the task of carefully rolling his blood-soaked shirt-sleeve down over his arm.

Rockliffe smiled faintly and went on, 'He also, for

211

some reason I cannot quite grasp, was convinced that he was in no danger from you; and so, because he has some strange notion that he owes you something – but more because he happens to be very much in love with your sister, he decided to forgo his options on your person and delope. Anyone else,' he concluded tolerantly, 'would have been content simply to shoot wide. But I suppose everyone is entitled to one vanity.'

'Have you quite finished?' asked the Marquis glacially, rising unsteadily to his feet. 'Or do you want to add that I like dogs and am kind to my aged mother?'

'Thank you, no,' mocked his Grace. 'I am merely waiting to hear you deny any part of what I have said.'

There was a long, dangerous silence and then Amberley bent shakily to retrieve his ruined coat. 'I'm going home,' he said with audible restraint. 'Will you drive me – or shall I ask Harry?'

Chapter Sixteen

Rosalind's second day of solitude was an ironic travesty of her first – for where, yesterday, she had avoided her brother in order to think, she now wished for his presence the better not to do so. But the hours dragged slowly by and Philip showed no sign of returning; and when, at around five o'clock, she received word that his Lordship would be dining at his club, she smiled wryly and reflected that she was merely being repaid in her own coin.

She was on the point of retiring to her room in the listless expectation of passing another sleepless night when the pealing of the doorbell and sounds of commotion in the hall brought a painful resurgence of hope that tensed her nerves and stopped her breath. Then the door was thrown impetuously open, she heard a flurry of taffeta and Isabel's voice, sharply questioning; and bitter disappointment lashed over her with the savagery of a tidal wave. She bent her head, arms folded tight over the actual physical pain inside her and tried to swallow the sudden, choking sobs that crowded into her throat.

Isabel saw the anguish in every line of that hunched figure but, already too anxious to be touched by it, she cast aside her loo-mask and fan and, oblivious of the danger to her ruffled ballgown, knelt swiftly at Rosalind's side.

'Rose!' she snapped, urgently shaking the other girl's arm. 'This is important! *Where is Philip?*'

Very slowly, Rosalind lifted her head. 'At White's,' she said dully. And then, 'Someone is with you.'

'Yes – Robert. We were at the Anstey's masked ball – and still are as far as Mama is concerned,' came the rapid reply. 'But I had to know it if was true so I made Bob bring me here. Have you spoken with Philip today?'

'No.' Rosalind made an effort to concentrate. 'If what is true?'

Isabel's hands fell away and she stood up.

'That he is to fight Amberley. Everyone is talking of it. They say he challenged him last night. He's said nothing to you?'

The pit of Rosalind's stomach fell away with a sickening lurch and for a moment she felt too ill to reply. Then, in an odd voice, she said, 'No. He went out this morning with Harry Caversham and hasn't been back since. We didn't even have breakfast together.' Then the implications of this dawned on her and she drew a long, unsteady breath, 'Oh God, no – he couldn't't!'

Irritated by the ease with which they ignored him, Robert strolled across to the fire saying flippantly, 'Well, it sounds to me as though he has. Ansford said that Caversham was to be Phil's second and, since everyone knows of it, I daresay they wanted to get it over as quickly as possible.' He grinned at Broody dozing quietly on his perch and added brightly, 'Only think; Amberley may be dead by now – and all because of a silly parrot!'

'Be silent,' said Isabel, her usually gentle voice harsh with strain. 'You make me sick.'

Gripping her hands together, Rosalind continued to behave as though Robert did not exist.

'What does he mean?' she asked Isabel tensely. 'They surely can't have quarrelled over Broody!'

'They didn't,' replied Isabel briefly. 'Or so I think. They quarrelled over you and, perhaps, a little because of something foolish I said to Philip yesterday. But they couldn't do it openly so they had to have an excuse. Gentlemen,' she finished sardonically, 'are very finicky about things like that. And, as excuses go, this one is superb because everyone thinks it a huge joke.'

'Do they indeed?' Rosalind was very white and her hands felt damply unsteady but the decision was back in her voice. 'Well, I don't. I think it's stupid and dangerous. Pull the bell.'

Startled, Isabel did so. 'What are you going to do?'

'Find out what is going on,' said Rosalind curtly. And then, lifting her head as the door opened, 'Porson?'

'Yes, madam?' The butler bowed.

'I wish you to send a message to White's asking my brother to return here immediately,' she said crisply. '*Immediately*, you understand?'

'Yes, madam.' Another bow and he was gone.

Isabel sank weakly into a chair but before she could speak, Robert said petulantly, 'Well, if you think I'm going to hang around waiting for Vernon to come back, you much mistake the matter. You can either come with me now, Bella – or else get your precious Philip to escort you. Well?'

'I'm not going until I've seen Philip,' said his sister flatly. 'And you can't return to the ball without me.'

'You think not?' He gave a short laugh and walked towards the door. 'Just watch me!'

Rosalind waited until she heard his hand on the latch and then said gently, 'It's entirely your decision, of course – but I think that if I were you I would stay and . . . guard my rear.'

He swung to face her. 'From what?'

'From me,' she replied dulcetly. 'You see, if you go now, I might not be able to resist telling Isabel about Vauxhall.'

It was checkmate and, for once, Robert had the sense to realise it. He said sulkily, 'Very well. Since you are so eager for my company, I'll stay.'

Rosalind's tone lost every vestige of sweetness. 'As far as I am concerned, Mr Dacre, both you and your manners belong in the nursery. You will stay in order to escort Isabel back to Anstey House and for no other reason – and if you have any intelligence at all, you will sit down and refrain from furnishing us with further proofs of your spite, your rudeness and your immaturity. I assure you that we know them only too well.'

Never, in all his twenty short years, had anyone spoken to Robert like that and, furiously, he made the mistake of saying so.

'Then it is high time that someone did,' retorted Rosalind coldly. 'If they had done so sooner, you might have stood some chance of becoming a man; as it is, you'll be hanging on to coat-tails and apron-strings all your life because you haven't the backbone to take responsibility for yourself. Now sit down and be quiet – I'm tired of you.'

And, thoroughly deflated, Robert sat without a word.

Rosalind turned towards Isabel. 'I think, while we are waiting for Phil, I'd like you to tell me exactly what it is you heard. All of it.'

Mistress Dacre sighed, folded her hands and repeated the little she knew. Then she said wretchedly, 'And I am so very afraid that it's partly my fault. If one of them gets hurt, I'll never forgive myself.'

'What did you say to Phil?' asked Rosalind curiously. And then, remembering Robert's presence, 'Or no. I imagine I've a shrewd idea of the sort of thing – and I can't say I blame you. It's a pity that you had to choose Lord Amberley – but I can understand that the opportunity must have been hard to resist. Phil can be a terrible fool at times.'

'No.' Isabel smiled sadly. 'He just wants a marriage of convenience. And, do you know – so long as he is alright, I don't think I mind.'

216

'Rubbish!' snapped Rosalind with irritable ambiguity. 'And I don't know why you should worry about Phil – if he wasn't alright he wouldn't be dining at White's. And if he *has* met Lord Amberley and – and any damage has been done, then it clearly wasn't to him.'

There was a long pause and then Robert said casually, 'Amberley is supposed to be a crack shot – and quite a reasonable swordsman too.'

'Which is presumably why you didn't challenge him after he knocked you down,' she responded swiftly, reducing him to silence again. And then, tilting her head, 'At last! Now we shall know.'

Isabel listened but it was several seconds before she heard the sounds betokening Lord Philip's arrival; and then, almost immediately, he was in the room.

He looked different; tired was the first word that sprang to Isabel's mind – then older. But, realising that neither was right, she could only think that he was subtly changed; and wonder why. His frowning gaze scanned the room and then came to rest on her own face with a sort of questioning intensity that made her heart turn over.

'Are – are you alright?' she asked hesitantly.

His expression altered and he gave a brief sardonic laugh. 'Perfectly. Is that why you sent for me with such haste?'

'No.' It was Rosalind who spoke. 'That may be all Isabel cares for but it wasn't she who sent for you. And I imagine you can guess what it is *I* want to know.'

'Yes. You want to know if I've killed your white knight – and the answer, of course, is no.' He laughed again and turned away to pour himself a glass of wine. 'It seems I'm not a good enough shot – so fear not, little sister, he'll live to fight another day. I only winged him.'

The blood drummed unpleasantly in Rosalind's ears and she clung tightly to the arms of her chair. 'What do you mean?'

Philip looked defiantly back across the room. 'I mean,' he said kindly, 'that I put a bullet through his arm. Painful, messy and visually dramatic – but a mere flesh wound.'

Unable to remain silent any longer, Robert said incredulously, 'He never missed you?'

Some of Philip's apparent bravado deserted him and he frowned into his glass. 'No. He deloped.'

'He what?' asked Rosalind, recovering a little.

'Fired in the air. What else would he do?' demanded Philip bitterly. And then, bowing mockingly to Isabel, '*He was a verray parfit gentil knyght*. You see, I've managed to place your quotation.'

Isabel flushed . 'Why did you challenge him?'

'Don't you know?' For a moment the satirical blue gaze continued to taunt her and then he ran a fingernail noisily along the bars of Broody's cage, jerking the somnolent bird into sudden wakefulness.

'Wark!' screamed Broody indignantly. He seized a seed and spat.

'That's why,' smiled Philip brightly. 'Don't tell me you hadn't heard?'

'You are angry with yourself,' said Rosalind disconcertingly. 'Why? Because you didn't kill him . . . or because you didn't miss?'

There was a long silence and then, 'Rot the Captain! Rot him, rot him *rot* him! Scabby landlubber!'

'Oh hell!' swore Philip, pulling off his cloak and casting it over the cage. 'One of these days I'll wring that blasted bird's neck!' There was another pause, punctuated only by a series of muffled, reproachful squawks and then he said, 'Alright. The truth is that I feel quite unreasonably guilty and wish I hadn't done it. Never having been in this situation before, I don't know if that's normal or not. But until this morning, I disliked Amberley with completely satisfactory thoroughness – and

218

thought that I knew why. Only then he sat on the grass, bleeding like a pig, and made a stupid joke and everything seemed different. It's absurd and illogical but I don't think I understand anything any more – and all because he could look at me and laugh.'

A tiny smile lit the violet eyes. 'Of course he *would* do that,' said Rosalind reflectively. 'I'm only surprised it's taken you so long to see it.'

'Not so fast,' replied her brother grimly. 'I said it *seemed* different – but it isn't. It can't be, for nothing is materially changed. He's still the man who is indirectly responsible for your blindness and who has tried to hide it; the man who fleeces drunken youths at dice and raises false hopes in the breast of any girl unwise enough to let him do so. And if you still doubt the last two, you have only to ask Robert. Ask him, for example, about Mistress Irwin.'

'I wouldn't ask Robert for the time of day!' said Rosalind frankly. 'And if these were your only reasons for challenging Lord Amberley, then I think you made a big mistake.'

'She's right.' Isabel came abruptly to her feet. Her face was very pale and her hands were gripped so tightly that her knuckles gleamed white. 'You *have* made a mistake – and a much graver one than you know.'

Philip's mouth twisted in a bitter smile. 'My God – are you in love with him as well?'

'No! And if you'll listen, I'll explain. You've been under a misapprehension from the very beginning and the Marquis knows it. He . . .'

'Be quiet, damn you!' Robert erupted violently from his seat to seize her wrist. 'You gave me your word!'

'And you gave me yours – but it wasn't worth much, was it?' She directed a resolute brown gaze at his Lordship. 'You appear to think Lord Amberley a hardened and destructive flirt. Did Robert tell you so?'

219

Robert's fingers tightened like a vice on her arm. '*Bella . . .*'

'Be silent!' she snapped. And then, to Philip, 'Well?'

His Lordship appeared faintly dazed. 'Yes.'

Isabel looked full into her brother's smouldering eyes. 'Take your hands off me,' she said in a tone of such flat contempt that he took an involuntary step back. 'You are despicable. You lie and cheat and twist the facts to suit your own ends – and the only reason you hate the Marquis is because you are jealous. He is all that you are not and so you hate him for it. Dear God – you make me ashamed of my name.'

'It's a lie!' shouted Robert. He was as white as his shirt and shaking. 'I'm *not* jealous – I'm *not*! And you don't know what you are saying, you bitch!'

'Some time ago,' continued Isabel as steadily as if he had not spoken, 'you persuaded me to give you a promise; I should never have done so and I bitterly regret that I did. But when I gave it I had no notion just how far your mischief-making would go – that, because of you, a man might have been killed. And now I'm going to tell the truth before it is too late – and there is nothing that you can say to stop me.'

Philip frowned at her. 'Isabel – what is all this about? That I fought Amberley has little enough to do with Robert.'

Isabel shook her head and took a couple of uncertain steps towards him. She said, 'It has everything to do with him. It was precipitated, in the end, by whatever happened at Vauxhall the night before last – and, later on, I think Rosalind should tell you precisely what that was – but your dislike of the Marquis has always stemmed from your belief that he won three thousand guineas from Robert at dice.'

'Hardly a belief,' commented Philip dryly. 'I saw him do it.'

'No. You saw him *win* – you did not see him accept his winnings. And, in fact, he never did so. He returned Robert's notes for nothing . . . and your three thousand guineas paid for a curricle and pair.'

Rosalind leaned back in her chair and closed her eyes. 'Well, well,' she said softly, not in relief but in mild interest. There was no place for relief since she had never believed the Marquis guilty of dishounour; and, instead, she found herself thinking of Rockliffe and wondering how much of this he had guessed.

It was a long time before Philip spoke and when he did so, it was to Robert. 'Is it true?'

Badly frightened, Robert slumped into a chair and floundered in a quagmire of unintelligible extenuations.

'*Is it true?*' repeated Philip, like the report of a pistol.

'Yes,' muttered Robert. 'God damn you, *yes*! But I . . .'

'Don't say anything else.' His Lordship's voice was restrained again but far from reassuring. 'If you do, I may not be able to keep my hands from your throat. I could forgive you the money – but not the deceit. Isabel is right; you are beneath contempt.'

'I'm glad that you think that,' remarked Isabel sturdily, 'because I haven't finished yet. Not unless you are prepared to present your apologies to the Marquis and agree to his marrying Rosalind.'

Rosalind's eyes flew open and she sat up.

'I shall apologise for misjudging him, naturally,' said Philip stiffly. 'But as for the rest – I don't know yet. There are other considerations.'

'I don't understand,' said Rosalind unevenly. 'He hasn't asked me to marry him. He didn't even come.'

Isabel raised enquiring brows at Lord Philip and, when he did not reply, turned back to his sister. 'He would have come,' she said simply, 'but that he thought you would not receive him. Philip called on him yesterday morning and told him that you knew of his part in your accident.'

'Philip?' The violet eyes were wide and dark. '*Why?*'

His Lordship flushed, suddenly ashamed. 'I thought . . . it seemed to be for the best.'

'For whom?' Rosalind rose unsteadily to her feet. 'Not for me – or only if he really *was* trifling with me. Was he?'

Again Isabel waited for Philip to speak before saying, 'No. He wants to marry you. But because Philip believed him guilty of every conceivable villainy, he used the only weapon he had and . . . *implied* . . . that you blamed his Lordship for your blindness.'

Rosalind did not know whether to laugh or cry. Shivering a little, she stretched out a groping hand to Isabel and felt it taken in a warm, comforting clasp.

'I don't understand,' she said childishly. 'How could he possibly think I would blame him?'

Isabel discovered that she felt suddenly very tired – as if all the life had drained out of her. She said, 'I think you had best ask him that question yourself. I must go. I never meant to stay so long.'

'No.' Rosalind smiled mistily at her. 'But I'm so very glad that you did. There is still a lot I need to know . . . but you don't know what you've done for me.'

'Oh I think I do,' replied Isabel dryly. And thought, I've betrayed my brother and disgraced myself in the eyes of yours. I only hope it was worth it. Releasing Rosalind's hand, she stooped to pick up her mask and fan and then retied the strings of her cloak; and when it was no longer possible to evade Philip's eyes, she looked up and said flatly, 'I'm sorry if you are angry but I had to tell her – and I am far guiltier than you for I should have told you the rest of it long ago.' Her eyes travelled fleetingly to her brother. 'Don't forget to ask Rosalind about Vauxhall. Goodnight.' And with a small curtsey, she walked towards the door.

'No – wait.' Philip stepped impulsively after her. He did not know what to say – only that he must say something. 'I've got to talk to you.'

'Yes.' Wearily she turned round. 'But not now, if you don't mind. I'm tired and I want to go home but I can't because I've got to go back to the Anstey ball. I'm sorry – but I don't think I can cope with you as well. Come, Robert.'

Philip flinched as though she had slapped him and said nothing more. He managed a slight bow, avoided looking at the Honourable Robert and a minute later they had gone. For a long time he remained where he was, staring at the closed door and then he turned abruptly away to lean his hands on the mantel. The seconds ticked by in silence as he tried to master his hurt and come to terms with the shock of Isabel's disclosures. Then he said curtly, 'I seem to have made an utter fool of myself.'

'Yes,' agreed Rosalind, completely without rancour. 'But it wasn't entirely your fault and you acted in good faith. And it can be put right. Fortunately.'

Philip frowned down into the fire, thinking how nearly he had come to making it horribly and finally wrong.

'You love him, don't you?' he asked.

'Yes.' She smiled a little.

'So much that nothing else matters?'

'Yes. As much as that – and more.'

'I see. He is to be envied.' His hands fell to his sides and he turned to face her. 'I'll visit him tomorrow and do what I can to set matters right – the rest will be up to him.' He grinned crookedly. 'Do you suppose he'll kick me down the steps – or fall on my neck?'

'Neither,' laughed Rosalind shakily. 'He's much more likely to make a joke of it. You know he can't help it – not even when he's bleeding like a pig!'

There is nothing very funny about having to confess yourself a dupe to the man you have insulted in every conceivable way and Philip was not looking forward to his interview with the Marquis. He could remember with distressing clarity all the unjust accusations he had hurled at Amberley's head and there was no reason, he thought gloomily, to suppose that Amberley would not remember them too; he had lied, not openly, but by implication, about Rosalind's feelings and would now have to admit it; and yesterday, adding injury to insult, he had put a bullet through the fellow's arm.

It did not augur well for their future relationship and Philip would not have been human if he had not wished that his sister had chosen to bestow her heart elsewhere. But since there was no help for it, since he owed both Rosalind and her Marquis some reparation and had come, at last, to understand how they felt, he duly left Great Jermyn Street on the stroke of eleven the following morning and set off to do his endeavour in Grosvenor Square.

His resolution was wasted for the Marquis was not at home. He had left very early that morning for Richmond, said his butler; and he was not expected to return until the end of the week. Unable to decide if he was glad or sorry, Philip went reluctantly home to tell his sister.

Under all the vicissitudes of the previous evening, Rosalind had remained reasonable and understanding; today, she was neither. She demanded to be taken instantly to Richmond.

Philip stared at her. 'Don't be an idiot, Rose. I can't go chasing the man all over the countryside – neither can you. It isn't sensible.'

'*I* won't be sensible if I have to wait for three whole days,' she retorted flatly. 'And it isn't all over the countryside – it's only to Richmond. It can't take more than an hour.'

'That isn't the point. I look a big enough fool as it is without charging uninvited into someone else's house. I'm . . .'

'It will be his mother's house – Mallory Place. He told me about it. I shouldn't think she'd mind.'

'Oh wonderful!' said Philip. 'As if it's not bad enough having to face Amberley, you want me to call on his mother and explain how I came to shoot her son. No thank you!'

Rosalind swallowed an infelicitious reply and tried what coaxing would do. '*Please*, Phil,' she begged. 'It's such a *little* thing to ask!'

'That's all very well for you to say. Your part is easy!'

'Not necessarily,' she replied dryly. 'And don't you . . .'

'*No*! God knows I'll be lucky to come out of this with any dignity at all and I certainly don't intend to sacrifice what little I *do* have by running after him like a damned tyro. I'll leave a letter in Grosvenor Square asking him to receive me when he comes back to town – but that's all I will do. And if,' he concluded wisely, scanning her flushed, stubborn countenance, 'you're going to fly into a temper, you can do it on your own. I'm off to see Isabel.' And without staying to hear the blistering reply that was doubtless brewing, he made a timely exit.

As soon as he turned into Clarges Street he realised that all was not well. The door of Lord Linton's residence stood wide open and through it, to the evident delight of the small group of urchins, maidservants and passers-by gathered on the pavement, came the loud, blustering tones of the Viscount demanding that some person or persons should immediately vacate his house.

'Oh Lord!' thought Philip irritably, as he pushed his way through to the steps. '*What now?*'

The scene in the hall was one of noisy confusion. Facing the Viscount and all talking at once were some seven or eight soberly-dressed individuals all clutching sheets of paper which they brandished militantly in his Lordship's alarmingly suffused face. And, behind his

225

father, pale, shaking and striving not to be noticed, stood the Honourable Robert. The situation, thought Philip savagely, was suddenly crystal clear.

'Stop this infernal din!' he shouted in a voice any soldier would have recognised.

It had its effect; the hall fell abruptly silent and every eye swung round to stare at him. Philip nodded curtly to the Viscount and fixed a derisive blue stare on his son. 'Your creditors, I presume?'

Robert fidgeted and turned away.

'Yes, young sir – we *are* his creditors!' volunteered a portly gentleman in brown. 'And we are here to . . .'

'I asked you to be quiet,' rapped Philip. 'It doesn't take a genius to see why you are here – or that you are wasting your time. I take it,' he said, looking at Lord Linton, 'that, as usual, your son is unable to meet his obligations?'

'Of course he can't meet 'em!' the Viscount snorted. 'And *I'll* not settle 'em. Couldn't even if I wanted to – which I don't!'

'I see.' Philip smiled coldly at Robert. 'Then it looks as though you are about to take up residence in the Fleet, doesn't it?'

A murmur of dissatisfaction rippled through the ranks of assembled merchants.

'Much good that'll do *us*!' grumbled one.

'And that's if the young puppy don't skip off to Foreign Parts,' added another.

Lord Linton eyed Philip speculatively. 'Don't suppose *you'd* think of helping the boy out?'

'I already have,' replied Philip. 'Frequently.'

'Ah.' The Viscount rocked back and forth, nodding wisely at the floor. 'But just once more? For Bella? Poor girl won't like to see her brother in the Fleet, I daresay.'

'But then she *won't* see it, will she?' objected Philip pleasantly. He was deriving a certain grim enjoyment

226

from repaying Robert for some of the trouble he had caused. 'You could hardly expect Isabel to visit the debtor's ward, after all. And I wouldn't be surprised if she wasn't rather glad to have Robert safely out of harm's way.'

This aspect of the matter had not previously occurred to Lord Linton and he appeared to consider it. Then he shook his head and said, a shade regretfully, 'No. Too much scandal. Got the name to think of, y'know. And it's Bella's name too.'

'It won't be when she is married to me,' Philip pointed out. And then, tiring of the game, 'But I might be willing to help – upon certain conditions.'

His Lordship brightened. 'Ha! Anything you like, m'boy. Only to name it.'

The prospect of a reprieve put new life into Robert. 'Don't you think,' he asked sullenly, 'that we should discuss this in private?'

The sapphire gaze travelled along the row of silently hopeful spectators and came to rest on Robert.

'Oh no,' said Lord Philip sweetly. 'These gentlemen have a vested interest and I . . . I am anxious to avoid committing a murder. So here and now will do very well indeed. Do I have your undivided attention?'

Robert coloured and toyed nervously with his quizzing-glass. 'Yes. Get on with it.'

Philip nodded. 'Very well. I have no intention of putting money in your unreliable hands – but if these gentlemen will present their accounts to me, I will discharge them . . . along with any others you may have. I shall also purchase you a commission in any regiment I can find that will take you out of England – and after that I shall never do anything for you again. Those are my terms; take them or leave them. Well?'

There was a long, nerve-racking pause and then Robert said furiously, 'Damn you – what choice do I have?'

'None,' replied Philip, coldly indifferent. 'But whose fault is that?'

At about the time that Lord Philip arrived in Clarges Street, his betrothed who had no idea of the stirring events taking place at her home called on Rosalind and found her pacing restlessly up and down the parlour in an orgy of frustration.

'Isabel – just the person!' Rosalind exclaimed, abruptly ceasing her perambulations. And then, anxiously, 'Philip isn't with you, is he?'

'No.' Isabel looked faintly mystified. 'I've been to Phanie's for a fitting of my wedding dress. Why?'

'It doesn't matter. It's just that he went to Clarges Street to see you.'

'Oh!' Isabel turned rather pink. 'Then perhaps I ought to go home – or do you think it would be better to wait here?'

'Neither,' said Rosalind firmly, her eyes sparkling with determination. 'If you go, you'll probably miss him. And when he finds you are out . . . I imagine he'll go to his club. He certainly won't come back here.' She laughed oddly. 'Yes. It's perfect – couldn't be better!'

'*What* couldn't?' asked Isabel, baffled. And then, with dire foreboding. 'Oh no – you're plotting something, aren't you? Something awful.'

'Yes – and no.' Rosalind's smile was tinged with brittle brilliance. 'I just thought that you might like to go for a little drive with me. Will you?'

Isabel regarded her with amused suspicion. 'I might. Where to?'

'Richmond,' said Mistress Vernon casually. 'Phil wouldn't take me there but I think that, if we left him a note, he might follow us.'

'But why?'

'Because you are with me.'

228

'I meant,' said Isabel dryly, 'why are we going?'

Rosalind laughed again and the sound had a recklessness that was strangely disquieting. 'To see Lord Amerbley – and exorcise a ghost. I hope.'

Chapter Seventeen

'*Mon fils* – I do not at all mind if you do not wish to talk to me,' lied the Dowager Marchioness of Amberley with an apparent placidity designed to cover her inner anxiety, 'but the roses you are scraping off the plate are what make it part of a set. And also, I do not like the noise.'

Starting slightly, the Marquis frowned down at the knife he had been running absently back and forth across the gleaming surface of a small Sèvres plate and laid it aside.

'I beg your pardon,' he said with a smile that did not quite reach his eyes. 'I was thinking of something else. I am a poor guest, am I not?'

'*Affreux*,' she agreed frankly, her gaze on the black silk sling that supported his left arm. It lent him a romantically heroic appearance that accorded rather well with the bleak pallor of his face but Louise appreciated neither; and still less did she appreciate the phrase 'a slight accident' – which was all the explanation he would give.

He said wryly, 'Perhaps I should have gone to Amberley.'

His mother rested her chin on one slender palm and surveyed him enigmatically across the table. 'Why did you not, then?'

And that brought him up short. Why had he not?

Because he had not wanted to go that far? Because he had hoped against hope that something might change? Folly. One had as well try grasping the moon's reflection in a pond. The only solid truth was that he could not stay in London for everyone to see that his duel with Lord Phillip had been no joke – and could not yet face the prospect of meeting Rosalind. So he had come to Richmond in time to sit over a late breakfast with Louise and tell her none of the things she wished to know.

She was an unusual woman, his mother, and always had been; she would sooner bleed to death than burden him with her concern and her questions. But they were there nonetheless and he found himself vaguely regretting that he had come.

The word vague, he thought detachedly, seemed to say it all – to describe his every thought, word and deed; he even felt *vaguely* unwell for the dull throbbing of his arm was echoed by a nagging ache in his head that would not go away. He was used to none of it and it produced a distant irritation that occasionally prompted him to cut through the cocoon of mists and shadows with the lash of his tongue. It did so now and he stood up, saying abruptly, 'I thought I might go abroad again.'

Dismay clutched at the Dowager's heart but she merely said, 'Oh? And where to this time?'

He shrugged and his mouth twisted in something not quite a smile. 'Beyond the edge of the world. I don't know. And it isn't really important.'

It was too much for Louise and, colouring faintly, she said, 'It is Mademoiselle Vernon, *n'est-ce-pas*? I do not like to ask – but if it is to take you away again, I think I must. She will not have you, *la petite*? *C'est ça?*'

'*Oui – c'est ça.*' There was no attempt at amusement now and his face was as hard and expressionless as a carved mask.

'Oh. I – am sorry. You told her?'

231

'Not I, no. Her brother.' And for all I know he may even be regretting it – thanks to Rock. But it's too late now; the damage is too great. And she'd as soon wed a leper. He looked frozenly at Louise's bent head and said, 'I'm sorry, Maman. I can't discuss it. Have you anything in your stables that is up to my weight?'

She nodded. It occurred to her that he was unwise – in this mood and with only one arm – to go riding but she knew better than to say so. 'Ask them to saddle Vulcan.'

'Thank you.' Again that tight, meaningless smile. Then, 'Don't worry, my dear. I'll try to come back in a more civilised humour.' And he was gone.

For a long time Louise sat quite still looking at a rather blurred image of the closed door and then, with an air of quiet desperation, she picked up her hat and walked resolutely out into the sunshine of her garden.

She was still there when her major-domo came to inform her that she had visitors. Two young ladies, he said with bristling disapproval, who had asked first for Monsieur le Marquis.

The Dowager laid down her trowel and thoughtfully pulled the gloves from her hands. Then she said quietly, '*Merci*, Gaston. I will see these young ladies.'

Gaston sniffed. '*Oui, Madam.*'

Louise regarded him with a twinkle of mischievous sympathy.

'I know, *mon vieux* – I know. But we are no longer young, you and I – and things are not as they were. Also, two young ladies are better than one, so it could be worse.' And on this somewhat obscure utterance, she drifted away into the house.

Isabel turned apprehensively as the door opened and received the confused impression that this small, elegant lady in apple-green could not possibly be the Marquis's mama. Then she recognised the line of cheek and jaw, realised that the delicate skin was no longer young and the white hair perfectly natural; and, looking into the Dowager's clear, green eyes, said impulsively, 'Oh – but you are so like your son!'

Louise gave a sweet rippling laugh but, even as she replied, her gaze was already on Rosalind. '*Merci du compliment, mademoiselle* – I am happy that you think so. But it seems that you have the advantage?'

Isabel flushed and wondered foolishly why no one had thought to mention that the Dowager Marchioness was French.

'I – I beg your pardon, Madame,' she said haltingly. 'It must seem odd to you but I – that is, *we* – have come to – to . . .'

Rosalind's fingers tightened on Isabel's arm and then fell away as she took a small, uncertain step forward.

'We came because I hoped to speak to his Lordship,' she said baldly. 'And Mistress Dacre came with me because I am blind.'

'Ah.' Louise's gaze became positively owlish. 'And what you have to say to my son, Mademoiselle Vernon – it will not wait?'

'No. It will not wait,' came the tense reply. Then, differently, 'You know who I am?'

'*Bien sûr*,' nodded Louise. You are the one for whom my son is in purgatory. And you look as though you are sharing it with him. 'Monsiuer Le Marquis has gone out riding but he will be back. You will await him, yes?'

'Yes please – if we may.' The violet eyes grew dark with anxiety. 'How *can* he ride? It was only yesterday he had a bullet through his arm!'

The Dowager's slim shoulders stiffened and she said flatly, 'A bullet, you say? *Vraiment*? I think we should sit down.'

'It's alright, Madame,' said Isabel helpfully, as she guided Rosalind to a chair. 'Philip said it was not serious – just a flesh wound.'

'Philippe?' queried Louise. And then, 'But yes! I have it now – he is your brother, is he not, Mademoiselle Vernon?'

'Yes. He is also,' replied Rosalind reluctantly, 'the gentleman responsible for shooting Lord Amberley. You didn't know?'

'Me – I know nothing!' said the Dowager, shrugging emphatically. 'Denzil is never communicative – and today less so than ever. But Milord Philippe – he was *not* shot?'

'No.' Rosalind's cheeks gained a little colour. 'I – I understand that Lord Amberley fired in the air. It was all a – a mistake and Philip deeply regrets wounding him but he thought . . . he thought . . .'

'*Oui, mademoiselle?*'

Rosalind clasped and unclasped her hands nervously. 'It is all rather complicated,' she said, 'Perhaps I should start at the beginning?'

A hint of laughter gleamed in the green eyes.

'Well if *you* do not, it is very certain that no one else will and me, I am consumed of a curiosity quite remarkable. But one does not, of course, wish to pry.'

The unmistakable note of levity in the attractively-accented voice was so strongly reminiscent of the Marquis that it brought an ache to Rosalind's throat and an answering gleam to her eyes. She said, a fraction less awkwardly, 'Of course not. But I think I would like to tell you.'

'*Eh bien.*' Louise smiled encouragingly. 'Then tell me.'

It was, as Rosalind had said, a difficult tale to tell – and was made the more so by her determination to deal fairly with everyone concerned. But when the threads showed signs of becoming tangled, the Dowager sifted them with some brief and beautifully direct questions that enabled Rosalind to explain and move easily on. Isabel said nothing and, indeed, hardly listened; instead, she wondered, hopefully, if Lord Philip would follow them and tried to calculate how soon he might possibly arrive.

'So you see,' finished Rosalind quietly, 'Phil realises his mistake and means to acknowledge it to Lord Amberley – so I beg you will not judge him too harshly, Madame.'

'I do not judge him at all, *ma fille*,' said the Dowager blandly. 'You had better address that request to my son.'

Rosalind smiled faintly. 'I do not need to. It is not in his nature to be less than generous.'

There was a long pause and then Louise said bluntly, 'I make you my compliments, *mademoiselle*; it seems you know Denzil very well. Do you love him?'

A slow flush stained Rosalind's cheeks and, bending her head, she said simply, 'Yes. Too much to let him live through three more days of believing that I blame him for what happened twelve years ago. It is enough that he appears to blame himself.'

'I see.' The Dowager's green stare rested consideringly on her guest's tightly clasped fingers. 'And if he asks you – you will marry him?'

With a slow, painful smile, Rosalind lifted her head. 'That would depend on why he asked me.'

Louise drew a long, bracing breath and came to her feet. 'I think,' she announced buoyantly, 'that we should have some tea – and you will both take off your hats and be comfortable, *non*? Then we shall enjoy a cosy *tête-à-tête* and make these foolish men very sorry that they have left us alone to do it. *D'accord*?'

'*D'accord*,' responded Isabel shyly. It was very easy, she reflected, to see where the Marquis had acquired his charm. His mother had it in abundance.

The tea was sent for and, over it, in the process of telling her sympathetic hostess all about her troublesome brother, Mistress Dacre unwittingly revealed a good deal of the situation between herself and Lord Philip – all of which the Dowager found much more interesting than the Honourable Robert's vagaries. Indeed, Louise was just beginning to think that it would be a pity if she were not to meet the erstwhile Captain when, from the hall, there came sounds of an arrival that was clearly not that of the Marquis. And then a tall, dark and exceedingly dusty young man erupted into the room.

'*Oh!*' said Isabel, blushing furiously. 'Ph-Philip!'

'*Oh Isabel!*' retorted his Lordship irascibly. 'I don't know why you sound so surprised – for, having troubled to leave me a note, you must surely have expected me. Oh – get your hands off me, man!' This to an affronted Gaston who was still trying to perform his duty of announcing this hasty guest. He was brushed briskly aside in a cloud of dust from Philip's coat and shut firmly out. 'Don't tell me I've ridden all this way for nothing!'

'We don't intend to,' said Rosalind, sighing. And then, to the Dowager, 'I must apologise for my brother, Madame. It seems he is fated to be continually at a disadvantage with your family.'

'*Ça se voit,*' agreed Louise. She stood up and directed a twinkling smile at his Lordship. '*Toutefois* . . . I am very happy to see you, my Lord. I have been hoping I might do so.'

That smile was so uncannily familiar that it was a moment or two before Philip recovered sufficiently to bow over the thin, shapely hand she extended to him. He coloured hotly and said, 'I b-beg your pardon, Madame. For my intrusion and also for my appearance.'

She laughed. 'Do not! One sees that you have ridden *ventre à terre* in pursuit of . . . your sister – and are a little out of temper. I do not regard it, *je vous assure!*'

Philip's mouth relaxed a little as he responded involuntarily to her charm. 'I thank you, Madame – but the truth is that I followed my bride-to-be. I have spent altogether too much time worrying over Rosalind's concerns and, save that I have a number of apologies to deliver presently to your son, intend, in future, to leave them in her own charge. It's high time I began putting my own house in order . . . and, if you will permit me, I should like to ask Mistress Dacre to walk with me in your garden.'

Louise shook her head decisively. '*Mais, non* – the garden is much too public! Your sister and I, we shall leave you here – and Mademoiselle Isabelle shall pour you a cup of tea.' She smiled encouragingly at Mistress Dacre. 'Tea, I have noticed, has a very beneficial effect on the temper and *monsieur le Capitaine* will appear much less formidable when he is seated. Come, *ma fille*.' And, taking Rosalind's hand, she led her quietly out of the room and closed the door behind her.

Philip showed no sign of sitting down and nor did he speak, so at length Isabel said hesitantly, 'Would you l-like some tea?'

'No,' replied Philip curtly. And then, drawing a deep breath, 'I'd like to know what you expect of our marriage.'

Startled brown eyes flew to meet his. 'I – I don't know what you m-mean.'

'Yes, you do. When it was first arranged, we scarcely knew each other but that is no longer true, is it? And, although I know you accepted me for the sake of the money, I want to know if . . . if you have come to like me at all for myself.'

Isabel stared fixedly down at her hands, her heart beating very fast. 'Does it matter?' she asked wistfully.

'Yes, damn it – it does!' Philip dropped romantically on one knee beside her chair and took her shoulders in an unromantic and somewhat exasperated grasp. 'Because if you are looking for a fashionable alliance where you can do as you please, you'd better not marry me – and so I warn you! It's true that I didn't expect to be jealous, didn't think I *could* be – but I am. And, once you're my wife, if I catch you flirting with any man under eighty, I'll knock his teeth down his throat!'

'Oh!' breathed Isabel, entranced. All her longings for a gentle and poetic courtship melted into the realm of things forgotten and unregretted and she said, 'W-would you really?'

'Yes. Why do you think I blew a hole through Amberley? And *don't* say it was because of Rosalind! I'm sick to death of the whole tedious business and it's bad enough that I'll have to let *him* think that it was that; but I can hardly say that I felt like killing him because you seemed a good deal fonder of him than you were of me, now can I?'

'No – I suppose not.' A sweet radiance settled on Isabel's face and she smiled shyly. 'B-but you were quite wrong, you know. And it would never have happened if you had f- flirted with me yourself.'

'Oh?' Philip grinned suddenly. 'Then I'd better take care to do so in future, hadn't I?'

She nodded and stared in apparent fascination at his cravat. 'You've been m-mistaken about other things too – such as the money. I never . . . I never . . .'

'Yes?' The sapphire gaze sharpened suddenly. 'You never what?'

'I never cared about it,' she replied simply. 'Papa did – but not me. I – I would have married you anyway but I thought that you wanted a . . . a *convenient* wife.'

Philip's hands tightened hard on her shoulders and he stood up, pulling her with him. 'I did – then,' he said unsteadily. 'But that was before I knew you and came to love you so. *Oh my dear* . . .'

And then she was in his arms and the need for words was gone as she lifted her face to his.

'Oh *God* – why doesn't he come?' said Rosalind as if the words had been wrenched from her. 'It's been *hours*!'

Sympathy mingled with satisfaction in the Dowager's eyes and she patted Rosalind's hand with absent affection. 'Yes. But that is nothing so extraordinary and no reason to suppose him lying dead in a ditch.'

'Isn't it?'

'No. Denzil is a very good horseman and quite able to take care of himself – even with only one hand. He will come when he is ready – and, when he does, it will be to this room for always he enters the house from the garden when coming back from the stables. It is his habit, you understand; and, me, I think it will be better that he first sees you and *not* Milord Philippe – who is, one hopes, more happily engaged.' She got up and shook out her skirts. '*Voyons* . . . I am enjoying myself today! And now I think I shall enjoy myself some more and tell *mon pauvre* Gaston that we shall be five for dinner. He will make me a sour face and say it cannot be done – which I find *fort amusant* for secretly he is pleased and knows that it can. You will not mind if I leave you, *ma chère?*'

'Not at all,' replied Rosalind politely. And wished it were true.

She also wished, as she sat quite alone and straining every nerve to hear any sound that might warn her of the Marquis's approach, that she could remember any of the things she had planned to say. But they had vanished beyond recall, along with a large measure of her composure, and she had the nasty feeling that when the time came, she might find herself blurting out something so hopelessly gauche that he would be unable to answer it truthfully.

And the truth was important. Before listening to Isabel it had not seemed possible that his Lordship could hold himself responsible for her blindness but now it appeared the most likely explanation. And it was as dangerous as it was ridiculous for it meant that Philip might well have been right.

'*How do you know it isn't from pity or guilt?*'

Or a quixotic but misplaced attempt to make amends in the only way open to him, thought Rosalind miserably; and, knowing the Marquis, this was by far the most likely of the three. Unless . . .

And then there were light footsteps on the stone terrace outside and she stiffened, her hands clenched tight in her lap.

Deep in his own unpleasant thoughts, Amberley had closed the door behind him and was several steps into the room before he realised that she was there. He froze, unprepared either for the sight of her or what it did to him; and then, with a kind of groping gesture, stretched out his hand to close his fingers hard on the solid back of a chair. The seconds ticked by in silence while he stared wordlessly at her from eyes that were full of shock and disbelief – and a queer, desperate hunger.

Rosalind's throat tightened with the agony of waiting in her endless, intolerable darkness and then she said stupidly, 'You are surprised to see me here, I suppose.'

The lame futile words echoed on and on in the stillness that followed them and, because she had no way of knowing that the reason he did not speak was because he could not trust himself to do so, she bent her head and said flatly, 'I shouldn't have come. I'm sorry.'

With an effort, he tore his eyes from her downcast face to study his own whitened knuckles. 'Why did you?' he asked.

The sound of his voice, harsh, brittle and stripped of its customary lightness, hit Rosalind like a blow for it was that of a stranger. She shivered, feeling suddenly and coldly alone. His voice was all she had to rely on and, without it, there seemed to be nothing left.

'I came to ask you something I had thought important,' she said unevenly. 'But I think that I may have been . . . mistaken.'

240

'Oh I doubt it.' He stood straight, his hand falling clenched at his side. 'You would like me to explain myself – isn't that it? To tell you why I never thought fit to mention the small matter of it being my coach that – that took away your sight? Well, I can do so if you wish – but there seems to be little point since you'd be quite mad to believe me.'

The flippancy was back but with a bitter and razor-edged vengeance.

'No – it's not that.' She made a tiny hurt movement that made him turn away, scalded.

He said, 'What then?' And had to wait a long time for her reply.

'I wanted to ask you if it's true that you blame yourself for the accident. I should have thought of it before . . . only it didn't seem possible that you could. Do you?'

'Yes,' he replied tersely. 'And that, of course, is why I – or no. It won't cure anything, so why say it? And my high regard for your intelligence suggests that you have already worked it out for yourself anyway.'

Rosalind's heart turned to stone and she discovered that she felt rather sick. 'Yes. I – I think so,' she said tonelessly. 'And there is no need for you to sacrifice yourself. I believe Philip allowed you to understand that I – that I held you responsible, but it isn't so. No blame attaches to you for you weren't driving, were you? And if the fault is to be laid at anyone's door, then it should be mine for failing to heed Phil's warning.' She came slowly to her feet and tried to smile. 'So you owe me nothing and are quite free . . . and that is all I wanted to say. W-will you pull the bell, please? I'm afraid I don't know where . . .'

'In a moment.' He turned to look at her and for the first time became aware of her pallor and the utter desolation in her eyes. He frowned and said sharply, 'What do you mean – that I am free and need not sacrifice myself? Did you suppose I intended to?'

Her smile went sadly awry. 'Didn't you?'

'No. Indeed, I'm hard-pressed to see how I could.' And there he stopped as the answer drove the breath from his body. Then, in a very odd tone, he remarked, 'I detect the fell hand of Lord Philip. What exactly has he said to you?'

'Nothing that you haven't said yourself – or as good as!' she retorted desperately. Her control was in shreds and she knew it. '*Please* let it alone. I want to go home.'

'Presently,' came the inflexible reply. 'First I want an answer. Just for a moment you had me wondering if you didn't suspect me of offering you my hand and heart in an orgy of expiation or some such thing – but, from what you've just said, it can't be that. Oh – I know that I've made you no such offer but you must have been aware that I was going to. And though I can well imagine Philip misdoubting my motives, I can't say I'd have expected you to believe him – and I'm bloody sure that I never said anything to help you do so. So what in hell's name is it?'

'But – but you *did*,' averred Rosalind, shaking and faintly dazed. 'Or you would have done so if you hadn't thought better of it.'

He stared at her helplessly, forcing down the desire to take her in his arms – anything that would stop her looking like that. Then, quite without warning, he realised what she meant. He said '*Oh God* – yes. I see.' And foolishly, breathlessly, he began to laugh at the unparalleled irony of it.

Rosalind listened, felt something wet on her cheeks and simultaneously discovered that she could endure no more. She turned, took two swift steps and collided painfully with a table.

The laughter ceased as if cut with a knife and there was suddenly a hand on her arm and an achingly familiar voice saying unsteadily, 'My dear – don't. I can't stand it.'

But it was too late for the choking sobs were already escaping from her throat; and, bending her head over the polished wood where her hands lay, she stopped fighting and gave way to them.

The sound of it tore at Amberley's heart and, freeing his left arm from the sling, he gathered her close against his chest, his right hand cradling her head with quiet protectiveness. He did not try to speak; indeed, he could not have done so and, above her hair, his eyes were full of anguished tenderness, his face white and set. He remained quite still until the broken sobs lessened and died and then, producing a handkerchief from his pocket, he proceeded to dry her wet cheeks.

Rosalind submitted docilely to these ministrations, her breath still catching faintly and, when he put the dampened cambric into her hand, she used it for the prosaic and unselfconcious purpose of blowing her small nose, before saying huskily, 'That was very stupid of me. I'm sorry. I can't think what made me do it.'

'Can you not?' He drew her gently to sit beside him on a sofa and possessed himself of both of her hands. 'And I thought it was my crassly ill-timed hilarity.'

His voice was bitter and she flinched at the sound of it.

'Don't – please! I know you didn't mean it.'

'Do you? I'd be happy to think so – but it isn't true, is it? You are doubtless thinking me all manner of things but never that what I failed so lamentably to say just now was not that my sense of guilt prompted me to marriage . . . but that it was responsible for making a coward of me.'

She tilted her head and a grave, considering expression entered the violet eyes. 'A coward? You? I don't think I understand you.'

'No,' he agreed, taking the handkerchief from her and turning it over and over between his hands. 'But that is why I couldn't quite bring myself to tell you about the accident. I was afraid, you see, of what your reaction might be . . . afraid to hear you say all the things I've been saying to myself.'

A strange sense of tranquility entered Rosalind's heart. She said, 'That was . . . foolish of you.'

He smiled faintly. 'Possibly. But not as foolish as proposing marriage in an attempt to placate one's conscience.'

'Then you didn't mean to do so?'

'No. Coward I may be – lunatic I'm not.' He rose and walked away a little, Then, looking at her, 'Aren't you going to ask what my reason was? No – I can see you're not. Perhaps you don't care . . . or would rather not know. I'm sorry if it's the latter because, having come this far, I think we must finish it – and the truth is that you were right the first time. I love you . . . *à corps perdu,* as my mother would say.' He gave a crooked smile. 'And you have no idea how much that is.'

'Oh, I think I have,' replied Rosalind with a tiny wistful laugh. 'But are you quite sure? It isn't – you aren't . . .'

'Sorry for you?' he finished crisply. 'I thought you knew me better.'

'I did . . . I *do*.'

'Then why ask it? If you married me I'd make no more allowances than I did at Oakleigh – less, perhaps. I'm not proposing to be your eyes – though I'd give you mine if I could. But I can't. And unless you love me, I've nothing at all to offer. For the simple fact is that it's I who need you and not the other way about. But only,' he repeated, 'if you love me. I don't think I can settle for less.'

Very slowly, Rosalind came to her feet. 'You don't need to,' she said simply, stretching out an unsteady hand towards him. 'You'll never need to. But I wish . . .'

The grey-green eyes blazed but he did not move. 'Yes?'

'I wish you weren't so far away,' she complained gently.

His fingers closed around hers with careful restraint. He said, 'It seems only fair to warn you that, if I come any closer, I am likely to behave with a deplorable lack of propriety.'

'Oh?' She flushed and stepped towards him, smiling. 'Then . . . why don't you?'

And, as though that had been all he had waited for, she was drawn inexorably into his arms, so close that she did not know if it was his heart she could feel beating or her own and with her head tilted easily back by his hand sliding up into her hair. A second passed, then two, three . . . and in a voice that was no more than a breathed caress, he murmured, '*Darling, darling* . . .' before his mouth came down on hers and the floor beneath her feet lost its solidity.

Her bones dissolved and she clung to him, lost and drowning under the slow, sweet delight of his kisses; darkness and doubt ceased to exist and the world shrank to the compass of his arms where nothing mattered except the drugging wonder of his nearness and the feel of his hair beneath her fingers. And when at last his mouth left hers and she felt the lean hardness of his cheek against her own, she said the thing which, above all others, he had waited to hear.

'My heart, my soul . . . I love you.'

It was long before they were ready to leave privacy behind them and join the others. But the future was theirs and nothing could dim it; so, at last, they went together to receive the blessing that they knew Louise would give them. And later, with joy still wrapped about them, Rosalind went confidently in the curve of Denzil's arm to find her brother.

Philip released Isabel's hand and came unhurriedly to his feet, watching the Marquis bring his sister across the room. And suddenly, seeing the expression in the grey-green eyes as they rested on Rosalind, all the tensions and misunderstandings of the last few weeks seemed to fade into fantasy. It was hard to know how he had been so blind; but, because Amberley was Amberley, he knew it need not matter. He smiled and said easily, 'You appear to have found something you thought lost. Are congratulations in order?'

Quite slowly, the Marquis withdrew his gaze from Rosalind and turned it on his Lordship. 'They are. But I think we would both prefer your happy consent.'

'They're both yours.' Philip walked half-way towards him and then stopped. 'And my most sincere apologies, too, for everything I said and did. And thought. I don't offer you excuses for any of it – I don't think there can be any. But you may like to know that I've learned a valuable lesson. And I beg your pardon – Rosalind's too.'

His sister smiled. 'Mine you have.'

'And mine.' The Marquis removed a reluctant arm from about Rosalind's waist and went to meet Lord Philip. 'You had every justification for what you thought – more, perhaps, than I had for not explaining myself. But, unlike you, I doubt I shall be found to have profited from the experience so I can only be grateful that others,' he smiled at Isabel, 'have better sense than I do myself. And, in any event, I should be happy to count myself your friend.'

And, when he held out his hand, Philip grinned and took it without hesitation.

It was the end of formality and soon the new freedom

from constraint was as evident in their silences as in their talk.

Then, her hand once more securely in Philip's, Isabel said lazily, 'Tell them about Robert.'

Philip laughed and met Amberley's eye.

'I found him hovering on the brink of being clapped up for debt,' he explained, 'and so I solved all our problems by acting on a very good piece of advice you once gave me.'

'Oh?' The Marquis raised one enquiring brow and settled his arm more closely around Rosalind. 'And what was that?'

'I've made a present of him . . . to the army. I thought,' said his Lordship innocently, 'that they might be better able to deal with him.'

The Marquis laughed appreciatively and Rosalind raised her head from his shoulder to say resignedly, 'And I suppose you also paid his debts?'

'Oh – that.' Philip shrugged. 'Well yes, I had to. And that reminds me . . . the silly fool owes Rockcliffe a thousand from some wager or other.'

'Does he?' Amberley drew Rosalind's head back to its resting place. 'Then you can leave that to me. I feel sure that Rock will be happy to contribute his mite to the general cause . . . and I really don't see why he should come off unscathed. Do you?'

'No,' replied Philip amicably. 'I can't say I do.'

'*I* think, quivered Rosalind, sotto-voce, 'that you are both quite unscrupulously devious.'

'But clever,' added Isabel winsomely. 'In a ruthless sort of way.'

The Marquis looked cheerfully across at Philip.

'How fortunate we are to be so perfectly understood. But . . . there is just *one* small detail that troubles me.'

'And what is that?' asked his Lordship, his exquisitely polite tone belied by the laughter in his eyes. 'You know, I hope, that if there is anything I can do . . ?

The Marquis grinned.

'I'm so glad you said that,' he replied pleasantly. 'Because I was just wondering which of us was going to have custody of Broody.'